THE STITCHING HOUR

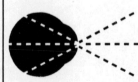

THE STITCHING HOUR

AMANDA LEE

WHEELER PUBLISHING
A part of Gale, Cengage Learning

GALE
CENGAGE Learning·

Farmington Hills, Mich • San Francisco • New York • Waterville, Maine
Meriden, Conn • Mason, Ohio • Chicago

LIBRARY OF CONGRESS CATALOGING-IN-PUBLICATION DATA

Names: Lee, Amanda, 1967– author.
Title: The stitching hour : an emdroidery mystery / by Amanda Lee.
Description: Large print edition. | Waterville, Maine : Wheeler Publishing, 2016. | © 2015 | Series: Wheeler Publishing large print cozy mystery
Identifiers: LCCN 2015050971| ISBN 9781410488220 (softcover) | ISBN 1410488225 (softcover)
Subjects: LCSH: Embroidery—Fiction. | Murder—Investigation—Fiction. | Large type books. | GSAFD: Mystery fiction.
Classification: LCC PS3620.R4454 S755 2011 | DDC 813/.6—dc23
LC record available at http://lccn.loc.gov/2015050971

Published in 2016 by arrangement with New American Library, an imprint of Penguin Publishing Group, a division of Penguin Random House LLC

Printed in the United States of America
1 2 3 4 5 6 7 20 19 18 17 16

To Tim, Lianna, and Nicholas

CHAPTER ONE

I reached down and patted the head of my Irish wolfhound, Angus. At only two years old, he still had a lot of puppy in him, but he was mannerly and well behaved. The patrons of my embroidery shop, the Seven-Year Stitch, loved him.

"Can you believe we've been here in Tallulah Falls for almost a year?" I asked him. I jerked my head in the direction of Jill, the mannequin-slash-Marilyn-Monroe-look-alike that stood by the cash register. "Jill says she can't." I looked at her, as if she'd actually said something. "What's that, Jill? What you can't believe is how I haven't dressed you in a beautiful new dress befitting the occasion?" I blew out a breath. "All in good time, Jill. All in good time."

Okay, so maybe having a mom who was a Hollywood costume designer led me to do more than my fair share of play-pretend as a child, and maybe . . . just *maybe* . . . that trait had followed me over into adulthood. But I got lonely when I was the only person in the store. And when the only "people" around to talk with were Angus and Jill, I made do. Besides, I was pretty sure that Angus not only understood every word I said but that he communicated with me too. He had such expressive eyes. And that smile! With Jill, you just had to make it all up as you went and hope she wasn't one of those cursed paranormal items that would come to life and try to kill you one day.

So on *that* creepy thought, I gazed around the store and firmly directed my thoughts back to my upcoming anniversary open house. Since it was October 1, Jill was wearing a witch costume. She wasn't scary — she was more of a Samantha from *Bewitched* type. Before the open house, I planned to change her into either a white or pink dress — more Marilyn than Sam.

Everything else in the store would probably be all right *as is,* other than tidying up and borrowing a few folding chairs from the library. Since I was good friends with the librarian, Rajani "Reggie" Singh, I didn't think that would be a problem. Under normal circumstances, I had plenty of seating in my sit-and-stitch square — two navy sofas that faced each other across an oval maple coffee table, a red club chair at either end of the table, and ottomans matching the chairs. I wondered briefly if I should shampoo the red-and-blue braided rug that lay beneath the table, but I decided a thorough vacuuming would be fine.

I turned to the merchandise part of the store, where I'd been marking down prices and placing specials on the shelf nearest the door. I looked over the embroidery projects that lined the walls with a critical eye. Should I add more? Take a few down? There was the redwork swan . . . the Celtic cross . . . the sampler I'd made from Louisa Ralston's original . . . the bunny done in crewel-work . . . the Bollywood-inspired elephant . . . the pirate map tapestry . . . the cross-stitched bride. . . . With a slight smile, I decided to leave them all. I didn't think it was necessary to add another one . . . yet . . . but there weren't any I wanted to take down.

I went over to the sit-and-stitch square, moved aside one of the candlewick pillows, and plopped down on the navy sofa facing the storefront window. I'd come a long way in the past year, professionally and personally. Just before I moved here, I'd adopted Angus, and we were living in an apartment in San Francisco where I worked in an accounting office. Then Sadie MacKenzie had called and urged me to come to Tallulah Falls and open my own embroidery shop. Sadie had been my best friend and roommate in college. She and her husband, Blake, had a coffee shop called MacKenzies' Mochas right down the street from the Stitch. She hadn't had to twist my arm; and despite my ups and downs in Tallulah Falls, I was happier here than I'd ever been.

I'd barely sat down when Vera Langhorne came through the door.

"Good morning, Marcy," she said.

"Hi," I said as Angus trotted over to greet Vera.

She scratched his head and cooed to him for a minute before joining me on the sofa. Vera had also come a long way in the year that I'd known her. She was no longer the mousy brunette in baggy clothes that I'd met when I'd first arrived in Tallulah Falls. Now she wore her hair blond with subtle highlights, and she always dressed with style and class. Today she wore gray slacks, black pumps, and a royal blue short-sleeved sweater twinset.

"You'll never believe what's coming in next door to you," she said.

"Please tell me that whatever it is won't be operated by a relative of Nellie Davis," I said with a groan.

Nellie Davis owned the aromatherapy shop down the street, and she and I had never been friends. Heck, we'd hardly been civil. I'd tried over the past year to warm up our relationship, but Nellie was convinced that all the mishaps that had befallen Tallulah Falls had coincided with my arrival and that either I or my shop — or both — was cursed. She'd been so antagonistic toward me that she'd recently talked her sister, Clara, into renting the space next to the Seven-Year Stitch — a knitting shop, no less, where she'd also planned to sell embroidery supplies! Unfortunately, Clara had met with a bad end, and the shop was once again for lease. Well, not anymore, it seemed.

"It's gonna be a haunted house!" Vera clapped her hands in excitement. "Won't that be fun? They're only here for the month of October, but from what they told Paul, they plan to do it up right."

Vera was dating Paul Samms, a reporter for the *Tallulah Falls Examiner.*

"They're going to take the first few days of the month to decorate and move in all their creepy crawly stuff, and the actual haunted house is going to open the following weekend," she continued.

I frowned. "Are they only going to be open

11

during the weekends? If so, how will they make enough to justify renting the building?"

"According to Paul, after that opening weekend, they're going to be open every night," said Vera. "So they believe — and so do I — that they'll make their rent back many times over. They'll have special events throughout the month to draw repeat business, like themed costume contests, local celebrities — news anchors and people like that . . . Paul might even be one. *And* they're having concessions!"

"They're having concessions at a haunted house? That seems a little odd."

"I'm surprised Sadie hasn't mentioned it to you. She and Blake are in charge of the food."

"Neither of them has said a word to me," I said. "How will that work? I can't imagine where they'll find the time to run a concession stand on top of operating a busy coffee shop."

"Paul says they're going to do fairly simple stuff — caramel apples, popcorn and kettle corn, cookies, some hot chocolate and a couple of other beverages maybe — and the patrons have to eat outside of the actual haunted house," said Vera. "The haunted house operators don't want to wind up with a colossal mess. And one of the MacKenzies' Mochas waitresses will work the haunted house each night. So it really shouldn't interfere with Sadie and Blake's schedules all that much."

"Cool."

"You don't look like you really feel that it's all that cool," Vera said. "What's wrong?"

"I'm just concerned about how it will affect my evening classes," I told her. "Some of my students are a little older — like Muriel — and I wouldn't want her to be frightened or put off if she hears a ton of screaming going on next door."

Vera laughed. "Sweetie, you know Muriel can't hear herself think. And I don't know that it'll be *that* disruptive. Maybe you could put on some music or something."

Oh, sure, I thought. *That would be great — blaring music to drown out the screaming teenagers next door.*

"Besides, you might enjoy going to the haunted house with Ted." Vera winked.

"I'm not saying it won't be fun," I said. "I guess I'm just being selfish. How will this affect me . . . Angus . . . my students . . . my open house?"

"That's right! Your anniversary's coming up!" Vera clasped her hands together. "What are we doing for that?"

"I thought I'd have special sales and markdowns for the two weeks leading up to the open house. And I want to have gift bags for open house attendees." I leaned forward. "But I'm struggling with what to put into the bags. Any suggestions?"

Vera looked up at the ceiling. "Well . . . you could put something different into every bag . . . like a coupon. Each coupon would be for a different amount off a particular item or the customer's entire purchase. And you could have *one* coupon for a free item within a particular price range."

"That's a fantastic idea," I said.

She smiled at me. "Don't sound so surprised, darling."

"I'm not surprised." I laughed. "Honest. I've simply been pondering over what I can give out that will appeal to everyone and not break the bank. The coupons are a wonderful idea."

"Sure," she said. "And you can put candies . . . teeny little sewing kits . . . maybe those braided friendship bracelets the kids like. . . ."

"You have a ton of fantastic ideas, Vera Langhorne! You should be an event planner."

Vera laughed. "I'll take that under advisement."

Just then, Reggie hurried into the shop. Although she was beautifully dressed in an Indian-style coral tunic with matching slacks, Reggie's normally elegantly coifed short gray hair looked as if she'd barely taken time to brush it this morning.

"Have you heard?" she asked us. "Somebody's doing a haunted house next to your shop, Marcy!"

"That's what Vera was telling me," I said, my smile fading. "I'm getting the feeling you're not in favor of haunted houses?"

She dropped onto the sofa across from Vera and me. Angus came and placed his head on the arm of the sofa closest to Reggie. She patted his head absently.

"I'm in favor of the *library's* haunted house," she said. "It's one of our biggest annual fund-raisers. And now this fancy group is going to come in and ruin it for us."

"No, they won't," Vera said. "Their haunted house isn't geared for small children. It's more for teens and adults. Paul interviewed the event organizers, and they told him all about it. Your haunted house is supposed to be funny and sweet. Theirs is supposed to be scary as heck!"

15

"You truly don't think their haunted house will have an impact on our fundraiser?" Reggie asked.

"I know it won't," Vera said. "In fact, I'll insist that Paul give the library equal time. I'll see when he can drop in at the library and do a story on *your* haunted house. I'll make sure he emphasizes the importance of the fund-raiser on the library's annual budget. How does that sound?"

"That sounds terrific, Vera. Thank you." Reggie smoothed her hair. "I'm sorry that I allowed the news of the new haunted house to upset me so badly. It isn't like me at all." She turned to me. "How do *you* feel about having a fun house right next door, Marcy?"

"I'm not terribly happy about it," I said. "I'm afraid it'll drive Angus and my students crazy."

"She was particularly concerned about the effect all the screaming might have on poor Muriel," Vera said. "I told her Muriel probably wouldn't even notice, no better than she can hear."

"True, but I see Marcy's point," said Reggie. "At least, they won't be disturbing your business during daylight hours."

"That's true," I said. "And it's only for a month. What real harm can it do?"

When would I ever learn to stop asking that

My sweetheart, Ted, came for lunch. Ted was the head detective for the Tallulah Falls Police Department. He worked for Reggie's husband, Manu, who was the Chief of Police.

Broad, strong, and well over a foot taller than me, Ted was a walking dream. He had black hair with a few flecks of premature gray and the bluest eyes I'd ever seen. He wore suits for work, and he favored gray and navy. Today he wore light gray with a royal blue shirt and a blue, gray, and lavender striped tie. He looked yummy.

On top of looking so mouth-watering, he brought my favorite lunch — chicken salad croissants from MacKenzies' Mochas. I had bottled water in the minifridge in my office. I didn't have a customer in the shop when Ted arrived, so I put the cardboard clock on the door, indicating that I'd be back in half an hour so we could go into the office and eat undisturbed.

After we kissed hello, I got us each a bottle of water, and we sat at my desk to eat.

"How's your day going?" I asked, as I opened the box containing my croissant.

"Fine. I'm guessing you've heard the news about the Horror Emporium that's moving in next door to you."

"Is that what they're calling it?" I frowned. "That seems like a mouthful . . . especially for kids."

"Well, from what I hear, the Horror Emporium isn't designed for children. It's more for adults," said Ted. "I've even heard that they plan to make visitors sign waivers before they buy their tickets, saying that if they're harmed in any way, suffer a heart attack or seizure, that the Horror Emporium will not be held responsible."

"Good grief! What're they planning on doing in there?"

He shrugged. "I'd say the waiver is more for publicity than anything. All the tough kids will want to come to prove they can't be scared by whatever some local haunted house can dish out."

"I suppose. . . ." I uncapped my water bottle and took a drink.

"You wanna go?"

I grinned. "Of course! Do you?"

"They can't scare me." He winked. "But I'll go with you so you'll have someone to hold on to."

I batted my eyelashes at him. "My big strong hero!"

He leaned across the desk to give me another kiss. "I've missed you today."

"But we had breakfast together this morning."

"Yeah . . . four and a half hours ago." He tore off a piece of his croissant and tossed it to Angus, who caught it in midair. "Good boy!"

"About this haunted house," I said. "Do you think they'll cause a lot of ruckus?"

Ted grinned. "Why, Ms. Singer, the Tallulah Falls Police Department will do our dead-level best to keep all the hoodlums at bay."

I rolled my eyes. "I guess I did sound like a grumpy old lady, didn't I?"

Angus drank noisily from his water bowl.

"Maybe a little," said Ted. "But, seriously, I can see your point. It would be ideal if this Horror Emporium wasn't right in the middle of Main Street. It's going to be hard for you and your students to concentrate during evening classes while crowds of people scream next door. I'll check to see if they're doing anything to help muffle the sound."

"Thank you."

"Just everyday hero stuff, ma'am," he said. He bit into his sandwich as Angus sat near him expectantly.

I tossed Angus a bit of my croissant to give Ted a break. "Vera was in earlier. She's the one who told me about the haunted house, by the way. But she had some great ideas for the open house." I told him about the coupons she suggested for the goodie bags.

"You're excited about this anniversary party, aren't you?"

"I am," I said. "The last party I had here didn't turn out so well. And the day after was even worse."

"Hey, don't say that. That's the day I met you."

I smiled. "That was the only good thing about it."

"You didn't think so at the time," he said.

"You suspected me of murder."

"Only a little."

"A little was too much, in my opinion," I said.

"I know. But we found the real killer . . . and look at us now."

Indeed. Had Sadie had her way, I'd have been dating Todd, who owned the Brew Crew across the street. And yet it was Ted who'd captured my heart almost from the beginning.

"We've come a long way," I said.

"We sure have," he said. "And we have a lot further to go."

"I just hope we can keep the killers at bay

for this year's open house."

We held each other's gaze, both afraid to say anything. It had been our unfortunate experience never to underestimate the propensity for murder in this lovely small coastal town.

CHAPTER TWO

Right after lunch, a couple of sweet ladies came in looking for some needlepoint kits.

"I used to cross-stitch," said one. "But my eyes aren't good enough to count all those teeny, tiny squares anymore."

"I prefer painting myself," said the other. "I'm just here with my sister. You don't sell art supplies, do you?"

"I'm afraid not," I said as I led them to the needle-point kits and supplies. "I'm getting ready for my one-year open house. I hope you'll stop back in for a goodie bag and some special discounts. I'll give you a flyer with all the information. And today I'm happy to give you a ten-percent discount on your total purchase."

"Well, aren't you nice?" said the sister looking for needlework supplies.

"What a handsome dog," said the other, going over to the window where Angus lay.

I'd put him in the bathroom so often when

elderly patrons came in that he'd learned not to rush to greet them the way he did most every other visitor to the store.

"I'd love to sketch him sometime." She patted his head, and he sat up, wagging his tail.

"Come by anytime," I told her. "I'm not sure how cooperative he'll be about posing, though."

The bell over the front door jingled, signaling a new arrival. I turned to see a tall, lanky man wearing black slacks, a white button-down shirt, a red-and-black paisley vest, and a black top hat. Angus leapt to his feet.

"Hello, my good man." After greeting Angus with a pat on the head, the visitor tipped his hat to us. "Ladies."

"Hi," I said. "Welcome to the Seven-Year Stitch. I'm Marcy. How may I help you?"

"My wife will be joining us momentarily," he said. "Please continue assisting these fine gentlewomen."

Gentlewomen? How strange! Who talks like that?

My customers were apparently wondering the same thing. The one sister hastily made her decision, paid for her selection, and said she'd be back for the open house. The man held the door for them, and they murmured their thanks as they hurried past him.

"Ah, I see my lovely wife approaching," he said, still holding the door open.

I quickly came around to the front of the counter and took hold of Angus's collar in case he decided to bolt.

The man's wife swept through the door, and she was every bit as flamboyant as he. She, too, wore black slacks and a white shirt; but instead of the vest, she wore a red jacket with tails. She had long tangerine corkscrew curls, and I wondered if it was a wig or her real hair. She also wore a tiny purple top hat perched on the left side of her head.

"Hi, I'm Marcy," I said.

"Wonderful to meet you, Marcy," she said. "I'm Priscilla. Did Claude introduce himself already?"

"No, my love," said Claude. "Marcy was entertaining customers, so I thought it would be more prudent to await your arrival." He removed the hat and bowed deeply. "Claude and Priscilla Atwood at your service."

I didn't bow. "Marcy Singer and Angus O'Ruff at *your* service."

"We're enchanted to make your acquaintance, Marcy," said Claude, as he returned the hat to his head.

"Indeed we are," said Priscilla. "And aren't *you* charming?" She held her flat palm out toward Angus, and he planted one large furry paw in her hand. Priscilla laughed. "How delightful!"

"Ted — my boyfriend — has been teaching him a few tricks." Should I also mention that Ted was a detective? Although Claude and Priscilla seemed nice enough, there was something about them that set off my internal alarm bells.

"Ted should be commended," said Claude. He extended his right arm toward the sit-and-stitch square. "May we sit, my lady?"

"Of course," I said. "Where are my manners? Would you like some coffee or bottled water?"

"Not me. Thank you," said Priscilla. "I'm fine."

"As am I." Claude took his wife's hand and led her over to the sofa that faced away from the window.

I sat on the sofa across from them, glad that the maple table was between us and that Angus had come to lay by my feet. He didn't appear to be nervous about these two. Why was I?

"So . . . what brings you to the Seven-Year Stitch?" I asked.

"You might say we're getting the lay of the land," said Priscilla, tossing one of those long curls over her shoulder. "We leased the shop next door for the next month."

"The Horror Emporium," I said.

Claude beamed. "I'm delighted to find that our reputation has preceded us. Tell us — what have you heard?"

"Only that you're opening a haunted house soon," I said. "I believe you were interviewed for the local newspaper by Paul Samms. Paul's girlfriend, Vera, gave me the news. She's thrilled about it."

"And how do you feel about it, Marcy?" Priscilla asked.

"I'm looking forward to checking it out." I tried to choose my words carefully. The last thing I needed was another neighbor who hated me. Nellie Davis already fulfilled those duties to the best of her abilities. "I have to warn you, though, I might not scare as easily as some of your other patrons."

"Yes, we know," said Claude. "We did our homework on the shopkeepers, and we thought you might be quite the challenge."

My eyes widened. "What do you mean?"

"Only that we'll have our work cut out for us if we intend to frighten the daughter of Beverly Singer."

"You know my mom?"

Priscilla laughed. "We know *of* her, dear."

"We would love to make her acquaintance," said Claude. "Is there any chance she'll be visiting Tallulah Falls in the coming weeks?"

I shrugged. "Anything's possible with Mom. So, tell me — how did you become interested in costuming?"

"It's vital to what we do," said Priscilla.

"Critical," Claude agreed. "We have to make our monsters and creatures look as realistic and horrifying as possible. I create the costumes, and Priscilla performs the makeup enhancements."

"That's fantastic. Do you do this type of work — haunted houses, I mean — year round?"

"No," said Priscilla. "We're a couple of gypsies really, going wherever the wind blows us, doing first one thing and then another. Claude is an excellent illusionist."

Claude squeezed her hand. "You flatter me, my sweet. She is right about us being two leaves taken by the breeze, however. We've done magic shows, community theater, a few television appearances here and there. . . ."

"And don't forget that off-Broadway production." Priscilla smiled. "I did makeup and helped with costumes and props, and

27

Claude played the role of Petruchio."

"What fun," I said, wondering if perhaps they were trying to wrangle an introduction to my mother in the hope that she'd help them get into the movie business. It wouldn't be the first time.

"It was enjoyable," said Claude. "But, alas, the East didn't suit us as well as the West; and we were glad when the wind changed direction for us."

"Well, I hope you enjoy your stay in Tallulah Falls," I said.

"If all our neighbors are as appealing as you, Mr. O'Ruff, and the MacKenzies, I'm sure we shall," said Claude. He stood and held out a hand to his wife. "We must go. We don't want to keep you from your work any longer. I do hope we see each other again anon."

I rose and walked them to the door because it seemed the polite thing to do. Angus followed at my side.

"Thank you for dropping by," I said. "If you need my help with anything, please let me know."

"Likewise." Claude tipped his hat, Priscilla wished me a grand day, and they strolled up the sidewalk in the direction of their shop.

I pushed the door up and shook my head.

I looked over at Jill and could've sworn I heard her whisper, "It's better to be absolutely ridiculous than absolutely boring."

I went behind the counter to get the tote that held my current project, a bouquet of large pink and white ribbon roses, complete with stems and leaves. It was a stunning pattern. I hoped to finish two before the open house next week — one to frame and display, and one to give away as a door prize.

Angus lay down nearby. As I worked, he began to snore softly.

The old song "You Don't Have to Be a Star," made popular by Marilyn McCoo and Billy Davis, Jr., began to play from my phone. Mom had been working on a film set during the age of disco, and I'd changed her ringtone accordingly.

"Hey there, Mom. Were your ears burning?"

"No. Why? Were you telling someone how badly you want me to be there for your open house?"

"Not exactly. I mean, I'd love it if you could be here, but that's not why your name came up." I relayed to her the visit of Claude and Priscilla Atwood. "Have you ever heard of them?"

"Their names aren't familiar. What television programs did they work on?"

29

"I didn't ask, and they didn't say. I got the impression they were dying to meet you so that you might pull some strings and get them into the movie business."

"I don't mind helping people when I can, but I'd never blindly give out anyone's contact information or pass along any recommendations for someone whose work I hadn't seen firsthand."

"I know, Mom. Maybe it's a good thing that you won't be able to make the open house. You won't have to worry about sidestepping the eccentric Atwoods."

"But that's why I'm calling," she said. "The movie wrapped earlier than expected — there's a first — so I'll be able to make it to your party after all."

"That's wonderful! When will you be here?"

"Not until next Tuesday . . . unless you need me before then."

"Tuesday will be great."

"And don't worry about . . . what were their names again?"

"Claude and Priscilla Atwood," I supplied.

"I'll handle them tactfully," she said. "A haunted house, huh? This should be an interesting visit."

Angus got up, went to the door, and looked back over his shoulder at me.

"Mom, I've got to run. Well, actually, I have to take Angus up the street. Talk with you soon."

"Okay. Give him a hug for me . . . well, you know . . . *after.* I love you."

I told her I loved her too before quickly ending the call and grabbing Angus's leash. I turned the cardboard clock around to let people know I'd be back in ten minutes, clipped the leash onto Angus's collar, and led him — though observers might've said he led me — up the street toward the town square. As I passed by Nellie Davis's aromatherapy shop, Scentsibilities, Nellie was standing at the window. As I passed, she quickly ducked out of sight. I wondered what on earth that was about but didn't have the time, energy, or inclination to give it more than a passing thought.

Angus went to the tall black wrought-iron clock that stood in the center of the square. He sniffed at the base and then peed. Afterward, he nosed around a little more, paying particular attention to one deserted bench where he peed a bit more, and then he trotted to me. Our stroll back to the Stitch was more leisurely.

As we reached the shop, Todd Calloway jogged across the street.

"Hi," he said. He scratched Angus's head

with both hands. "Hey, buddy. How're you doing? Huh?"

Todd had wavy — not quite curly — brown hair and eyes the color of milk chocolate. When I'd first arrived in Tallulah Falls, Sadie had been determined that he and I would be perfect for each other. As it turned out, we preferred being friends.

"Come on in," I said. "Want a bottle of water or anything?"

"Nah, I'm good." He followed us inside, sat on one of the club chairs and stretched his long legs out on either side of the otto-man. "What do you think of this haunted house?"

I glanced at the door to make sure no one was coming. "Have you met the Atwoods yet?"

"No. Are they the people behind the Horror Emporium?"

"Yeah. They're pretty eccentric. They say things like *gentlewomen* and *alas.*" Angus had gone into the office, and I heard his water bowl banging against the wall. "Let me refill his water dish, and I'll be right back."

"Alas and yon, prithee hurry."

I raised a brow. "Alas and yon?"

"Yep, and I can prithee with the best of them, gentlewoman."

I giggled. "Whatever you say, Todd."

When I came back, Todd had his eyes closed and his head resting on the back of the chair. I eased closer and shouted, "Boo!"

He opened his eyes. "Really?"

"Eh, it was worth a shot." I smiled, sat on the sofa, and picked up the ribbon embroidery project I'd left on the table.

"Tell me about these eccentric haunted house people."

I shrugged slightly. "It's like they're from a different era or something. For some reason, they reminded me of circus folk . . . from the eighteen hundreds."

"Been to a lot of eighteen hundred–era circuses?" He grinned. "I've got to meet these people."

"I imagine you will sooner than later. I got the impression that they're making the rounds and trying to meet everyone," I said. "I suppose they're hoping to drum up business. And, I have to admit, after meeting them, I'm curious about what kind of show they'll put on in their Horror Emporium." I pulled the needle through the cloth and back through the green ribbon stitch I'd just made to form a leaf. "When you first came in, you asked what I thought about having a haunted house next door. Frankly, I'm afraid it will disrupt my classes this month."

"I'm thinking along those same lines," said Todd. "Will people shy away from the Brew Crew because they're put off by the haunted house's screaming fans? I guess we'll have to wait and see."

"Either way, it's only a month." I smiled. "If nothing else, maybe it'll give Nellie Davis something else to occupy her mind besides me for a change." I told him about her standing at the window and then ducking out of sight as Angus and I passed.

"That's weird . . . even for her," he said.

"I know. I wonder if she's met Mr. and Mrs. Atwood."

Angus brought a tennis ball to Todd and dropped it at his feet. Todd picked the ball up and tossed it to the other side of the room. Angus scampered after it.

"What's it worth to you for me to find out what's up with Nellie?" Todd asked.

"How about peanut butter fudge brownies?"

He clutched his chest. "You'll make me brownies? Just to find out what's going on with Nellie?"

"No, but I'll buy them for you from MacKenzies' Mochas."

"Deal." He stood. "Be back in a few."

When Todd came back, he was grinning and shaking his head. "Are you ready for this?" He dropped onto the club chair.

"I don't know. Am I?"

"I doubt it. Nellie Davis thinks the Atwoods are vampires."

My jaw dropped. "Vampires?" Then I scoffed. "If they're vampires, then how are they walking around in the daylight?"

Todd slapped his forehead and addressed Angus, who'd come to sit beside him. "*Then how are they walking in daylight?* she asks. Not, *Isn't that ridiculous because there are no such things as vampires?* Have a talk with her, will ya?"

Angus woofed.

"Fine," I said. "There are no such things as vampires . . . more than likely. But if there *were,* then how would they walk around in the daylight?"

"It depends upon whose mythology you embrace," said Todd. "These days werewolves and vampires can do pretty much anything they want."

"That's true."

"And what's with the *more than likely* crap?" he asked.

"I don't know. Too much *Supernatural*? I love Sam and Dean. They teach you not to discount anything."

"Angus, help me out here, would you, buddy?"

Again, Angus barked, excited to be made an integral part of the conversation.

"Remember whose bed you share," I said to Angus.

"She has a point there, buddy. That's a lesson all men must learn quickly."

Angus let out a low rumble.

"I hear ya," said Todd, nodding as if Angus had uttered a clever bit of banter. "And I agree a hundred percent."

"Will you two stop talking about me and tell me what Nellie Davis said about the Atwoods?" I asked.

Our conversation was delayed by a customer who came in and wanted to debate the benefits of linen over Aida cloth. I explained that it was really just a matter of preference, that I had both, and that the one I chose depended on the project I had in mind. The woman ended up choosing Aida cloth, and I noticed her eyes lingering on Todd as she paid. He never looked in her direction, so she left after I'd told her about the upcoming open house.

I went back to the sit-and-stitch square

and sat on the ottoman in front of Todd. "Now spill."

"How are the preparations for the open house coming?" he asked.

I plucked a candlewick pillow from the sofa beside me and tossed it at Todd's head. Todd laughed, caught the pillow, and Angus ran to get his tennis ball.

Todd lobbed the pillow back at me. "Where should I begin?"

"You left the Stitch and walked up the street," I prompted.

"That's right." He grinned. "So I went into Nellie's shop and I told her I was looking for something for Audrey."

Todd was dating Deputy Audrey Dayton of the Tallulah Falls Police Department.

"Nellie said she was glad I'd stopped dating you and was seeing someone else," he said.

I pursed my lips and narrowed my eyes.

He held up his hands in surrender. "Hey, her words, not mine! I thought you wanted the full 4-1-1."

"Yes, please. Leave nothing out, no matter how insulting it might be to me."

"After the dating dig, she asked what she could help me find. I said I'd just look around. And then I asked her what she thought about a haunted house moving next door."

Angus pawed at Todd's knee, urging him to throw the tennis ball. Todd complied with Angus's wishes before continuing his story.

"She said she wasn't happy about it," he said. "And then she asked me if I'd met the Atwoods. I told them I hadn't but that you met them this morning. She wanted to know what you thought about them, and I said that you found them eccentric. 'Eccentric, my eye,' she said. 'I believe they're vampires!' Oh, and you owe me brownies."

CHAPTER THREE

I'd just sold a customer a set of Japanese embroidery needles and invited her to the open house when Sadie walked into the shop. Sadie held the door as the woman left.

"How's it going?" Sadie asked, as she dropped a kiss on Angus's head before taking a seat in the sit-and-stitch square. She was dressed in a blue polo and jeans, and she still wore her brown apron with the tan MACKENZIES' MOCHAS logo. Her long, dark hair had been swept up into a messy bun; and when she sat, her brown eyes immediately closed.

"You look exhausted," I said.

"I am. I didn't sleep well last night, and the shop has been a madhouse all day."

"Would you like some water?"

"Please." She still hadn't opened her eyes.

I stepped into the office and got us each a bottle of water. I heard Sadie squeal, and I hurried back into the main part of the shop.

Angus had placed his front paws on Sadie's lap and was licking her face.

"Angus! Come here." I got his favorite toy at the shop — a Kodiak bear Vera had given him. "Here, Angus. Get your bear." I tossed the bear toward the window.

Angus loped over to the bear, picked it up, and lay down by the window.

"Sorry about that." I handed Sadie her water.

She giggled. "No problem. Every girl wants to be awakened with a kiss from a handsome prince, right?"

"I'm not sure those fantasies include doggie breath . . . but okay."

"I hear you've met the Atwoods."

"Who told you?" I asked. "Todd? How many brownies did he have you bill me for?"

"No, it wasn't Todd. It was the Atwoods. They think you're magnificent."

"How nice. Um . . . how did you and Blake get involved with providing concessions for the haunted house?"

"After they leased the building, Claude and Priscilla approached us and made us a great offer. We get to keep eighty percent of the proceeds of what we sell there, and it should be really good advertising for our business."

"You aren't having trouble with MacKenzies' Mochas, are you?"

"Oh, no," she said. "This deal simply seemed to be a win-win, and it's only for a month."

"That's true. It's just that you look so tired right now that I'm concerned about you doing even more work," I said. "Is there anything I can do to help out?"

"With the open house coming up, I'd say you have plenty to keep you busy. In fact, I came by to talk about food for your party. But, first, tell me what you thought about the Atwoods."

"They're eccentric," I said. "But I seriously doubt that they're vampires."

Sadie frowned. "What?"

"Nellie Davis thinks the Atwoods are vampires. At least, that's what she told Todd," I said. "I saw her acting weird — more so than usual — and he offered to investigate for peanut butter fudge brownies."

"If they were vampires, they couldn't be walking around in the sunlight . . . could they?"

I threw up my hands. "That's the very question I asked Todd."

"And what did he say?"

"He said it depends on whose mythology — literary mythology, I believe he meant —

that you embrace."

"And Nellie apparently subscribes to whatever mythology allows the Atwoods to be vampires and walk the streets of Tallulah Falls in broad daylight."

"I guess."

Sadie shook her head. "I agree that Claude and Priscilla are a bit strange in the way they dress and talk, but I'm guessing that's just all part of their act."

"Do they ever drop the act?" I asked.

"They haven't around me. Not yet anyway."

"What do you know about them?"

"Only that they like to travel, have done a number of odd jobs, and that they're leasing the building beside yours to operate the Horror Emporium through Halloween," said Sadie.

"Vera seems to think the haunted house will do really well. She said the Atwoods are planning costume contests and things like that periodically to keep the attraction fresh and new."

"They are." She smiled. "They might even ask you to participate in some way . . . you know, judge a contest or something."

"Really? That'd be fun."

"But enough about the Horror Emporium. Let's talk about your open house.

What would you like to serve?"

"Nothing too messy," I said. "Some cook-ies . . . a cheese platter . . . maybe some veggies and dip. What do you think?"

"Sounds good to me. And instead of punch this time, let's do coffee — regular and decaf — and peach tea."

"Super. Are you sure you and Blake can fit it in without too much inconvenience?"

"I'm positive," she said. "I think doing the concessions for the Horror Emporium will be fun. All the foods are easy to make, and one waitress will man the stand each eve-ning."

"I hope it goes great. I simply worry about you spreading yourself too thin."

She tilted her head. "Um . . . I thought I was *your* mother hen."

"Works both ways," I said. "Oh, by the way, Mom is going to be here for the open house."

"Fantastic! I know the Atwoods will adore her."

I smiled. "Doesn't everybody?"

After Sadie left, I got back to work on my ribbon embroidery project as Angus snored by the window. I should have known the peaceful afternoon couldn't last.

From the corner of my eye, I spotted Nellie Davis — puffy white hair sticking straight up in the breeze — walking down the street toward MacKenzies' Mochas. A few minutes later, she and her latte burst through my front door. The movement was so abrupt that Angus sat up and began barking. I set aside my project and hurried to put my arms around him.

"Everything's all right, Angus. Hi, Nellie. How are you?"

"I'm worried, that's how I am. And you should be too."

"About the Atwoods, you mean?"

"Yes, about the Atwoods." Nellie wore her typical all-black ensemble, offset by the paleness of her skin, the white hair, and her signature red-framed eyeglasses. "I've thought all along that you were cursed, but I didn't think you'd brought it on yourself. Those two are just asking for it."

"Would you like to sit down, Nellie?"

"No, I don't have time." She looked over her shoulder. "Mark my words — those people are inviting evil right into our midst! Have you seen the dreadful things they've been carting into that building?"

I shook my head. "What sort of dreadful things?"

"Skulls, mechanical witches . . . coffins." She took a dramatic pause. "Or maybe

44

those are their beds."

"You never know," I said.

Nellie peered at me. "I think I *do* know. It's like they're from another time . . . maybe even another world."

I decided to go ahead and throw out the *v*-word. "But if they were vampires, how could they walk around in daylight?"

"Not being able to walk in daylight is a myth they've perpetuated to trick us," said Nellie. "I looked up vampires on the Internet. What Hollywood tells us is a lie. Real vampires call themselves a *subculture*. I call them trouble."

"And you think the Atwoods are vampires because they brought coffins in for their haunted house?" I asked.

"That's only part of it. And they aren't calling it a *haunted house* or a *funhouse*. They're calling it a Horror Emporium." She shuddered. "Who knows what sort of horrors they have planned for the poor dumb souls who are willing to go in there? I won't be going — you can bet on that. Not of my own free will anyway." She raised a bony index finger. "But don't tell them that. I don't want to wind up cursed. So . . . that's all I came to say. You've been warned." With those comforting parting words, she left.

I was still hugging Angus, and I looked at

him. "Jinkies, Scoob. Is this Nellie's latest tactic to run us meddling kids out of Tallulah Falls? Or does she really believe the Atwoods are some sort of evildoers?"

He licked my nose.

"Jinkies," I told him again because I liked the sound of the nonsensical word. "And zoinks." I giggled, kissed his head, and went back to the sit-and-stitch square.

Angus stretched back out by the window.

As I resumed work on my project, my mind wandered . . . to vampires, of course. The handsome ones I'd seen on TV . . . then Nosferatu . . . then the Atwoods. . . . I imagined the Atwoods sashaying into the shop in their odd but dapper costumes.

"Miss Marcy," said Claude.

"*Magnificent* Marcy," Priscilla said, a purr in her voice. "We want you to join us."

"Yes, Marcy. Become a creature of the night." Claude extended his arms. "Be forever young, forever beautiful!"

"But all I can have to eat is blood, right? No chocolate?"

"We could mix a bit of chocolate syrup in with your O negative, I suppose," said Priscilla.

"That sounds disgusting." I wrinkled my nose.

"It is," Claude assured me. "I tried it

once. Terrible combo. Blood and Tabasco sauce isn't bad though."

"Ewww." The very idea made me queasy.

The bells over the shop door jangled, and I snapped out of my reverie to see Claude and Priscilla Atwood coming into the shop. I *had* snapped out of my reverie . . . hadn't I?

"Good afternoon," Claude said, tipping his top hat. "We've come to ask you to join us —"

My eyes widened.

"— for a sneak preview of the Horror Emporium!"

"We had this wonderful idea for a party while we were introducing ourselves to everyone. We're inviting all the neighbors," Priscilla said. "It's more or less a grand opening party."

"Even though we won't be opening to the public until this weekend," said Claude.

I found my voice at last. "That sounds wonderful. So when is the party?"

"Tomorrow evening." Claude frowned slightly. "Short notice, we know. Sadie informed us that you have classes every Tuesday, Wednesday, and Thursday, so we're starting the party at five just for you."

"I'm flattered, but you don't have to do that."

"Of course, we do," Priscilla said. "We realize you won't be able to stay for long, but at least you can get some idea of what we have in store for you and the other denizens of Tallulah Falls beginning on Friday night."

"Thank you," I said. "That sounds fantastic. I'm looking forward it. May I bring my boyfriend, Ted?"

"We'd be disappointed if you didn't." Claude winked. "We look forward to meeting the man who holds Marcy's heart, don't we, my sweet?"

"Indeed we do." Priscilla smiled. "See you at five tomorrow."

They left, and Angus came over to me and put his head on my knee. I stroked his head. Claude and Priscilla Atwood were a strange pair — that was for sure. I didn't think for an instant that they were modern-day vampires, but there was something odd about them. That, or else Nellie had forgotten to take her paranoia with her when she'd left the shop earlier.

Ted called as I was dusting the shelves before closing up shop for the day.

"Hey, babe," he said. "What do you want to do for dinner tonight?"

"Given the day I've had, I'd love a quiet evening at home."

"Are you hungry?" he asked.

"Not starving. You?"

"I can wait. Why don't I come and get you and Angus, and we'll go for a walk on the beach before we call it a day?"

"You always know how to help me relax."

When Ted got to the Seven-Year Stitch, he'd changed from his suit into a pair of khaki shorts and a white T-shirt. He patted his chest, and Angus jumped up and planted his front paws on Ted's shoulders for a hug.

"Hey, Angus. Have you had a good day?"

"We've had a very interesting day," I said.

"Tell me about it on the way."

"Would you mind driving?"

"Not at all," he said.

I locked up the Stitch, tossed my keys to Ted, and we all piled into the Jeep. I was glad the Atwoods weren't around when we left because I wanted to warn Ted about them before I introduced them to him.

On the way to the beach, I rested my head against the passenger seat and relayed the day, from lunch on, to Ted. So by the time we got there, he knew all about the Atwoods and their invitation to their grand opening party; he knew that Todd was willing to work for brownies; he knew that Nellie Davis believed the Atwoods to be vampires who were going to bring some sort of evil down upon Tallulah Falls; and he knew that Mom was coming for the Seven-Year Stitch anniversary.

"You're being awfully quiet," I said after I'd finished.

"I'm trying to let all that sink in." He squeezed my hand. "And here I thought we were about to have a dull moment in good old Tallulah Falls."

"Not on your life, sweetheart."

"Please don't say that. Don't you realize the Atwoods are devising some evil plot even as we speak?"

I laughed. "Oops. I forgot."

Ted pulled into a parking spot, and we got out of the car. He got Angus's leash, and we walked down to the beach. Angus was pulling at his leash, and Ted unsnapped it and let the dog run. Then he took my hand and we strolled along at a leisurely pace.

"It's so beautiful today," I said.

"Yeah . . . unseasonably warm . . . no rain. I wish it would last."

"Me too."

Ted raised my hand to his lips and kissed it. "Look at the ocean. Was today really that bad?"

I smiled. "No, actually, it was pretty wonderful. I had lunch with a handsome guy, met with Sadie about the refreshments for the open house, got to meet the new neighbors, and learned that Mom is coming for our anniversary party. I'm a very lucky woman."

"And I'm a very lucky man." He let go of my hand. "Climb on." He turned his back and I hopped on for a piggyback ride.

We laughed as Ted ran down the beach toward Angus. He spotted us and came to run with us. We had such fun.

In little more than twenty-four hours, I'd be berating myself for ever thinking this day was the slightest bit stressful. I'd remember what a truly stressful day felt like.

CHAPTER FOUR

I headed to work the next morning cheerful and looking forward to the Atwoods' sneak preview. I unlocked the door, turned on the lights, unleashed Angus, and then went back to MacKenzies' Mochas for the brownies I owed Todd. As I started back up the street, I could see Angus lying in the window chewing on his Kodiak bear, so I slipped over to the other side of the street and ducked into the Brew Crew.

Todd's day manager, a beefy young man with a beatific smile, was behind the bar putting away new stock.

"Morning, Will," I said.

"Hey, Marcy. What can I do for you?"

I placed the bakery box on the bar. "I'm here to make good on a debt I owe Todd. Peanut butter fudge brownies. Make sure he gives you one."

"I'll do it," he said. "Are you going to the Atwoods' party this evening?"

"I am. I can't stay long — I have a class — but I'm looking forward to seeing what they have in store for us."

"Me too. Pam's not going, though. Everything still makes her sick." Will's wife was pregnant.

I smiled. "Give her my best."

"I will. See you later."

I hurried across the street, and Angus met me at the door and began sniffing my pant legs.

"Yes, I've been to MacKenzies' Mochas and the Brew Crew," I said. "I'll make it up to you." I went into the office where I keep a stash of dog treats in my desk. I took out a granola bone. I started to take it back into the shop, but when I turned around, Angus was right there waiting for it. I handed it to him. He took it, turned, and scampered back to the window where everyone passing by could see that he had a treat.

Before the shop got busy, I called Reggie at the library.

"I won't keep you but a second," I said. "I just wanted to invite you and Manu to go with Ted and me to the Atwoods' sneak peek of the Horror Emporium tonight. I thought you — well, all of us — could get a better idea of what they're doing, and you can explain the differences between their exhibition and yours to your patrons."

"I don't know," Reggie said. "If they're having some sort of special showing, I don't want to be a party-crasher."

I saw the postal carrier approaching with a box.

"If I get their okay, would you and Manu go with Ted and me this evening? We don't have to stay long."

Angus rose and sounded the alarm.

I covered the mouthpiece of the phone. "Shhh. It's all right."

"I hate to be intrusive."

"You aren't being intrusive," I said. "If anyone is, I am. And trust me — with the Atwoods, I don't think there's any such thing as a party-crasher. I'll call you back as soon as I talk with them."

I ended the call and held open the door for the postman while Angus continued barking and stomping his feet, overcome with excitement. Sometimes my mom sent care packages from San Francisco that always included something for him. I knew that with Mom coming to visit us next week, the box wasn't from her.

The postman put the box on the floor and then turned and spoke to Angus. "Hey, pal! Whatcha doing? Huh? Think there's something in one of these boxes for you?" He took a small dog biscuit from his pocket and tossed it to Angus. "There's a little something."

"Thank you, Mel," I said. "Have a good day."

"You too!" He left as Angus noisily crunched the biscuit.

I opened one box, and Angus hurried to peer inside. It was skeins of embroidery floss. He snorted with disgust and went back to lie by the window. The other box contained key rings with the Seven-Year Stitch logo. I planned to put them in the open house goodie bags. I took the box of floss into the storeroom and began sorting the floss into the proper bins.

The bells over the door alerted me that someone had entered the shop. I went to greet them and found Christine, one of my regular customers there. She was stooped down, hugging Angus around the neck. Christine is rail thin, and I hoped Angus didn't tip her over.

"Hey, there, Christine. How've you been?"

"I've been great. What about you?"

She had face-framing light gray hair and bright eyes, and she seemed to radiate kindness. I was always happy to see Christine walk through the door.

"I'm good. I'm excited about the open

house next week. Even my mom is coming. I don't think you two have met yet," I said.

"I'll look forward to meeting her." She smiled, straightened, and brushed off her jeans. "I dropped in because, frankly, I'm nervous about this hardanger class. I've never done it before."

"You'll do fine," I assured her. "It looks harder than it actually is."

"If I have any trouble, will you work with me during the days?"

"Of course, I will." I put an arm around her. "It isn't like you to be nervous about a class. What else is going on?"

Her smile faded, and she sighed. "You know my son Jared has been dating that waitress from MacKenzies' Mochas?"

I nodded. "Keira."

"Right. Well, she sure had me fooled. I thought she was the sweetest thing! But it turns out, she has a mean streak half a mile wide."

"Oh, no. What happened?"

We walked over to the sofa that faced away from the window. Angus came and sat beside his friend.

"After Jared's first marriage was such a disaster, I was truly hoping he could find somebody sweet and wonderful and who would love him as much as he'd love her,"

56

said Christine. "But it seems he keeps making bad choices. This Keira was as nice as pie at first. Then she started making all these demands — on his time and then on his money. And if he couldn't afford to buy her something she wanted, she'd pout for days. Plus, he wasn't supposed to question anything *she* did, but he had to report in where he was and who he was with."

"I'm sorry." I'd known Keira was a nasty piece of work when Jared had taken an interest in her. I'd started to say something, but I'd felt that it wasn't my place. I'd thought that maybe Keira was so hateful to me because she simply didn't like me. Back when Sadie had been trying to fix me up with Todd, Keira had her eye on him. She saw me as a threat and had despised me. "So have they broken up?"

"He's been trying to break things off with her for weeks," she said. "But Keira keeps calling and pleading with him to take her back. 'And, oh, by the way, my rent is due and I'm short this month.' It makes me furious."

"Surely, Jared can see that she's using him."

"Of course he can. But he's so bighearted that he feels sorry for her." Christine gave Angus another hug. "He tells me that he'll help her out *just this one last time,* and then he'll be rid of her for good. And he is . . . until she calls again." She looked at the dog. "You're excellent therapy, you know that?"

"Isn't he, though? He's probably saved me a fortune in counseling." I laughed.

"You're good therapy too. It's nice to have someone you can trust to share your feelings with."

"And to try to come up with eligible ladies Jared might take an interest in," I said.

"That too," she said with a giggle.

Angus stood and went to the door.

"Uh-oh. Somebody needs to walk up the street. Christine, we'll be right back." I went to the counter and grabbed Angus's leash.

"I have to run, sweetie. I'll talk with you later. Thanks for the shoulder."

"Anytime," I said. "Here." I handed her one of the key rings from the box on the counter. "You're the first to own an original Seven-Year Stitch key ring."

She smiled as she looked at the key ring. "This is adorable. Thank you!"

"You're quite welcome." I snapped the leash onto Angus's collar, and we went up the street toward the town square. Christine headed toward MacKenzies' Mochas. I wondered if she planned to give Keira a piece of her mind.

I took Angus up to the town square. Dark clouds were gathering overhead, and I was glad he made this a quick trip.

When we walked past the Horror Emporium, I poked my head inside the door. "Claude! Priscilla! It's Marcy Singer."

"Good day, Marcy," Priscilla said, coming from behind a curtain that divided the shop in half. Her tangerine hair was piled on top of her head, and she wore a black carpenter's apron over her slacks and frilly blouse. She wagged her finger at me. "No peeking yet!"

"I didn't intend to . . . honest. I just have a question for you and Claude. Would you mind if I bring Rajani Singh — Reggie — and her husband, Manu, to the party this evening?"

"I would be delighted to have them accompany you."

"As it happens, Reggie is our librarian," I said. "The library puts on a haunted house each year for the children — nothing that could possibly compare with Haunted Emporium, I'm sure. It's an annual fundraiser. I wanted Reggie to be reassured that the Haunted Emporium won't be for the faint of heart."

"Not even for the tremulous of heart. We pride ourselves on catering to brave —

somewhat foolhardy — adults." Priscilla laughed. "Our wicked exhibits are not for the eyes of innocent children. We turn away anyone under fourteen years of age. But we'll happily post a flyer for the library's event for our patrons who have small children."

"How nice of you! Thank you. I'll certainly pass along your generous offer to Reggie."

"I'd love to chat longer, Marcy, but I must get back to tonight's preparations," Priscilla said.

When Angus and I walked back into the shop, Sadie had taken Christine's spot on the sofa. Before I could greet her, she began talking.

"I'm beginning to regret signing on to do the Horror Emporium's concessions. It seemed like such fun, you know? It wasn't going to be that much work. One waitress each evening would get to leave the hassle of her regular shift to work the stand. It would be great, right?"

"I'm thinking . . . not . . . right?"

"Right! I mean, yes. Correct." She growled, and Angus gave her a wide berth as he went to the office to get a drink of water. "The Atwoods called yesterday and informed me that they'd decided to have an impromptu party this evening. Naturally, they need food for that. Plus, one of our waitresses called in sick this morning, so the rest of the staff is swamped. I've asked Keira to oversee the Atwoods' party, and you'd think I'd asked her to volunteer for a root canal."

"I'm sorry. It appears that Keira has put herself at the top of everybody's hit list for the day."

"What do you mean?" she asked.

I told her about Christine's visit and Jared's drama with Keira.

She rolled her eyes. "That sweet boy should've known a shark like Keira would eat him alive. I mean, she's a decent waitress, but she's manipulative, narcissistic, and selfish."

"I told Christine I'd try to help her come up with eligible bachelorettes for Jared."

She smiled slightly. "I'll help. As a matter of fact, you think he might be interested in running the concession stand at the Horror Emporium? He might meet some girls working there."

"Hey, that's not a bad idea."

"I'm kidding . . . kind of." She groaned. "I'm going to slip out the back. It'd would be just my luck to run into the Atwoods on the street and have them ask me to cater the renewal of their wedding vows tomorrow morning or something just as outrageous."

"Okay." I smiled. "I'm here if you need me later."

"Thanks." She hurried through the shop and out the back door of the building.

After Sadie left, I got out my phone and called Reggie. She didn't answer, so I left her a voice message letting her know that the Atwoods would be delighted to have her and Manu join Ted and me at the sneak peek and that they would even post a flyer for the library's haunted house.

A young woman came in. Angus pegged her for a dog lover right away and bounded over to welcome her.

"Oh, my goodness! What a huge dog!" She laughed and petted his head.

"Welcome to the Seven-Year Stitch," I said. "I'm Marcy, and that's Angus, our goodwill ambassador."

"He's gorgeous," she said. "I've never seen a dog this big. Are people ever put off by him?"

"If he makes anyone nervous, I put him in the bathroom," I said. "He's a sweetheart, but some customers do get intimidated by his size. May I help you find anything in particular?"

"I'm actually looking for cross-stitch pattern books. I've only recently discovered embroidery, and I'm eager to do new projects." She smiled. "I think I might've finally found a hobby I can stick with."

"I hope so. What other hobbies have you tried?"

"Well, let's just say baking didn't pan out for me. But I *did* meet an awfully nice fireman."

I laughed. "Every cloud does have its silver lining." I pointed her in the direction of the cross-stitch pattern books and told her about the current classes being taught on Tuesdays, Wednesdays, and Thursdays. "The beginning hardanger class is tonight, and although it has been going on for a couple of weeks, I'd be happy to help you get caught up."

"I appreciate that, but for now I'll stick with cross-stitch."

As she perused the books, I went over to the counter to let her browse in peace. I saw Todd jogging across the street. I figured he was going to MacKenzies' Mochas, and I waved at him. Instead of turning in the direction of the coffee shop, though, he came on into the Stitch.

The young woman looked up when the bells over the door jingled, and Todd winked at her. Her cheeks pinkened.

He was an incorrigible flirt. I wondered if Audrey knew and how she felt about that. Not that it was any of my business. Todd was Todd, and he needed a woman who would accept him the way he was.

"Hey, there," I said. "How are you this morning?"

"Probably five pounds heavier, thanks to you," he said. "I'd have said six if you hadn't told Will to make me share. Thanks for the brownies."

"I owed you."

"Indeed you did." He double tapped the counter, so Angus would jump up and put his paws on it. He then turned and talked with Angus as if they were the only two in the store. "Is she behaving herself today? No? I thought not. But . . . hey . . . whatcha gonna do, right? Play ball, I guess. Where's your ball? Huh? Let's go get it!"

Angus dropped back onto all fours and loped over to the other side of the shop to retrieve his tennis ball. He came back and dropped it at Todd's feet. Todd took the ball into the sit-and-stitch square. He sat on one of the club chairs and rolled the ball toward Angus. Angus leapt on it and took a victory lap with the ball in his mouth.

My customer laughed at their antics and

then paid for the pattern book she'd chosen. I invited her to the Seven-Year Stitch one-year-anniversary open house.

"Would it discourage you from coming if I told you both of those clowns are likely to be here?" I asked.

"Not at all," she said. "I'll look forward to it."

She took the periwinkle bag containing her purchase and went smiling off down the street.

"I should have you and Angus perform the halftime show for the open house," I teased, joining him in the seating area.

"We'll sing, won't we, Angus?" Todd asked. He began to howl, and Angus barked.

"Please! You're giving me a headache!"

"You wound us," Todd said. "So . . . are you going to the Atwoods' shindig this evening?"

"Yeah . . . are you?"

"Wouldn't miss it. I have to say, I owe you an apology. Until I met those two yesterday, I thought you were exaggerating."

I grinned. "And now what? Are you with Nellie — do you think they're vampires?"

"They might be. They're . . . something."

"More than anything, they remind me of Gomez and Morticia Addams from that old show *The Addams Family*," I said. "By the way, I have to warn you. Sadie was here earlier, and she said Kiera will be doing the concessions for the party this evening. Keira isn't happy about it, but —"

"When is Keira ever happy with anything?" he interrupted. "Hey, Audrey has to work tonight. You and I should go to the party together. It would drive Keira nuts."

As he spoke, Ted walked in with lunch. "It would drive me nuts too, Calloway." He came over and dropped a kiss on my lips.

"Howdy, Wyatt Earp," Todd said. "Didn't mean to get caught poaching on your land."

Ted and Todd had a somewhat friendly relationship, which was good albeit a little odd given past circumstances. But that was all water under the bridge . . . pretty much.

Ted arched a brow. "You aren't poaching. You're more than welcome to tag along to the Atwoods' party with Marcy and me. I'll even let you hold my hand if you get scared."

"Thanks, man. I appreciate that." He stood, patted Angus's head, and waved good-bye to Ted and me.

I smiled at Ted before walking over to the counter to get my BE BACK IN _____ clock to put on the door. "You're awfully generous today. You'd just better keep one of those hands free for me. Priscilla made me a little nervous today with her talk of their *wicked exhibits.*"

"I'm intrigued."

"I'm more intrigued with what you have in the bag at the moment." I set the clock hands for thirty minutes from the present time and followed Ted into my office. "What's for lunch?"

"Burgers and fries — compliments of Captain Moe."

CHAPTER FIVE

Ted arrived at five o'clock. I finished tidying up the shop, and then we put Angus in the Jeep and drove him home. Ted gave Angus his dinner as I hurried upstairs to freshen up.

On our way back to the Atwoods' party, I mentioned to Ted that Manu and Reggie were supposed to meet us there.

"At least, I hope they will," I said. "I invited them, and then Reggie didn't want to impose, and then I cleared it with the Atwoods, and then I called Reggie and left her a voice mail telling her the Atwoods were all for it and would even help promote the library's haunted house . . . which I think is really nice of them."

"What're you nervous about?" he asked. "This party?"

"A little. Keira is doing the concessions, and she's never liked me."

Ted shook his head. "I know you better

than that. What is it really?"

"I don't want to disappoint the Atwoods." I blew out a breath. "I mean, they're eccentric, but they seem nice and I want to act really, really frightened and awed by their exhibits. But with Mom being a costume designer, I've grown up seeing some of the best special effects work in the business — along with some pretty lousy effects."

"But you also grew up around actors." He squeezed my hand. "*Act* scared . . . blown away . . . awed by the entire spectacle." He raised my arm, kissed my hand, and then went up my arm as far as our seat belts would allow while I giggled helplessly. "Let's make it an evening to remember, *cara mia.*"

Yes, of course, I'd told him that the Atwoods reminded me of Gomez and Morticia.

Manu and Reggie were standing on the sidewalk near the Seven-Year Stitch when we arrived. It had started to drizzle, and Reggie held an umbrella over her head. She looked as glum as the weather. Manu, on the other hand, seemed ready to enjoy the show. Unlike his wife, Manu preferred Western clothing. This evening, he wore jeans, a plaid shirt with a brown leather vest, and a brown cowboy hat. Reggie wore a turquoise smock, with white Indian embroidery called *chikankari,* and matching pants.

We got out of the Jeep, and I hurried over to Reggie. I hadn't bothered with an umbrella. I guessed my short platinum hair would go in every direction regardless. The Oregon weather was one of the reasons I hadn't let it grow out into a style that would've been more difficult to manage.

"Did you bring a flyer for the library's haunted house?" I asked.

She nodded. "I have to say, though, I'm still uncomfortable about this whole thing."

"She feels threatened by it," said Manu. "She's afraid it'll be some spectacular thing that will outshine the library's efforts in every way."

"They go from one extreme to another," Ted said, slipping an arm around my waist. "Marcy is afraid she won't be able to act suitably impressed and will insult the Atwoods."

We all laughed.

"Let's just go in with the resolution to have fun," I said. "No matter what."

"No matter what," Reggie agreed.

Todd joined us and asked what we were doing "no matter what."

"Having fun," I said.

"All right." He took Ted's hand. "Shall we?"

"Get that hand away from me, Calloway. God only knows where it's been."

"I've just been picking my nose is all," teased Todd. "Besides, you said I can hold your hand if I get scared."

"If you're scared at this point, you'd better go back to the pub and have a juice box, Junior," said Ted. "Maybe Reggie's kiddie funhouse is more suitable for you."

Todd dropped Ted's hand and looked at me. "I feel slightly insulted."

"Then you'd better suck it up, Buttercup," I said. "Let's go on inside before we all get drenched."

"I must be adorable for you guys to keep calling me nicknames," he said.

"Yeah," Ted said flatly. "We can hardly stand you . . . you know, because you're so cute."

We all walked into the Horror Emporium, which was filled with familiar faces. Claude and Priscilla greeted us with the exuberance and style I'd come to expect.

Priscilla was dressed in an Elvira-Mistress-of-the-Night-type gown with her tangerine hair piled high on her head. She wore long black opera gloves and had a large square emerald ring on her left hand. It fit perfectly atop the glove, so I thought it must be part of the costume.

"Welcome!" Priscilla did a curtsy that I supposed the men appreciated, given the amount of cleavage she was showing.

Claude tipped his top hat and bowed. This evening, he wore a black tux and tails. He took Reggie's hand and kissed it. She slid her eyes in my direction, and I stifled a giggle. He kissed my hand next and told us all ever so gallantly that he was delighted we could attend their soiree.

Ted and Manu were practically gaping at each other. Todd, naturally, went right along with the madness.

"Claude, my good man," he said. "What a delight to see you and the lovely Priscilla again." He even made a show of kissing Priscilla's hand.

"May we offer you some refreshments?" Priscilla asked. "Please come and join the others."

We went over to a long, tall table where Vera, Paul, Blake, and a couple of other shop owners stood. As we made small talk, Keira sullenly dumped popcorn kernels into a popping machine.

"Hi, Keira," Todd said. "I haven't had a chance to talk with you at MacKenzies'

Mochas lately. How've you been?"

"Lovely. Absolutely lovely." Her monotone and lack of smile belied her words.

"Glad to hear it." Todd spotted Will and walked away to chat with him and Paul.

"What's with Keira?" Ted asked me quietly, as we took our plates of food to the side to eat. "I know she's generally not the most chipper person on the planet, but she's usually able to muster a fake smile."

"Sadie said Keira really didn't want to be here," I whispered. "One of the waitresses called in sick this morning, and Sadie was having a rough day earlier. She was even put out with the Atwoods for springing this on her at the last minute. I'm surprised Blake is here."

"He'd about have to be here to help kick off the Horror Emporium and make sure it all runs smoothly, especially given Keira's attitude." Ted dabbed at his mouth with his napkin, and then spoke at a normal volume. "These sandwiches are really good."

"They are," I said. "And the seasoned pita chips are wonderful."

Claude rang a tiny bell. "May I please have everyone's attention? As soon as you finish eating, please make your way into" — dramatic pause — "the Lair of the Serpent." He turned with the precision of a military marcher, presented his arm to Priscilla, and together they went behind the curtained portion of the Horror Emporium.

Vera sat her nearly empty plate down on the counter. "Well? What are we waiting for?"

Paul smiled. "After you, my dear."

Blake followed Paul inside.

Reggie, Manu, Ted, and I looked at one another. None of us wanted to be the first of our crowd to go in. Of course, Vera had already blazed the trail, but the rest of us were hesitant.

Todd grabbed my hand. "Come along, Marcy Lou!"

"Marcy Lou?" I asked.

"Yeah, well, I had all these nicknames so . . ." He nodded at Ted. "You, too, Teddy Bear."

"I'm going to kill you before this night is through," Ted said.

I put on my game face, ready to seem terrified, and stepped with Todd behind the heavy draperies. I found myself in a shadowy room. I could barely see Todd's silhouette in front of me.

I could hear a rattlesnake. I imagined the sinister sound came from a speaker. Then a spotlight flashed on, and I saw an actual, live Western rattlesnake. It was slithering over a branch. I shivered slightly, hoping that the snake was enclosed somehow. Although it certainly didn't appear to be, I knew the venomous snake couldn't be allowed to leave the exhibit. I'd have to ask the Atwoods how they'd managed the effect.

Other spotlights dimmed and brightened, illuminating other snakes in the "lair." Claude's voice came over an intercom, and it sounded surprisingly like that of Vincent Price.

"Good evening, and welcome to the Lair of the Serpent," he said. "It's only one room in our Horror Emporium, so don't get *too* comfortable here. Follow the yellow arrows on the walls in front of you to escape the serpent and to see what awaits you as you move along our maze."

We walked along as indicated by the yellow tape. Suddenly, a huge mechanical serpent with yellow eyes sprang out at us and hissed.

I squealed and jumped back. Ted laughed and caught me.

"Oh, come on," I said. "You weren't surprised by that?"

"Sure," he said. "But Manu and I are officers of the law. We're trained to handle surprises."

"Tell that to my stomach," said Manu. "It just jumped into my throat."

We went on through the maze of horror exhibits, and I had to admit, the Atwoods did an impressive job. There were actors in costume popping out at us with prop weapons, and there were various mechanical beasties as well as dummies and other aspects of staged scenes. I knew the younger adults — and some of the older ones, judging by Vera's screams and peals of laughter — would adore the Horror Emporium.

There was a point at the latter part of the journey through the maze where a door opened, a scaly witch flew out toward us on a broom, and a camera snapped a photo of our frightened faces. Claude and Priscilla presented us each with a copy of the photo, and I swore I would treasure it forever. They wouldn't allow us to pay for the photos, even though they planned to charge regular customers for them. I thought I should at least leave a sizable tip.

The Horror Emporium's exit was at the back of the building. To return to the concessions, one had to go back to the front of the shop and reenter. Rather than go through the back door to the Stitch, I told Ted I wanted to go back around the front and express my appreciation to the Atwoods personally.

"I'd even like to leave them a tip or something. These photos are priceless," I said.

"I agree. The look on Manu's face alone is worth a mint." He laughed.

"I'd like to speak with Mr. and Mrs. Atwood as well," said Reggie. "I forgot to give them the flyer they so graciously offered to display."

"I've got to get to work," said Todd. "Marcy, would you mind letting me go through the Stitch so I won't have to go all the way around the buildings to get back to the street?"

"Sure," I said. I stepped over and unlocked the door to the Stitch. "In fact, it would be easier for all of us to simply go through my shop."

We went through the Seven-Year Stitch and stepped out onto the sidewalk. We were still talking about the exhibition as we walked toward the Horror Emporium, when I noticed a woman lying facedown on the sidewalk. Was it another prop? One last *gotcha!*?

"That's Keira," I said.

"Stay back," said Manu.

He and Ted went forward to investigate. Todd, Reggie, and I did not stay back as instructed. We moved forward. Either Keira was suddenly awfully game to play the role of victim for the Atwoods, or else there was something seriously wrong.

Manu rolled Keira onto her back. Her eyes were open, but they were glassy and staring. On her neck were two small puncture wounds.

"Her pulse is really weak," Manu said.

None of us noticed Nellie Davis walking toward us from the opposite direction. At least, we didn't until she shrieked *vampires* and fainted.

Ted was already calling for an ambulance and for some backup. Reggie, Todd, and I hurried to check on poor Nellie, who'd hit the pavement pretty hard when she'd fallen. Thank goodness, she'd fallen to the side and not directly onto her face or she'd have been hurt worse than she appeared to be. Todd gently moved her onto her back. Her red-framed glasses were broken. I hoped she had another pair handy somewhere.

After making his calls, Ted joined us. He took Nellie's pulse and called her name. Her eyes fluttered open.

"Wh-what . . . happened?" she asked.

"You fainted," he said. "I've called for ambulances, and they're on the way. Until the paramedics get here, I want you to lie still. All right?"

"Okay." She held a trembling hand up to her face.

"I have your glasses," I said. "They broke when you fell."

Claude and Priscilla hurried out of the Horror Emporium.

"What on earth is happening?" Claude asked. "We heard some sort of commotion and looked outside, and two people are lying on the sidewalk!"

Manu and Ted exchanged glances.

The rain began to pick up, and Reggie opened her umbrella and held it over Nellie's face. "Are you sure we can't move her inside?" she asked Manu.

"I'd rather not do anything until the EMTs arrive," he said. "She took a rather hard fall. They're only about two minutes out."

"Okay," Reggie said. "I'm sorry, Ms. Davis."

"It's all right," Nellie said. "It's not your fault."

"So Ms. Davis fell? Did she trip or something?" Priscilla asked.

"She fainted," Ted said.

"What happened to our waitress?" Claude asked. "Did she faint as well?" He sniffed the air. "There isn't a gas leak or anything, is there?"

"Was our exhibit *that* frightening?" Priscilla asked lightly.

"Actually, we're not sure what happened to Keira," said Manu. "She was lying here unresponsive when we came outside."

Priscilla gasped. "And here I was making jokes. I'm so sorry. It wasn't my intention to be insensitive."

Manu motioned for Ted and the two conferred quietly. Ted glanced at me before looking back at Manu. A muscle in his jaw worked, and I realized he was gritting his teeth. Uh-oh.

As soon as the ambulance arrived, Ted came over and took me by the elbow. "Your students will be arriving, and we need to get ready for them, don't we?"

"Well . . . under the circumstances, I thought maybe I'd cancel class." I looked down at my soaked clothing.

"Come on." He propelled me into the Seven-Year Stitch.

"What it is?" I asked. "This isn't about my class, is it?"

"No, it isn't. Let's go into your office."

"All right." I slowly led the way into my office. "Please tell me what's going on. You're making me worry."

"There was a key ring found beneath

Keira's body. It had the Seven-Year Stitch logo on it."

I gasped.

Ted closed his eyes. "Where did she get it?"

"I don't know. I had a box of them on the counter earlier, but after Christine left and I got back from walking Angus, I put the box in the storeroom. The key rings are going to be put in the goodie bags for the open house."

He opened his eyes but pinched the bridge of his nose between his index finger and thumb. "You didn't give one to Keira? To Sadie?"

"Christine Willoughby," I said. "I gave one to Christine."

The bells over the door jangled. The students had begun to arrive.

"I'll tell students as they get here that we're canceling tonight's class given what's happened to Keira and to Nellie," I said. "I'm too nervous to concentrate on hardanger tonight."

"You'll have to go into the station along with everyone else and give a statement anyway."

When we walked into the shop, we saw that it wasn't a student who'd come in but Manu.

"Keira's dead," he said. "Her heart stopped, and the paramedics were unable to get it started back."

I gasped, and Ted put his arm around my shoulders and pulled me close.

"Suspected cause of death?" Ted asked.

Manu shook his head. "There'll have to be an autopsy."

"Those marks on her neck," I said. "You don't think that rattlesnake . . . ?"

"No," said Manu. "I'm fairly certain it was secured. That will, however, be one of the topics I discuss with the Atwoods and the other actors to ensure that they knew where the snake was at all times."

Christine walked in. "Hey, what's going on outside?"

Ted, Manu, and I looked at one another and then at Christine.

"Someone collapsed — and later died — outside the Horror Emporium this evening," Manu said. "Another person came upon the scene and fainted."

"Wow. That must be some scary haunted house, huh?"

"Where were you prior to arriving here, Ms. Willoughby?" Ted asked.

Her eyes flew to mine. "Excuse me?"

Ted nodded to Manu, who took a small evidence bag from his pocket.

"The victim was Keira Sherman, the waitress from MacKenzies' Mochas," Ted said.

Christine's hands flew to her mouth. "Keira?"

"Also, this key ring was found beneath her body." Ted held up the Seven-Year Stitch key ring.

Christine went to feeling her pockets. "I have a key ring like that. Marcy gave it to me this morning." Tears filled her eyes as she turned her pocket wrong side out. "There's a hole in my pocket. I must've lost it."

"Ms. Willoughby, I'm going to have to ask you to come with us to the police station to answer a few questions," said Manu.

"But I didn't do anything!" she said.

I felt so helpless. "Everything will be all right. I know you didn't hurt anyone."

"I didn't," she told me. "I swear I didn't."

"I know. Just go with Manu and answer his questions. In fact, we're *all* going. Everything will be fine."

Vera and Paul walked into the shop. Vera's eyes widened, and I could practically see the questions forming in her mind.

So did Ted, apparently, because he gave both her and Paul a stern look that indicated now was not the time or place to try to get a story for tomorrow's paper.

Chapter Six

Everyone who'd been at the Horror Emporium party voluntarily went to the police station to give their recorded statements. We all crowded into the small lobby to wait our turns. Vera and Paul had been fortunate enough to snag a couple of the orange industrial chairs that lined the wall across from the reception desk. At least, I thought they were fortunate until an unkempt, obviously intoxicated man sat beside Vera and placed his hand on her thigh. She gave out a little yelp, leapt to her feet, and hurried a few feet away. Paul glared at the man and then followed Vera.

Since Manu and Ted had gone to separate interrogation rooms while another detective I'd never met manned a third room, I walked over to Blake. He didn't see me approach him and started when I touched his arm.

"Sorry," I said. "How're you holding up?"

He sighed and ran a hand down his face. "I don't know. I'm not trying to give you a short answer . . . I'm just . . . numb? Confused? I'm sad . . . especially for Keira's family. Man, I dread seeing her parents."

"Have you told Sadie?"

He nodded. "I called her on the way here. She was going to give the police time to notify Keira's parents, and then she was going to take some food over." He shook his head. "I should be there with her. What if the parents blame us because we had Keira working at the haunted house tonight?"

"Actually, I think it's best that you not be there to visit the parents yet," I said. "You need time to process everything and to deal with your own emotions first."

He put an arm around me and pulled me against his side in a brotherly hug. "I keep thinking that if I'd stayed out there with her instead of going through the Horror Emporium, she'd still be alive right now."

"Stop, Blake. You can't blame yourself. We don't even know what happened to Keira."

"I know, but —"

Before I could interrupt Blake with more *it's not your fault* platitudes, a female deputy called my name. I told Blake I'd see him in a few, and then I followed the deputy into the interrogation room.

I was ushered into the room with the detective I'd never met. There was a small metal table with two of the orange chairs the department seemed to favor placed on either side. The detective sat facing the door. There was some digital recording equipment to his left, a water bottle on his right, and an old-fashioned notepad and pen directly in front of him.

"Ms. Singer, my name is Mark Poston. I'm with the Tallulah County Police Department, and Chief Singh called me in to help take statements in this matter." I'd later learn that he'd taken Manu's, Ted's, and Reggie's statements in addition to mine. Manu thought it would be wise to have an outsider interview us so no one could later claim that any one of us was shown impartiality by the police department.

I told Detective Poston that it was nice to meet him. He turned on a recorder and asked me to state my name for the record.

"My name is Marcy Singer."

"How did you happen to be at the party at the Horror Emporium?" he asked.

"Since my shop is right next door to the Horror Emporium, Claude and Priscilla Atwood extended an invitation to me," I said, feeling the need to be very formal and precise with this middle-aged detective with the suspicious gray eyes. "It was my understanding that the Atwoods were inviting all the merchants on the block."

"Did you know the victim?"

"Not well. I knew her from MacKenzies' Mochas, but she and I didn't socialize."

"Are you aware that a key ring bearing your shop's logo — the Seven-Year Stitch — was found *underneath* the victim?" he asked.

"Yes, I am aware of that. Detective Nash showed me the key ring and asked me about it."

"How did that key ring get beneath the body of the victim?"

"I have no idea."

"May I see your key ring please?"

I opened my purse and fished out my I ♡ MY IRISH WOLFHOUND key ring and placed it on the table between us. I supposed he was trying to see if he could tell whether or not the key ring found under Keira's body could've fallen off or been torn off my set of keys during a struggle or something.

"You do realize I was with the Tallulah Falls Chief of Police and head detective the *entire* time this . . . ordeal . . . was taking place, don't you?" I asked.

"I do, Ms. Singer, and that's why I was brought in on this case — to make sure this is an uncompromised investigation. Do you believe that what happened to the victim found lying outside the Horror Emporium was an accident?"

"Given the fact that she had two puncture wounds in her neck, I don't see how it could've been an accident. Do you?"

He pursed his thin lips together. "I'm the one doing the interrogation here. I'll ask the questions. Why do you think it wasn't an accident, Ms. Singer?"

"I didn't see anything to indicate foul play except for the two bite marks, but that was enough to indicate that Keira had suffered some sort of attack," I said. "The obvious culprit would be a snake . . . and I'm pretty sure that the Atwoods took every precaution to secure their Lair of the Serpent." I shrugged. "I didn't examine the wounds myself. They could've been fake. Keira might've put those marks on her neck at the Atwoods' suggestion, for all I know. When we first came upon the body, I think everyone in our group thought the discovery was part of the production — one last gotcha."

"You talk about the victim as if you knew her personally," said Detective Poston.

"As I told you, I knew her from MacKenzies' Mochas. She'd waited on me several times."

"Was that the extent of your relationship with the victim?"

"Although I didn't have a beef with Keira, she'd made no secret of her dislike of me. She'd once viewed me as a rival for a man's affections."

"But you didn't share her animosity?"

"I didn't. Nor did I see myself as her rival," I said.

"Did you see the victim upon your arrival at the event?" he asked.

I replied that I had.

"What was she doing, and what was her demeanor?"

"She was serving food, and she didn't appear to be terribly happy about it," I said.

"Why do you say that?"

Again, I shrugged. What was I supposed to do? Act out how miffed Keira had seemed? I guessed I could've stood, swiped his water bottle off the table, and then huffed as I tossed it into the garbage can. No . . . there was no garbage can in this room.

"The recorder cannot see your shrug," Detective Poston said. "Would you please verbalize your response?"

"She just didn't seem to want to be there," I said. "Granted, I knew from Sadie that the Atwoods' last-minute request had caused extra work for everyone at MacKenzies' Mochas — especially since they were short a waitress — and that no one was particularly thrilled with the situation."

Detective Poston scribbled a note, but I couldn't see what he'd written because it was hidden by the notepad cover. "Do you think Sadie and the victim might've argued about the party?"

"They might have." My eyes widened. "No! I mean, no more than any employer instructing an employee to do something she didn't want to do. I'm sure that whatever was said, Sadie handled the situation diplomatically."

"You're awfully quick to jump to your friend's defense, Ms. Singer. What was her working relationship with the victim like?"

"I've never seen Sadie treat Keira or any of her employees with anything other than respect."

The detective wrote something else on that stupid notepad, making me want to snatch it away from him to see what he was writing.

He coolly met my eyes. "Tell me what you know about this key ring bearing your shop's logo that was found near the victim."

"I ordered a box of those key rings to give away at my anniversary open house next week," I said.

"Had you already begun distributing the key rings?"

"I gave one to Christine Willoughby. She'd come into the Seven-Year Stitch just after I'd opened the box."

He scribbled furiously in that notebook. "And did you give away any others?"

"No. Right after that, I had to take my dog up the street."

"And do you lock the door when you take him for a walk?"

"No. I'm usually not gone more than about five minutes . . . certainly no more than ten."

"Was anyone in the shop when you returned?"

I brightened. "Yes. Sadie was there. So it's possible that someone could've come in and taken a key ring while I was gone." I was delighted to be able to throw suspicion off poor Christine. I just knew she wasn't guilty of harming Keira, and I *had* left the open box on the counter unattended. Anyone could've picked up one of the key rings and been gone before Angus and I returned.

"Did you give Sadie a key ring?" asked Detective Poston.

"No, I didn't."

"But she might've helped herself to one

while you were out. Isn't that correct?"

My heart sank. "She *could* have, but she didn't."

"You know this for certain?"

"Well, no . . . but I know Sadie. Had she taken one, she'd have told me so," I said. "She was flustered over the last-minute request from the Atwoods, and I doubt she even noticed that box on the counter."

Detective Poston didn't comment. He merely wrote in his notebook while I prayed I hadn't unintentionally sacrificed Sadie to save Christine. Of course, I had no doubt Detective Poston had me at the top of his suspect list as well. None of us were innocent until proven not guilty.

I'd driven Reggie home and had arrived at my house about an hour and a half before Ted got there. I'd just put Angus into the backyard when I heard Ted at the door. For a couple of minutes, we merely stood there in the foyer holding each other. Then we moved to the white overstuffed sofa in the living room. My living room was almost completely decorated in white — sofa, matching chair, mantel, accent pieces. . . . It was very light and airy, a welcome contrast to our current dark moods.

After we sat on the sofa, Ted removed his

shoes and loosened his tie. He stretched out, and I lay down beside him.

He kissed my temple. "Are you all right, babe?"

"Just tired." I rested my head against his chest. "That Poston guy seems to be a tough customer."

"He is. He's one of the best interrogators in the region, though. That's why Manu sent for him. With all of us being at the scene of the crime when it occurred — in a social capacity — it was imperative to bring in an outsider to ensure that every *t* is crossed and every *i* dotted."

"I understand. I just hope I didn't mess up." I raised my head and explained that I was afraid I'd incriminated Sadie somehow.

Ted shook his head. "Poston's fair. Everybody is a suspect, and he won't give anyone more weight than anybody else until the evidence starts mounting up."

"Still, he makes me nervous . . . like he's in a hurry to implicate someone. And right now, I'm afraid he's set his sights on Sadie, Christine, and me."

"Hey, he interrogated Manu and me too," he said. "No one is given any preferential treatment . . . and that's how it should be." He caressed my face with the back of his hand. "We'll find out who did this. There won't be anyone framed for a crime he or she didn't commit."

"I know. I just hate that this happened. Is the medical examiner certain Keira was *murdered*?"

"Given the fresh puncture wounds on her neck, the ME is ninety percent certain it was murder. We'll know more following the autopsy."

"Don't you think it was strange that she had the puncture wounds but that there wasn't very much blood?" I asked.

"It depends on what made the wounds."

The thought of how the neck wounds might've been made brought Nellie to mind. "How's Nellie Davis? Has anyone checked on her?"

Ted nodded. "Officer Moore went by the hospital and took her very brief statement. He said she must've been loopy from pain meds because she kept insisting that Keira was killed by the vampires."

I smiled slightly. "Poor Officer Moore. . . . Little does he know."

"That's what I thought. I didn't say it though. I'll go by the hospital in the morning and see Ms. Davis before going to the station."

"She was hurt badly enough for them to admit her?" I asked. "I knew she was bruised up, but I didn't think it was that serious."

"I doubt it is," Ted said. "They're simply keeping her overnight for observation."

"That's good . . . especially since she lives alone. I wonder if she has a spare pair of glasses and, if so, anyone took them to her."

"Officer Moore took care of that. Ms. Davis said she kept a pair at home and another at work. She gave him her shop key and he retrieved the ones she kept there."

"He's a good kid," I said.

"He is. He'll make a fine detective one of these days."

"Do you have any theories about who might've killed Keira?" I asked.

He shook his head and pulled me closer. "I have no idea. Manu and I — and, likely, Poston — will tackle the case tomorrow. Learning the cause of death should help narrow down the suspects."

I didn't say so, but I desperately hoped Keira's cause of death didn't implicate any of my friends . . . or me.

I went to work early the next morning with the hope of speaking with the Atwoods. I knew how devastating it was to have your business labeled a crime scene immediately after your grand opening.

I unlocked the door to the Seven-Year

Stitch and let Angus inside. The Horror Emporium was dark, but I knocked on the door anyway. No answer. Of course, if the crime scene techs hadn't finished with the building last night, the Atwoods wouldn't be allowed inside yet.

I went back to the Stitch, but I locked the door behind me. There was still at least an hour before I was scheduled to open, and I wanted to check on Priscilla and Claude before customers started coming in. I went into the office with Angus on my heels. I gave him a granola bone from my stash in the desk drawer and then called Sadie.

"MacKenzies' Mochas; Sadie speaking."

"You sound rushed," I said. "I won't keep you but a second. Could you give me a phone number for the Atwoods? I'd like to call and see how they're doing after last night."

She huffed, said she'd have to look it up and would call me back.

"Wait. I don't open until ten. Let me come over and help you and Blake out until then."

To my surprise and dismay, Sadie began sobbing.

"Oh, Sadie, I'm so sorry. I'll be right there."

I grabbed my keys, told Angus where I

was going, and promised to be back as soon as possible. Then I hurried out the back door and down the alley to MacKenzies' Mochas.

Sadie opened the door and joined me in the alley. I hugged her as she continued to weep.

"Do you want to go back to the Stitch and hide out in my office until you feel better?" I asked. "I can take over for you in the shop, and you can go hang out with Angus. Or I can go with you — whatever you want."

She shook her head and took a couple of deep, shuddering breaths. "I . . . c-can't. W-we're too busy." She took another breath. "I have to . . . pull myself together . . . and get back to work."

"You take a break and let me help Blake man the counter for a few minutes."

"N-no. I . . . I'll be all right . . . in a second. It's j-just . . . Blake is so upset about Keira."

"I know. We all are," I said softly.

"B-but that detective . . . Poston. . . . He thinks . . . maybe . . . Keira and Blake . . . were having an affair!"

"That's ridiculous, and you know it. Blake is just concerned because he feels responsible. He told me last night that he should've stayed outside with Keira instead of going through the haunted house. He thinks he could've prevented her death."

"I . . . hope you're right."

"I am," I insisted. "Talk with Blake. He'll confirm what I've told you."

She nodded and said she needed to go back inside. "Oh . . . here." She handed me a piece of paper with the Atwoods' phone number.

"I'm here if you need me."

"Thanks." She turned and went back into the coffee shop, and I went back to the Stitch.

CHAPTER SEVEN

I went back to the Stitch where Angus was still lying in my office eating his granola bone. I sat down at my desk and fished my cell phone out of my pocket. Instead of calling the Atwoods, though, I called Ted.

"Good morning, babe," he said in his sexy voice that almost made me forget why I was calling.

"I'm so mad at that Detective Poston! I want to punch him square in the nose!"

"Please don't. I'd hate for you to be arrested for assault. What has he done?"

"He has Sadie thinking that Blake and Keira were having an affair!"

"What?"

"You heard me," I said. "I just came from Sadie, and she's crying her eyes out."

"I'll look into it and see why he gave her that impression. He has been known to throw theories out right and left in order to see what rings true with the suspect. What about Blake? What does he have to say about all of this?"

"I don't know. I don't think Sadie has confronted him with it yet."

"Maybe you should talk with him," he said. "It would be less threatening coming from a friend rather than his wife."

"That's true. I'll think about it. It's just ridiculous . . . isn't it? I mean, Blake and Keira didn't even seem to like each other. Did they?"

"Like I said, I'll check into it and get Detective Poston's reasoning behind his line of questioning."

"Thank you," I said. "I'm sorry I took out my anger on you."

"You can take anything you want out on me anytime."

I laughed. "I love you."

"I know. And I love you, Inch-High Private Eye."

After talking with Ted, I readied the coffeepot and then went into the shop to tidy up before opening. I dusted the shelves and fluffed the pillows on the sofa. Angus went to lie by the window. It was clouding up outside.

As I unlocked the door, I noticed an Angus-nose print on the glass. I got a window cleaning wipe from behind the counter and went to work on the smudge. I'd just got it removed when I saw the Atwoods drive up. I stepped out onto the sidewalk and invited them inside.

They were dressed as flamboyantly as ever. Claude wore a white tuxedo today with a blue sequined vest. Priscilla wore black leather pants with red over-the-knee stiletto boots, a lacy white blouse, and a black leather vest. Had these people ever heard of jeans, T-shirts, and sneakers? Or even regular business attire?

"Would you like some coffee?" I asked.

"I would, yes," said Claude. "It smells wonderful."

"Freshly brewed," I said with a smile. "Priscilla?"

"Please."

I went into the office and brought the coffeepot, three cups, an assortment of sweeteners, and creamer out on a tray. I placed the tray on the oval table in the sit-and-stitch square. Claude and Priscilla had already taken a seat on the sofa facing the window. Angus was observing them from his spot near the door.

I poured the coffee and then sat on one of the red club chairs. "I'm terribly sorry about what happened last night."

"So are we," said Claude.

"We're heartsick," added Priscilla. "And everyone who gathered on the sidewalk saw many of our characters! How will they be effective now?"

Claude looked at his wife sharply. "Of course, we're saddened for the poor girl and her family. It's just that we're a smidge concerned about our business also."

"I'm sure the characters will still scare everyone who goes through the Horror Emporium," I said. "They were very good."

Priscilla smiled. "Really? You think so?"

"Yes, I do."

"We're delighted to hear that," said Claude. "We consider you something of an expert, given your mother's profession."

"Well, that would make *her* the expert," I said. "But I have been around a lot of special effects, and yours were terrific."

Claude gave Priscilla's hand a squeeze. "See? I told you so."

She smiled at me. "Men adore those four words, don't they?"

I tightly returned her smile. "So . . . when will you be able to reopen?"

"We have to clean up the mess left behind by the crime scene technicians and then get the crew together to do a run-through, and then we'll be back in business," said Claude. "We should be open tomorrow night."

"We could probably open tonight," said Priscilla. "But we want to build suspense. We know people will be anxious to come to the Horror Emporium after hearing about poor Keira's demise."

I tried to hide my surprise and repulsion about how cavalier the Atwoods were being over Keira's death. "Have you heard any more about what might have happened to her?"

"We have no clue," said Claude. "If the police know, they're being mum about it to us. They did a thorough examination of the Lair of the Serpent last night and then had us remove the snakes so the crime scene technicians could study the inside of the room. They appeared to be satisfied that none of the vipers had escaped."

"So they are no closer to finding the cause of death?" I asked.

"Of course, they are." Priscilla took a sip of her coffee. "They have eliminated snake bite as a cause."

"Right," I said, shifting in my seat. I didn't care for their attitude in the least. Didn't they care that a girl was dead?

Claude must've noticed the chill that came from my direction because he said once again, "We *are* saddened for the poor girl and her family."

I simply nodded.

The bells over the door jingled, signaling that someone had come in. I welcomed the chance to turn my attention to someone else. The woman who came through the door was young and slender. I'd never seen her before. Angus trotted over to greet her.

"Hi," I said. "Welcome to the Seven-Year Stitch."

"Thank you," she said, a chuckle in her voice. "Your dog is gorgeous."

"Thanks. Is there anything in particular you're looking for this morning?"

"Yes. As a matter of fact, there is." She patted Angus's head. "My granny is looking for some pillowcase kits."

"I have several," I said. "Follow me."

"We'll be taking our leave now, Ms. Singer," said Claude. "My lovely wife and I have much to do."

"Thank you for the coffee," Priscilla said.

"You're welcome," I said. "Come again."

I noticed the girl was watching the Atwoods leave instead of looking at the pillowcase kits.

"Those are two of the tamer outfits I've seen them in," I said softly.

She giggled. "Are they circus folk or something?"

"Something like that," I said.

She found two kits she thought her grandmother would like — one with butterflies and flowers, and another that featured lacy, open fans. I invited her to come to the open house next week.

"I'll be here!" she said. "And I'll bring Granny with me."

I rang up her purchases and secured them in one of the periwinkle Seven-Year Stitch bags. When she'd left, I took away the coffee tray. I emptied the cups into the sink, placed the pot back on the burner, and put away the sweetener and creamer.

I returned to the sit-and-stitch square and flopped down onto the club chair with a sigh.

Vera came in. "Wow, honey, why the long face?" She kissed Angus on the nose and then sat on the sofa.

"It's the Atwoods," I said. "I'm beginning to think Nellie was right about them being vampires." I went on to tell Vera about how cold they'd acted over Keira's death. "I realize they didn't know the girl, but to look at her murder as a convenient publicity stunt for the Horror Emporium is flat-out wrong!"

"Oh, I agree. That's dreadful." She frowned. "And they seemed so *nice* too. Eccentric, to be sure, but nice."

"I thought so too." I rested my chin on my fist. "What's Paul saying about everything?"

"Not much," she said. "We were so tired when he dropped me off at my house last night that he didn't even come in for a nightcap."

"You know that I wasn't Keira's favorite person — and vice versa — but I didn't want anything bad to happen to her."

"Of course, I know that. Everyone knows that."

"I don't think Detective Poston does," I said.

"He interviewed Paul. Paul didn't particularly care for the man . . . said he was brusque and tried to be intimidating." She straightened her spine. "But he didn't intimidate Paul."

"I thought he seemed like a bully too. Ted says he's one of the best interrogators in the region." I drew my brows together. "Who interviewed you?"

"Manu. I told him what I knew — which wasn't much. None of us were really in a position to know what was going on out in the lobby area. We were all going through the maze of horrors . . . or whatever they were." She shrugged. "The Atwoods did an admirable job, I think — you know, giving the devil his due and all."

"They did . . . and I felt terribly sorry for them — you know, because their grand opening was spoiled by Keira's death. . . . At least, I did until they came in and spoke about the publicity her death would generate for their business." I shook my head. "Would you like some coffee?"

"No, thanks, dear. I'm fine. But, by all means, don't let me keep you from having some if you'd like."

"I had some earlier." I recalled how the beverage had seemed to turn bitter in my mouth as I'd listened to the Atwoods talk. "It kinda made me sick."

"It's likely your nerves. Last night took its toll on us all."

"Tell me something," I said. "Did Paul interview the character actors hired by the Atwoods?"

"I don't believe he did. The piece focused on Claude and Priscilla and their vision for the haunted house," she said. "I don't think he featured any of the actors in the article. Besides, the Atwoods didn't want any of their characters or props photographed. They wanted everything to be a surprise."

"Priscilla was concerned about the actors this morning. She was afraid that too many people who'd gathered on the sidewalk had seen the characters and wouldn't be frightened by them." I stretched my legs out on the ottoman and folded my hands behind my head. "So Paul didn't interview the actors, huh? Are you up for some detective work?"

She grinned. "Am I? You should know me so well that you don't even have to ask."

"We need to talk with those actors . . . see if any of them knew Keira. One of them could've easily disappeared sometime during the performance and then slipped back in. The place was pitch dark."

"It was. Had I not been holding on to Paul's hand, I'd have tripped a time or two." She folded her arms and pursed her lips. "How are we gonna pull this off? They all know we aren't with the police department. For one thing, they've all been questioned by the actual police. Why should they want to talk with us?"

I thought a few seconds. Then my eyes widened. "Mom!"

"What?"

"Mom — she's coming in on Tuesday. If these people applied for jobs acting in a haunted house, then they're probably interested in *other* acting jobs," I said. "We'll tell them about Mom's upcoming . . . scouting trip. . . ."

Vera barked out a laugh. "*Scouting* trip? Really?"

"Well . . . we'll come up with *something*. We don't want them to think she's actually casting a movie or anything — I mean, I don't want to *lie* to these people — but we'll somehow use Mom and her connections as a way to chat them up."

"You're really something — you know that?"

"Still in?" I asked.

"You know I am."

"Good. I have to find out who murdered Keira and why before every friend I have comes under Detective Poston's microscope." I glanced at her from the corner of my eyes. "Can I tell you something in complete confidence?"

"Sure."

"You won't tell Paul?"

She hesitated. "No . . . not if you ask me not to."

"I'm asking you not to."

"Your secret is safe. Spill it."

"Sadie was beside herself this morning," I said. "She couldn't stop crying. That stupid detective made her think that Blake and Keira might've been having an affair."

Vera lowered her eyes.

"Vera?"

She wouldn't look up at me.

"Vera, you don't think it's true?"

She reluctantly raised her eyes. "I don't know, hon. I do know that Blake and Keira had been seen together on more than one occasion — and they weren't at the coffee shop."

"Then where were they seen?" I asked. "Was it a motel? Was it in Blake's van? I mean, maybe he was just giving the girl a lift home or something. Maybe her car broke down. It could've been completely innocent."

"It could've been," Vera said.

"Where were they seen together?"

"At her house once. . . . Another time they were at a shop in Depoe Bay together."

"What shop?" I asked.

"I don't know. I'm just telling you what I heard."

"From whom?"

"From more than one person. I hope there was nothing to it, but where there's smoke. . . ."

"No. Not in this case. I refuse to believe it," I said. "I'm going to ask Blake about it myself."

"Be careful there, sweetie. If there *was* something going on, you don't want to find yourself in the middle of it — especially given your relationship with the MacKenzies."

I took a deep breath. "It can't be true. It just can't."

"I hope you're right." In an obvious attempt to change the subject back to something less daunting, Vera asked, "Now, how are we going to round up these actors to see what they know?"

I thought about this for a few seconds. "Maybe we could enlist Paul's help. He could tell the Atwoods that he's merely following up — I don't want them to know what we're doing — and then he could tell them we're interviewing actors here tomorrow morning before the store opens and to call me for an appointment. Do you think you can get Paul to do it?"

She smiled. "I can get Paul to do just about anything."

"Great. You and I will talk with the actors between eight and ten tomorrow, if that works for you."

"Eight's a bit early for me on a Saturday morning . . . but, for this, I'll make an exception."

CHAPTER EIGHT

After Vera left to persuade Paul to go along with our scheme, my mind turned back to Blake and Keira. I simply could not believe for an instant that the two of them had been having an affair. Todd was Blake's best friend. I decided to get his input before talking with Blake. Maybe Todd would have the simple explanation I was looking for, and I could pass that information on to Sadie, and everything would be fine again.

I took out my cell phone and called Todd.

"What's up, Marcy?"

"Hi! Um . . . how are you?"

"Better than you, from the way you're hemming and hawing," he said. "I'm just putting away some stock I got in today. You need me to come over?"

"If you have a second, I'd appreciate it."

"I'll be right there."

Within minutes, Todd burst through the door as if he expected me to be at the mercy of a deranged killer. Angus enthusiastically ran to greet him. Todd petted the dog and then brushed past him to where I was sitting on the sofa.

He sat beside me and took one of my hands. "Are you okay?"

"No. It's Sadie. She's beside herself because Detective Poston implied there was something going on between Blake and Keira."

Todd looked down at the floor.

"Please tell me it isn't true," I said.

He released my hand and ran both of his hands through his hair. "They weren't having an affair."

"Then what *were* they having, and why didn't Sadie know about it?"

"Keira's dad was interested in opening a MacKenzies' Mochas between Tallulah Falls and Depoe Bay," he said. "Keira was going to operate the store, and Blake and Sadie would get a small percentage of the store's net profit for the use of their logo."

"All right. I'm following you so far. Why would that entail Blake and Keira running around behind Sadie's back?"

"She wasn't entirely on board with the idea. Initially, Mr. Sherman came into the coffee shop and approached both Blake and Sadie."

Angus, who'd gone to retrieve his tennis ball, came to sit by Todd's side. He dropped the ball onto the floor. Todd picked it up and lobbed it across the floor. Angus quickly chased it down.

"Blake told Mr. Sherman that he and Sadie would discuss it," he said. "But Sadie was afraid that opening another shop would cheapen MacKenzies' Mochas."

"And Blake disagreed."

"He saw it as a way to make easy money." Todd shrugged. "Blake's reasoning was that if Mr. Sherman was going to open a coffee shop anyway, why not let him capitalize on the popularity of MacKenzies' Mochas so he and Sadie could enjoy a little profit from the venture."

"So he went through with it against Sadie's wishes?" I asked.

"Not exactly. He and Keira were sneaking around scouting locations for her dad's coffee shop. Blake thought that if they found the perfect spot and could make a more concrete proposal to Sadie that she'd be persuaded that it was a good idea."

"Then he needs to be up front with Sadie now. Todd, she's devastated. She thinks Blake is so upset over Keira's death because he had feelings for her."

"Blake is beating himself up over Keira's

death because he feels like he could've prevented it."

"So what do I do now?" I asked. "Sadie needs to know the truth."

"Let me go talk with Blake," said Todd. "I'll let him know what Poston told Sadie. I just hope he doesn't go medieval on the guy."

"You and me both."

I had a customer come in just before the three o'clock slump to get some blending filament. Needle crafters use blending filament to add light reflection to their embroidery, lace making, weaving, and knitting. This woman bought all of the silver I had in stock. After she'd left, I went into the office, booted up the laptop, and ordered more.

While I was on the computer, I reminded my social media network about my upcoming open house. That seemed a little cold given Keira's death, but the event was still taking place and I — and many of my customers — were looking forward to it.

Overall, it had been a depressing day. I called Ted. He'd had to work through lunch.

"Hey, babe," he answered.

"You sound tired," I said.

"A little. You sound down."

"A little. Let's do something fun tonight . . . something to lift our spirits."

"All right." He paused. "How about Captain Moe's?"

"Perfect. I haven't seen the captain in ages." It had been only a couple of weeks, but where Captain Moe was concerned, that felt like ages.

If you were to picture Alan Hale from the old sitcom *Gilligan's Island* with a snowy white beard, then you'd know what Captain Moe looked like. When Ted and I walked into the little Depoe Bay diner, Captain Moe came from behind the counter to encompass us both in a bear hug.

"It's been too long since I've seen wee Tinkerbell and her knight in shining armor," he said with a grin.

He and his brother, Norman Patrick — Riley Kendall's dad — have called me Tinkerbell since the moment they met me. I didn't know if it was because I was blond or short, but either way, it was a fun nickname and I didn't mind it . . . especially from Captain Moe.

After taking our order, he came back and sat with us at our table. "I've asked the chef to take over for me for a few minutes."

"I'm glad," I said. "We don't see enough of you. You need to come to Tallulah Falls more often."

"I'm there more than you think," he said. "But Laura keeps me busy."

Laura was Riley's baby daughter.

"Wait until she figures out that you're Santa Claus," said Ted.

Captain Moe laughed. "Somehow, I think she already has." His smile faded. "I'm sorry about that business outside the Horror Emporium the other night."

"So are we," I said. "When we came upon Keira, we thought it was planned . . . you know, part of the show."

"Is Ken Sherman hassling the police to find out who's responsible for his daughter's death?" Captain Moe asked, with a furtive glance in both directions.

"Probably," Ted said. "I don't know the man. If he's been in, I'm sure he's spoken with Manu."

"Oh, I imagine he has. I've known Ken for a long time. He's a bully during good times. It's hard to tell what something like his daughter's death would do to him."

"I feel sorry for the family," I said. "You say you know Mr. Sherman? Has he ever tried to open another Captain Moe's?"

He nodded. "That he has, Tink. He hasn't approached you about another Seven-Year Stitch, has he?"

"No. He was wanting to open a MacKenzies' Mochas though," I said.

"That sounds more up his alley," said Captain Moe. "He seems to be more into food establishments than anything else. I believe he dabbled in the gas station market in the late nineties, but that didn't go so well for him. So are Sadie and Blake considering his offer?"

"It's my understanding that they were," I said. "Blake was all for it, but Sadie was needing a bit more convincing. Of course, I think Mr. Sherman wanted Keira to run the business, so I doubt he'll still be interested."

"I don't know. If Ken wanted the business, he probably still will."

"I don't get it," said Ted. "Why does the guy open businesses based on other people's ideas? Why doesn't he just establish his own name or brand? Or franchise with a larger business?"

"In theory, he takes small local businesses that have already gained a solid reputation and clientele in the area," Captain Moe said. "He builds on that foundation to grow both businesses. . . . At least, that's what he pitches to potential customers."

"Then what's he really selling them?" I asked.

Captain Moe lowered his voice. "His

products and management skills are so shoddy that he winds up hurting the original business rather than helping it. I have a friend whose business Ken Sherman ran into the ground."

"How?" asked Ted.

"My buddy had a small but popular seafood place. People lined up down the street to get in on the weekends. It was called Jim's Lobster Shack. Sherman came in and talked Jim into letting him use the logo, menu, whatever, and said he'd give Jim ten percent of the net profits made by the restaurant Sherman planned to open. Jim thought he couldn't lose."

A waitress brought us our drinks. We thanked her, and so did Captain Moe.

"Cap, you want something?" she asked.

"No, dear, I'll be along in a few minutes," he said.

After she'd left, I asked Captain Moe what happened to his friend's business.

"Well, Sherman opened his place, and it tanked. The food wasn't very good, the service was terrible, and the restaurant didn't have the overall atmosphere of Jim's place." He stroked his beard. "People who had gone to the new place thinking it was managed by the same people were disappointed. But, rather than stop going to

Sherman's restaurant and returning to Jim's, they didn't eat at either establishment."

"They didn't trust Jim anymore," I said sadly.

"Right. He was out of business within six months," said Captain Moe. "Jim was close enough to retirement age that he said it didn't bother him . . . that he'd been meaning to retire anyway . . . but I know better. Tell Blake and Sadie to stay away from Ken Sherman."

"I will," I said.

He gave me a one-armed hug. "I'd better go see what's happening in the kitchen. Ted there looks hungry enough to eat a moose."

"Do I really?" Ted asked as Captain Moe returned to the kitchen. "I didn't have lunch."

I smiled. "You look gorgeous. And I think the only moose you would eat would be a chocolate mousse."

"You wouldn't happen to have any, would you?"

"Not on me. But I think Captain Moe will hurry with our food," I said. "That's a shame about Mr. Sherman — taking what's special about small establishments and then ruining them."

"I doubt that's his goal," said Ted. "He's a

businessman. I'm guessing he's trying to make the business run more efficiently, but in so doing — like you said — he strips away the small-town charm that makes it special."

"I hope Blake explained everything to Sadie," I said.

"I'm sure he did. I hope she'll forgive him for going behind her back. I mean, it's wonderful that he wasn't having an affair, but he was still keeping a secret from her."

"I think he was intending it to be more like a surprise, but you're right. He was keeping something from her."

When we got home, Angus happily accepted the grilled hamburger patty Captain Moe had sent him. Okay, he wolfed it down in just a couple of bites. Then he pawed at the back door to go outside. I hesitated because it was drizzling.

"I'll take him for a quick walk," Ted said, removing the leash from the hook by the door and snapping it onto Angus's collar. He kissed me. "Why don't you find us a movie to watch when Angus and I get back?"

"I can do that," I said with a smile.

The three of us left the kitchen. Ted and Angus went out the front door, and I walked into the living room, slipped off my shoes, and sank onto the sofa. It felt good to be putting this tiring day behind me.

I was reaching for the remote when my cell phone rang. It was Vera.

"Hi, Marcy. Hope I'm not interrupting anything. I just wanted to quickly let you know that Operation Act–Scam is a go."

I laughed. "Operation Act–Scam?"

"Yeah, well . . . I had to call it *something.*"

Actually, she didn't, but I didn't want to burst her bubble by saying so. Besides, she *had* found a way to put our plan into action.

"Rather than involve Paul, I let on that I was sort of an assistant to your mom," Vera continued. "The actors are coming in tomorrow morning in fifteen-minute intervals. That'll give us a chance to speak with all seven of them with a few minutes to go over our impressions of each one once they've left. I got us matching notebooks so we'll look official."

"Wow," I said. "You thought of everything."

"I know. Maybe after this, I'll open up my own detective agency. Wouldn't that be something?"

I agreed that it certainly would.

After talking with Vera, I turned on the TV to see what movies were playing. I saw that one of the earlier pictures my mom had worked on as a costuming apprentice would be on in ten minutes. I hurried to the kitchen to make popcorn and to pour Ted and me some drinks.

I heard Ted and Angus come in through the front door and Angus shake the rain off his coat in the foyer. I grabbed a handful of paper towels and was on my way to clean up the floor when Ted intercepted me and took the towels.

"Do I smell popcorn?" he asked.

"Yes, you do," I said.

"I'll take care of drying the floor while you finish up with the snacks. I take it you found us a good movie?"

I laughed. "I found us an *interesting* movie. It's an old sci-fi film — one of Mom's first when she was just an apprentice. The costumes are pretty good, but the story and special effects are lame."

"Sounds fun."

Ted wiped up the floor while I put our snacks on a tray and gave Angus a granola bone to keep him busy and not begging for popcorn or cookies for a few minutes. I carried the tray into the living room. Ted and Angus joined me. Angus stretched out in front of the hearth and began gnawing on his bone. Ted and I snuggled up on the sofa and began watching the movie.

"*Gor and the Saturnian Princess?*" Ted groaned.

"Did I mention that the costumes aren't bad?" I asked, with a giggle.

"You might've said something like that." He reached into the bowl for some popcorn. "This is gonna be good."

At the first commercial break, we'd both laughed so hard we could hardly breathe.

"Is this movie supposed to be so funny?" Ted asked.

"No. It's billed as a drama. Of course, they do tend to overact, don't they?"

He grasped my shoulders and stared into my eyes. "Yes . . . my beloved darling . . . they do . . . have a penchant . . . for theatrics."

I kissed him. "Come with me to the Casbah?"

"You . . . know I . . . will."

The movie started back, and I became semiserious. "Speaking of theatrics, what do think will happen when our moms meet?"

"They'll be cool. And civil." He grinned. "And they'll circle each other like a pair of she-wolves."

CHAPTER NINE

Since Vera had asked me to be at the shop by eight Saturday morning, Angus and I arrived at seven thirty to tidy up and make some coffee. Well, *I* was tidying up and making coffee. Angus was sniffing around to see if anything intriguing had happened while he was gone. It was a good thing we arrived early. Vera showed up at seven forty-five.

She wore a fuchsia pantsuit with taupe pumps and a white gardenia lapel pin. And she was positively glowing.

I, on the other hand, was wearing jeans and a powder blue sweatshirt with the sleeves pushed up. And white canvas sneakers. I didn't always embrace casual Fridays, but I glommed onto slouchy Saturdays with both arms!

"You look like you just stepped out of *Executive Vogue* or something," I said.

"Thank you." Vera dropped a kiss onto the top of Angus's head and came over to sit on the red club chair that faced the store. She reached into her tan leather tote and brought out our matching notebooks. They were pink, I supposed, to coordinate with her suit, and they had elegant *B*s on the front.

I frowned at mine. "What's the *B* for?"

She rolled her eyes. "For Beverly, of course. We're working on behalf of your *mom,* remember?"

"Oh . . . right."

"Come on, Marcy. Get in the game! The actors will begin arriving any minute."

"Should I run home and change?" I asked, half-seriously.

"No, hon. You're fine. You're her daughter. They'll know she won't hold you to the same standards she expects of the rest of the staff."

"Then they don't know Beverly Singer," I muttered. I smiled at Vera. "Since you're obviously the executive in charge, I take it you'll be running the show?"

"Please . . . I mean, if you don't mind."

"I don't mind at all."

"Just, if I start to falter or something, jump in," she said. "All right?"

"Will do. Would you like some coffee?"

She shook her head. Her hair — thanks to some really good hair spray — didn't move.

"Not yet. Let me get into character and get comfortable first."

I tried not to snicker as I went into the office for my own cup. This was going to be good.

The first person through the door was a tall, thin young man with straight brown hair that fell to the middle of his back. He had a full beard and kind hazel eyes. I tried to place him but couldn't remember seeing him at the Horror Emporium. He must have been wearing a mask.

Vera consulted her notebook. "You're Travis Stevens, correct?"

"That's right." He backed away as Angus approached. "I'm sorry. I didn't know there'd be a dog here. I've been afraid of dogs since I was a little boy."

"Let me put him in the bathroom," I said. "I'm terribly sorry."

"Why don't you take Angus up the street while Mr. Stevens is auditioning?" Vera inclined her head toward the door. "You know he'll bark so loudly we won't be able to hear Mr. Stevens if you shut him up in the bathroom."

That was true, but I didn't want to leave Vera to question our first suspect on her own. Not that I was an expert by any stretch of the imagination, but I knew what I wanted to ask.

Still, I took Angus's leash from beneath the counter and snapped it onto his collar. "We'll be back in about ten minutes. If you aren't finished by then, Mr. Stevens, I'll keep Angus on his leash so you'll feel more comfortable." I gave Vera a pointed look. "Please be sure and ask him everything *Mom* wanted to know."

Vera rolled her eyes and flicked her wrist. "Darling, you act as if I only started working for her yesterday."

All righty then.

I took Angus up to the town square. At least, he made the best of the situation so I wouldn't have to take him out again for a little while. Hopefully, the rest of the suspects would be more dog-friendly.

As I was walking back to the Seven-Year Stitch, Priscilla Atwood came out of the Horror Emporium. I couldn't swear to it, but I got the impression she'd been standing at her door waiting for me to walk past.

"Good morning," she said.

"Hi. How are you?"

"Fine. I'm glad it isn't raining and hopeful that the good weather continues into the evening."

"Me too." I tried to ease past her with a *have a good day,* but she stepped into my path. She was wearing green today and reminded me of an overgrown leprechaun.

"You aren't stealing my actors away from me, are you?" She smiled, but the expression didn't reach her eyes.

"No. Why?"

"I understand that they're all coming by your shop this morning for some reason."

"Oh . . . that. My mom is coming in for the open house, and I thought some of them might be interested in finding other gigs after the Horror Emporium closes up shop," I said.

"So might Claude and I."

"Of course. You'll have to pop in and say hello when Mom gets into town." I hoped Mom wasn't going to throttle me over this whole charade. Maybe when I explained my reasoning behind it, she'd understand. Maybe.

"Indeed we will." She gave me a more genuine smile this time and then went back inside her shop.

When I stepped into the Stitch, Travis Stevens was gone, and Vera was writing in her notebook as fast as she could. I un-snapped Angus's leash and put it back behind the counter. He ambled into the office to get a drink of water.

I waited until Vera looked up from her

writing to ask, "Well?"

"He's not that great of an actor and obviously didn't know Keira."

"What makes you so sure?"

"He said he was bummed that she died because he thought she was really cute and he'd wanted to ask her out," she said. "No guy who'd spoken with Keira for more than ten minutes would ask her out."

"Vera!"

"Well, the truth's the truth. Kiera being dead doesn't change that."

"No, I suppose not."

Our next suspect came through the door. Angus hurried from the back to see who'd come in.

"Oh, what a pretty dog!" The girl — a perky redhead — patted her thighs, and Angus trotted over to greet her. "He's so big! I *love* him!"

"You're Adalyn Daye?" Vera asked.

"Yes, ma'am."

"Where are you from originally?" I asked.

"Oklahoma."

I looked at Vera. "Keira had spent a little time in Oklahoma, hadn't she?"

"She might have," Vera said. "Adalyn, did you know Keira Sherman, the girl who was working the concession stand the other night? She worked for MacKenzies' Mochas."

"No, I sure didn't," said Adalyn. "I mean, I'd heard of her, but I didn't know her myself. But wasn't that the saddest thing?"

"It was," I said. I started to ask from whom Adalyn had heard of Keira, but she didn't give me the chance.

"Well, I know we're short on time. My monologue is from *The Glass Menagerie.*"

And so it went all morning. Vera and I watched audition after audition, and none of the actors admitted to knowing Keira.

Vera had gone, and I was waiting on a customer who needed some Persian yarn for her needlepoint project when Jared Willoughby walked in. I'd met the tall, athletic young man only once when I'd stopped in at his garage to have the oil changed in my Jeep. But it was through Jared that I'd met his mom, Christine.

I had a good idea why he was here.

"Hi, Jared. I'll be with you in just a minute."

"Take your time." He was petting Angus, who'd walked over to greet him. "So this is the famous Angus. I've heard a lot about you."

The woman with the Persian yarn made

her selections and paid for them. I placed her yarn, a sheet about our classes, and a flyer about the upcoming open house into her bag and wished her a good weekend as she left.

Then I joined Jared in the sit-and-stitch square where he'd taken a seat on the sofa facing the window.

I sat on a red club chair. "How's your mom?"

"She's holding up. It's no fun being a murder suspect. But then, you know that."

"I do." I offered him something to drink, and when he declined, I returned to our weighty subject. "And what about you? I know Keira's death had to be quite a blow to you. After all, you'd been dating for how long?"

He shrugged his broad shoulders. "We were off and on for two or three months." He ran a hand over his face. "I'm sorry for Keira — she was a better person than the one everybody saw — and I'm especially sad for her dad, but I'm really concerned about my mom right now. I'm scared that the cops are trying to pin Keira's murder on her."

"Your mom will be fine," I said. "Ted and Manu will find Keira's killer, and Christine will be cleared."

"I wish I was as sure of that as you are," he said.

I didn't say so, but I wished I felt as certain of that outcome myself. "Can you think of anyone who might've wanted to hurt Keira?"

He shook his head. "I've been racking my brain since the police talked with me the other night. I can't think of a soul who'd want to kill her. I mean, she didn't have a lot of friends, but no one was sending her death threats either."

"I didn't know Keira well. What was she like?"

He leaned back into the soft cushions of the sofa. "She was beautiful — that's what attracted me to her at first. As I got to know her, I saw that her prickly attitude came from her insecurities."

"Really? Gee, I wouldn't have thought Keira would have felt insecure about anything."

"She was insecure about *everything*," he said. "She has an older sister named Bethany who is not only gorgeous but brilliant. She has a doctorate in psychology as well as a law degree, and she's a criminal attorney in one of the largest law firms in Seattle."

"Whoa. I can see where having her for a sister could be intimidating."

"I kept telling Keira to be her own person and to stop comparing herself to her sister or to anyone else, but she said that was easy for me to say because my mom is crazy about me." He shook his head. "Keira couldn't see how much her family cared about her. I mean, her dad was even buying her a restaurant, for goodness' sake."

"What did she say when you pointed that out to her?" I asked.

"She said he wasn't buying the restaurant for her out of love but that he was buying it to make her appear to be more successful. She felt that her dad didn't think she was good enough . . . and that he never would."

"How sad that she felt that way."

"Even sadder is the fact that those insecurities worked their way into everything else in Keira's life," Jared said. "She refused to trust people, looked for everyone's ulterior motive, and believed that no one could truly care for her."

"Your mom told me that you and Keira had broken up but that Keira was having a hard time letting go. She said that Keira was even asking you to pay her bills. Why would she do that if her family had enough money to buy her a restaurant?"

Jared blew out a breath. "Money was just another manipulation to Keira. She would push me away and then chase after me. This last time, though, I'd had enough of her games. She wouldn't grow up and allow me to help her see her self-worth, and I didn't want her to keep dragging me down. I couldn't handle all that negativity in my life, you know?"

"I understand completely," I said. "We need people in our lives who help lift us up, not tear us down . . . or even try to hold us where we are."

After Jared left, the melancholy lingering in his wake cast a pall over the shop, including Angus and me. Angus stretched out by the front window and fell into a fitful sleep. Huge gray clouds had moved in, and I believed that the drizzle we were getting now was simply a precursor of what was to come. So much for Priscilla's weather holding out.

There weren't any customers in the shop at the moment, and I wandered into the storeroom to do a quick inventory. When I heard the bells over the door jangle to announce an arrival, I was noting the fact that I was running low on several floss colors — and in this company's case, floss *numbers.*

"Welcome to the Seven-Year Stitch!" I called. "Please make yourself at home, and

I'll be out in a second!"

As I snapped a photo of the depleted flosses' numbers with the camera on my phone, Ted came into the storeroom and slid his arms around my waist.

"I hope this is what you meant about making myself at home." He kissed the back of my neck, sending shivers down my spine.

"Ooh, let me take a selfie." I changed my camera setting to allow us to do the modern-day equivalent of a photo booth. I wouldn't be adding our goofy poses to any social media sites, but Ted and I could enjoy looking at them and laughing at ourselves.

Ted was dressed casually today in jeans and a navy blue sweater that played up his eyes. He was supposed to have been off today, but Keira's murder had everyone in the department working overtime.

"Are you having a good day?" he asked.

"It's better now."

Angus had followed Ted to the storeroom and was waiting patiently outside the door. The dog probably thought the three of us were getting ready to have lunch.

"I'm sorry, Mr. O'Ruff," I said. "But Ted and I worked through lunch today because we're planning on having a big dinner at the steakhouse near Lincoln City."

Angus cocked his head, and I looked at

Ted, hoping he hadn't come by to tell me he couldn't make it this evening.

He smiled. "That's absolutely right." He looked at Angus. "But don't worry, buddy. We'll bring you back a doggie bag." He went out to the counter where he'd left a small box from MacKenzies' Mochas. "In the meantime, I had to make sure you two were keeping your strength up today. I brought peanut butter cookies for everybody."

I grinned and shook my head at how cute they were — Angus waiting patiently for his cookie . . . Ted easing it slowly out of the box to tease him just a bit.

After treating Angus, Ted turned to me. "How about you? Would you like a cookie?"

"Not right now. But I'll make a fresh pot of coffee for you to enjoy with yours."

"Thanks. I'll take you up on that offer."

"So . . . um . . . how was the mood at MacKenzies' Mochas?"

"I think Blake must've taken Calloway's advice and talked with Sadie," he said. "There's a bit of coolness between them but nothing like what I'd expect if she still suspected him of having an affair."

"I'm hoping she'll find time to drop in later. I don't want to pry, but I would like to know that everything's all right with the two of them."

Angus, who had practically inhaled his cookie, sat waiting for another. When Ted and I walked into the office so I could brew the coffee, the dog trailed along behind us and flopped onto the floor beside my desk.

As I busied myself with the coffeemaker, I said as casually as I could, "I suppose I should tell you what Vera and I were doing this morning."

Ted put the box of cookies on my desk, slid his hands into his front pockets, and looked up at the ceiling. "Let's hear it."

"It's not that big a deal . . . really."

He lowered his eyes back to my face. "Of course, it's a big deal. Had it not been, you'd have said, *Hey, guess what Vera and I did.* This was a *I have a confession to make since you're probably gonna find out about it anyway and you're not gonna like it* thing. So give it to me straight please."

"Well. . . ."

He frowned.

"Okay," I said. "She and I got to wondering if any of the actors at the Horror Emporium could've known Keira prior to her death, so we . . . auditioned them."

"For what — the role of killer?" He affected an old-man-director voice. "Were you to be cast in the role of Keira Sherman's murderer, how would you do it?"

"Oh, my gosh! That's better than what we did. I should've talked with you beforehand."

"Marcy!"

"What? I mean, had we done it your way, we might've at least gained some insight into *how* exactly Keira was killed," I said. "As it stands, we've got nada."

He nodded toward the coffeemaker. "How much longer? I'm needing that caffeine more than ever."

I glanced at the aromatic brew streaming into the pot. "Any second now."

"So you and Vera held *auditions*? For what?"

"We left it open. See, Vera pretended to be Mom's assistant, and we let the actors think Mom is scouting for new talent."

"Babe, your mom is a costume designer. She has nothing to do with casting."

"Well, of course, you and I realize that, but they only know she carries some clout in the business and that she *knows* people."

He pinched the bridge of his nose between his thumb and forefinger. "And how exactly did you use these auditions to investigate Keira's murder?"

The coffee was down to an occasional drip, so I slid the pot off the burner and poured Ted a cup. Before I could return the pot, a drop of coffee hit the burner with an angry hiss.

"We let the actors perform a brief monologue and then asked them questions." I gave him the example of the girl from Oklahoma.

"But, sweetheart, if the killer *was* working undercover at the Horror Emporium in order to get an opportunity to murder someone — namely, Keira — he or she is *not* going to admit to having a prior connection to the victim."

"I know. Still, Vera and I got to meet the people behind the Horror Emporium masks and learn a little about them," I said. "If we find out anything new or see any of them acting suspiciously, we can fill you in."

"And what're you planning on telling your mom when all of these actors flock to the Stitch to see if she can help make them stars?"

I scrunched up my face. "I'm not ready to think about that yet."

I'd changed into a red dress and nude heels before my date with Ted. He'd dressed up too. He wore gray slacks, a white shirt, and a navy sport coat. So he looked great, but he didn't appear to be headed off to the police station.

And he brought me a single red rose. I put it in a bud vase and placed it in the center of the kitchen table. Ted gave Angus a granola bone — which I knew wouldn't be eaten until we returned — and again promised him a doggie bag.

On the drive to Lincoln City, Ted and I speculated about what Angus might be doing in our absence.

"First, he'll call all his friends from the dog park," Ted said.

"Don't be ridiculous. He'll send them a group text."

"Of course. I'd forgotten how tech savvy he is."

"So you think he's having several friends over instead of just one special someone?" I asked.

"Well, he hasn't given me the impression that he has his eye on anyone special. Has he said anything to you?"

"No . . . but then, he wouldn't." I took Ted's hand. "Too bad everyone can't find someone as wonderful as you." I groaned as soon as I'd said the words. "How sappy was that?"

"Pretty sappy. I might've gotten a cavity. In fact, I thought for a second there that we'd been transported into a corny movie of the week that would end in one of us tragically dying."

"I'm sorry. It's just that Jared Willoughby came by the Stitch today. He's really worried about his mom, and of course, he's upset over Keira. That poor guy has been so unlucky in love." I shook my head slightly. "First he had that disastrous short-lived marriage, then got into what — from all accounts — was a stormy relationship with Keira."

"He'll bounce back. And he'll find someone."

"Yeah . . . I know. I just hope you and Manu can keep his mom out of prison. I know she's innocent, Ted."

"We'll do our best, babe." He squeezed my hand. "Hey . . . we were laughing and joking about Angus planning a party, and now we're down in the dumps. This date is supposed to be cheering us up, you know."

"I know. Subject dropped. We'll put everything aside and have a wonderful night."

"All right," Ted said. "I do love how you're so compassionate, but tonight I don't want you to have the weight of the world on your shoulders."

"I won't." I wished I hadn't mentioned Jared, Keira, and Christine. The investigation was consuming so much of our attention, and we'd both wanted to put it out of our minds tonight. I resolved again to dedicate the evening to having fun and not being distracted by thoughts of something that — at least, for now — I could do nothing about.

That resolution, like most, turned out to be easier said than done. When we walked into the restaurant, we saw Jared Willoughby having dinner with the lovely young actress, Adalyn Daye.

CHAPTER TEN

As Ted drove us back home, I went ahead and acknowledged the elephant in the room . . . er, the backseat.

"Well, that was awkward . . . you know, trying to forget about the investigation when Jared Willoughby and his date are sitting at the table right across from ours."

"True. But I thought we did fairly well under the circumstances," said Ted. "When we passed by them, you greeted them both by name. Is the woman a Seven-Year Stitch customer?"

"No, she's actually one of the actresses at the Horror Emporium. Her name is Adalyn Daye."

After Ted and I had been seated, dinner conversation had been relegated to the mundane for us and for Jared and his date. Neither couple seemed to want to talk within earshot of the other. Jared acted as if I'd caught him doing something wrong, and

Adalyn seemed confused as to the weirdness that had settled between us.

"I don't know why Jared acted so strange," I said.

"It's not like it was wrong for him to be on a date . . . right? I mean, he and Keira had broken up."

"He *was* awfully jumpy though. In fact, he acted like a man with something to hide. You can bet I'll be looking even more closely into his whereabouts on the night Keira died and talking with their acquaintances about their relationship. I'll be going back and reviewing Ms. Daye's statement as well."

"You don't think they had anything to do with Keira's death, do you?"

He glanced over at me and raised a brow. "Now, Inch-High, what's my motto?"

"Everyone's a suspect."

Since Ted was working on Sunday — likely following the leads he'd gained on our date the night before — I called Riley Kendall to see if she was free for lunch.

"I'm thrilled that you called," she said. "Everyone decided I needed a day off — everyone, that is, except me. Mom took Laura, and Keith went to play basketball

146

with his brother. I'd love to have lunch with you."

"Wonderful. I'm having sort of a lonely day myself, and some girl time will do us both good."

"I'll bring a bottle of merlot."

"Does merlot go well with cheddar and bacon quiche?" I asked.

"Merlot goes well with *everything.*"

When I got off the phone, I went straight into the kitchen and got to work on that quiche. Of course, it was necessary to explain to Angus why I was rushing around, but he was delighted to hear that Riley was coming over.

I think he was happier still to learn that she wouldn't be bringing the baby. Not that Angus didn't like Laura — he did. And he wanted desperately to snuffle the tiny creature that smelled so intriguing from a distance. But every time Riley brought Laura around, both Riley and I shielded her from Angus's curiosity.

We knew — I more than Riley, naturally — that Angus would never purposely harm the child, but he was so large that we thought it best to wait until Laura was a little older and bigger before allowing the two to interact. Today, he didn't have to share Riley with the baby. He decided to take a nap so he'd be refreshed when she arrived. I deduced this from the way he lay down on the floor and fell asleep.

Even casually dressed, Riley had an air of sophistication and confidence about her. She made me feel as if she could step into a courtroom in the jeans and sweatshirt she wore and still sway a jury as if she was dressed in a designer suit. The adage *clothes make the woman* didn't apply to Riley.

"Mmmm. . . . something smells great." She gave me a hug and then handed me the bottle of merlot. "Don't think I forgot you, mister." She took a large cookie that was shaped like a peanut out of the small white bag she carried. "Did you know they're selling these at the pet shop now? They're organic and even gluten-free. What'll they think of next?"

I laughed and admitted that I had no idea. Angus took his cookie to the living room to savor it privately.

I'd already placed the quiche in the center of the table and had blueberry mini muffins in a napkin-lined basket on the counter. I moved the muffins over to the table before we sat down.

"It's nothing fancy," I said. "More of a brunch than a lunch, I suppose."

"I think it's super. Thank you again for inviting me. Maybe Mom and Keith were right about my needing a little time for myself."

I poured the wine into our glasses and served the quiche. As we ate, Riley asked me about Christine. "I don't know her all that well — only from the classes we've been in together at the Stitch — but she seems like a super-nice person."

"She is," I said. "I haven't spoken with her since the night Keira was found and we all had to go to the police station to give our statements, but she was terribly distraught about everything." I shook my head. "And you know the strongest piece of circumstantial evidence they have against her? A Seven-Year Stitch key ring."

I explained that I'd gotten the key rings in only on Thursday and that they were for the open house goodie bags.

"Christine was there in the shop right after the key rings arrived. She was upset about Jared — her son — and his relationship with Keira, so I handed her a key ring as sort of a pick-me-up. Then, lo and behold, the key ring was found beneath Keira's body."

"And Christine is the only person to whom you gave a key ring?" She'd clearly shifted into lawyer mode.

"Yes, but I took Angus for a walk and left the box open on the counter, so theoretically, someone could've come into the shop while we were gone and taken one," I said. "Not to say anyone would *steal* a key ring from the shop — they weren't all that valuable or anything — but someone could've come in, realized they were free, and —"

"Have you counted them?"

"What? No." I closed my eyes. "How dumb am I? That's the first thing I should've done Friday morning."

"Don't beat yourself up. You've had a lot on your mind," said Riley. "We'll go over there and count them now."

My eyes popped open. "No way! You can't spend your day sitting with me on the storeroom floor counting key rings. I'll go in early and do it tomorrow."

"Let's do it now. The two of us will be able to verify that the key rings weren't miscounted or that you didn't pocket one to help Christine." She smiled. "Besides, my curiosity has the best of me now."

Riley and I thought it best to leave Angus at home this trip. We shouldn't be gone long, and he was — as Riley had pointed out — another variable that could call the accuracy of our count into question. On the chance that more than one key ring was missing, the prosecutor could ask, "How can you be a hundred percent certain that your dog didn't carry off one while you were counting them?" Riley really did think of everything. I hoped I never found myself in trouble with the law but that, if I did, Riley Kendall was on my side of the courtroom.

I parked the Jeep at the back of the shop. When we started to go inside, Sadie came out of MacKenzies' Mochas with a bag of trash.

"Hey," she said. "Is anything wrong?"

"No," I said. "Riley and I are just here to count key rings."

Sadie frowned. "Key rings?"

"One of Marcy's promotional key rings was found underneath Keira's body Thursday night," said Riley. "The only person Marcy gave one to was Christine Willoughby."

"I did leave the open box on the counter when I took Angus for a walk Thursday morning," I said. "You were here when I came back. You didn't notice anyone coming into or leaving the shop around that time, did you?"

"No. I was so tired and frustrated, I don't think I even paid attention to a box being

151

on your counter that morning. And I certainly didn't take a key ring." She frowned. "So you guys are planning on counting the key rings because you're hoping it's the *only* one missing or because you're hoping more than one is missing?"

"I'm hoping there's at least one more missing," I said. "That key ring is the only evidence tying Christine to Keira's death. And I *know* she's innocent."

"Don't be too sure of that," said Sadie. "There's very little we know for certain." She lowered her eyes and shook her head slightly. "I need to get back inside. I'll try to come over later and help you if you need it."

"Um . . . okay . . . thanks." I unlocked the door, and Riley and I went inside.

I flipped on the lights and we walked into the storeroom.

"Sadie does have a point about not knowing everything about everyone," Riley said softly. "I've been an attorney too long not to realize that people are often capable of things we'd never thought them to be."

I realized she was probably thinking of her own father, who was currently serving time in prison for fraud.

She shook off her melancholy and smiled. "Sadie's gloomy mood must've been contagious. Let's put these grim thoughts aside and get to counting those key rings."

Thirty minutes later, we'd counted and recounted the Seven-Year Stitch key rings. Rather than the four hundred ninety-nine I'd expected there to be, there were four ninety-seven.

I looked at Riley. "So now what?"

"You let Ted know, and we'll both make a note of this on our calendars," she said. "That way, we have the exact date, time, and number of key rings logged. We don't know when the other two key rings were taken, and we can't even be a hundred percent sure that the company sent five hundred since you didn't count them upon arrival."

"But there's now reasonable doubt that the key ring found on the sidewalk beneath Keira's body is the one I gave to Christine?"

"Precisely."

We put the key rings back into the box, and I turned the lights off.

"I'll call Ted after we get back to my house," I said, opening the door.

I stopped when I heard angry shouting and shot Riley a questioning glance.

"Shh." She reached around me and pulled the door up, leaving it cracked so we could see who was arguing.

A short man with neatly trimmed black hair and a full beard was pointing his finger at someone. I eased the door open a tiny bit farther so I could see who the short man was pointing to. It was Blake.

"You'll pay for this!" the short man shouted. "My daughter's death is on your hands!"

"That must be Ken Sherman," I whispered.

Riley nodded.

"Should we do something?"

She shook her head. "This is something else you need to report to Ted . . . and then stay out of."

After Riley went home, I let Angus out into the backyard and sat on the porch swing. Angus typically liked to lie on the swing beside me, but he became interested in a squirrel and chased after it until it scampered up a tree. Angus lay at the bottom awaiting its return.

I breathed in the scent of the pine trees mixed with the briny sea air and wondered what to do with all the information I'd gathered over the past couple of days. This puzzle kept getting more and more complex.

While Christine Willoughby was the primary suspect due to the Seven-Year Stitch key ring I'd given her, Riley and I now knew there were three missing key rings from the box. Of course, Christine had said she lost the key ring, so the one found with Keira could very well have been hers. But what about the other two? Had someone taken them, or had I received only four ninety-seven from the factory? Should I contact the company to ask how certain they were that their shipments were a hundred percent accurate? Or would that make any difference in the eyes of the police?

And what about Jared and Adalyn? Had Keira known about their relationship? Had Adalyn known about Jared's relationship with Keira? Jared had to have known that with the two working in such close proximity — and with MacKenzies' Mochas doing concessions for the Horror Emporium — they would have to cross paths eventually.

My mind wandered back to Ken Sherman yelling at Blake. Why did he blame Blake for his daughter's death? Did he — like Blake — feel that Blake should've been helping Keira with the concessions rather than touring the Horror Emporium? Or was there something more to Mr. Sherman's accusations? I wondered whether I could find a way to casually talk with Mr. Sherman . . . or, if I should do as Riley had suggested and stay out of it.

There simply had to be *something* I could do to help find Keira's killer. I was completely lost in thought when my cell phone rang, and I started so violently that I almost fell off the swing. The ringtone was "You Don't Have to Be A Star," so I knew it was Mom.

"Hi, Mom. What's up?"

"I just had you on my mind. I'm really looking forward to seeing you on Tuesday."

"I'm looking forward to it too. But" — I took a deep breath — "there's something I need to tell you." I explained about the murder and how Vera and I had interviewed the Horror Emporium's actors to see if any of them had known Keira. "So now they think that you're scouting for new talent."

"You told them I'm a talent scout?" she asked.

"No. They know you're an acclaimed costume designer. But they also know that you have connections."

"Uh-huh."

"I'm sorry. I didn't know what else to do!"

"It's all right. We'll deal with it when I get there," she said. "Did your plan work? Did you find anyone who knew Keira?"

"I didn't think so, but then I saw Adalyn Daye — one of the actresses — with Jared

Willoughby."

"And Jared had been dating Keira."

"Right," I said.

"If I were you, I think I'd look at that a little closer," she said. "When you and Todd were going out, Keira was certainly aware of you."

"Yeah, and she hated me because she wanted Todd."

CHAPTER ELEVEN

After talking with Mom, I got to thinking about Keira and her obsessive behavior over Todd. I gave Todd a call.

"Hi," I said when he answered. "Do you have a minute to talk?"

"Sure. What's up?"

"When you dated Keira . . . what was she like?"

"I didn't go out with her but a time or two, and you *know* what she was like," Todd said. "I hate to speak ill of the dead, but Keira had problems. She was insecure, clingy. . . . Notice I'm *not* saying nuts."

"I did notice that." I told him about Jared Willoughby's visit to the Seven-Year Stitch the day before. "He said she was a better person than everyone realized but that he couldn't deal with her immaturity and negativity, so they broke up. He moved on quickly — Ted and I saw him at dinner last night with one of the actresses from the

Horror Emporium."

"Oh, I can imagine how happy Keira would have been had she known Jared was dating someone who worked right up the street from her," said Todd.

"Do you think she knew?"

He barked out a laugh. "Of course, she knew. She made it her business to know everything about every guy she was interested in . . . and about every girl *he* was interested in."

"I guess you're right. By the way, Riley and I went to the Stitch today. As we started to leave, we saw Ken Sherman yelling at Blake. He apparently blames Blake for Keira's death."

"Ken Sherman is probably blaming everyone except himself for his daughter's death. I don't know much about him, but he strikes me as that kind of guy." He paused. "I did talk with Blake, and he was planning on confessing everything to Sadie. He swore to me that there was nothing between him and Keira except a business relationship."

"I know," I said. "And I believe that's true. But he still went behind Sadie's back, and that'll take her a while to get over."

"You don't think Sadie suspected there was anything going on between Blake and Keira before Detective Poston put the thought into her mind, do you?"

"No. I believe she'd have come to me if she had. Friday morning, she was so hurt."

"I'd hate to think she killed the competition." He chuckled, but there wasn't his usual teasing warmth in the laugh. "Hey, I need to go. I'm picking Audrey up in half an hour."

"All right. Have fun."

I shook my head as I ended the call. There's no way that Todd Calloway would even *consider* that Sadie had something to do with Keira's murder. He knew better . . . and he *had* laughed. I was just being touchy.

So I was back to where I'd begun when I'd sat down — who *had* killed Keira and why? I mulled over everything that had happened and everything everyone had said. I wondered if Captain Moe knew more about Ken Sherman than he'd been at liberty to say in his crowded restaurant Friday night.

I called Ted.

"Hi, babe," he said. "I'm heading your way in just a few minutes."

"I wanted to ask you if you'd mind my asking Captain Moe to join us for dinner."

"I don't mind in the least, but I would like to know what you're up to, Inch-High."

I explained my feeling that Captain Moe could probably tell us more about Ken

Sherman here than he could at his restaurant. "And since Riley and I heard Mr. Sherman shouting at Blake today in the alley behind MacKenzies' Mochas, I'd like to know more about the man."

"You and Riley just happened to be lurking in the alley?"

"No. We'd gone to the Stitch to count the key rings. There were four hundred ninety-seven in the box."

"Good to know," he said. "If Christine Willoughby is innocent, then who was trying to set her — or you — up with that key ring?"

"That *is* the million-dollar question. And *why* runs a close second."

By the time Ted got to my house, I had oven-fried chicken baking, a tossed salad chilling in the refrigerator, green beans on the stove, and a turtle cheesecake thawing on the counter.

He gave me a kiss. "You sure have been busy."

"Does the house look okay? I cleaned before I began cooking. I gathered all of Angus's toys and put them in his basket in the living room, I mopped the kitchen, I —"

He silenced me with another kiss. "Everything — especially you — looks wonderful."

"Thanks. After all that cleaning, I had to shower and change, of course." I reached up to make sure my hair was dry. It was slightly damp but almost there. It occurred to me that I hadn't gone on my cleaning frenzy before inviting Riley over. But, then, Riley visits often. Captain Moe had never been to my house before.

"Is there anything you need for me to do?" Ted asked.

"You could tell me that Keira's killer has been arrested and that he or she gave a full confession and the case is closed."

"I wish I could, sweetheart. I'm working on it."

I rested my face against his broad chest. "I know."

He dropped a kiss on my head. "In the meantime, try not to worry so much."

"Easy for you to say."

"Actually, it's not. I want to find this killer every bit as much as you do."

"Let's hope Captain Moe can at least give us a little bit more insight into Ken Sherman," I said.

"I've only seen the man a time or two — when he's come into the station to talk with Manu — but there's something about him that gets my guard up. For one thing, he seems more angry than grief-stricken about his daughter's homicide," he said. "I know anger is one of the stages of grief and all, but something strikes me as not being quite right about that guy."

"You don't think . . . maybe *he* had something to do with Keira's death, do you?"

"I don't think he'd hurt his own daughter. Plus, he has an alibi for the time of her murder. But I wouldn't be surprised to learn that Ken Sherman has his fair share of enemies."

"Most powerful businessmen do," I said.

The doorbell rang.

"That must be Captain Moe." I hurried to the front door to find that I'd been correct in my assumption.

"Hello, Tinkerbell!" His voice boomed into the entryway and beyond as he handed me a bouquet of mixed fall flowers. "Thank you again for inviting me to dinner this evening."

"We're glad you accepted. Ted's in the kitchen. Come on back."

Ted and Captain Moe exchanged pleasantries while I put the flowers in a vase and placed them in the center of the table.

"Where's my friend Angus?" Captain Moe asked.

"He's in the backyard," I said. "He's been playing hide-and-seek with a squirrel for the majority of the afternoon. I'll bring him in to say hi after dinner."

"What're you drinking, my good man?" Ted asked.

"What've you got?"

Ted listed off the beverages we had, and Captain Moe settled on peach tea.

"I'll have the same," I said as I took the chicken out of the oven.

"This looks great, Tink. You've outdone yourself."

"Thank you. That's high praise coming from the best chef in Depoe Bay."

"Aw, I wouldn't say that," said Captain Moe. "I won't object if *you* say it, I just won't say it myself."

We all laughed.

I finished putting the food onto serving platters and placed them on the table. I did one last check to see if we needed anything else before we all sat down.

"I had lunch with Riley today," I told Captain Moe. I explained how she and I had gone to the Seven-Year Stitch to count the key rings left in the box I'd ordered.

"That sounds like Riley. When she gets something on the brain, she has to know immediately. So how many were in the box?"

"Four hundred ninety-seven. That accounts for the one I gave to Christine Willoughby, and as for the two others . . ." I shrugged. "Either someone came in and took a couple while the box was sitting on the counter, or the factory shorted me."

"I doubt the factory shorted you," said Captain Moe. "If it's a reputable company, they know it would come back on them if they didn't provide what they'd promised."

"The captain's right. Most factories have quality-control systems in place to ensure the customers get what they pay for."

"So now we just need to figure out who took them and why," I said. "We don't know whether someone is trying to set up me or Christine, or if it was simply a coincidence that a Seven-Year Stitch key ring was found with Keira's body."

"Captain Moe, you mentioned Ken Sherman the other night," said Ted. "How familiar with him are you?"

Captain Moe inclined his head and didn't look up from the chicken breast he was cutting. "I don't know him all that well, but I've heard plenty of rumors."

"You think it might be one of those *where*

there's smoke, there's fire type things?" Ted asked.

Captain Moe met Ted's eyes and nodded. "I don't think Ken Sherman is someone I'd care to do business with."

"What kinds of things have you heard about him?" I asked.

Captain Moe savored a bite of the chicken. "This is delicious, Marcy. Thanks again."

Marcy. Not Tinkerbell. He's dodging the question.

Ted ate a forkful of green beans. I got the impression that I shouldn't ask anything else about Ken Sherman . . . that Captain Moe would tell us whatever he wanted us to know if and when he felt like it. But I also resisted the urge to change the subject.

After a couple of minutes of eating in companionable silence, Captain Moe said, "I've heard he launders money for a drug dealer."

Ted was reaching for his glass and nearly knocked it over. "What?"

"Ken Sherman," he said. "I've heard that those businesses he franchises are fronts for money-laundering operations."

"That's why he doesn't really care whether or not they succeed," I said.

"Right," said Captain Moe. "Although I don't think that was his initial plan for the

MacKenzies' Mochas franchise — and I'd hate for it to get out that I'd said such a thing. I have no way of knowing whether or not the rumors are true. And you said he was opening the coffee shop for his daughter." He shrugged.

"Your secret's safe with us," said Ted. "We won't tell a soul. But I will discreetly look into Mr. Sherman's business operations. I mean, we're doing that anyway, but I'll look a little closer now to see whether or not Mr. Sherman might have had an enemy who could have hurt Keira to get back at her father for some reason."

"Just be careful." Captain Moe took a drink of his tea. "As I told you, I don't *know* anything, but I've heard that some of the people Ken Sherman deals with aren't very nice."

"When Riley and I were leaving the Stitch today, we heard Mr. Sherman yelling accusations at Blake MacKenzie," I said. "It seemed he was blaming Blake for Keira's death."

"Then that's another lead for our fine detective to pursue, isn't it, Tink?"

I smiled, glad we were back to my nickname and that the conversation appeared to have lightened. "Indeed it is. You know, sometimes you sound just like your niece."

He laughed. "Hopefully, some of the lessons her father and I taught her served her well."

"Are you going to see the baby while you're in Tallulah Falls?" I asked.

"Now, do you honestly think I'd miss an opportunity to see wee Laura?"

"No, I don't believe you would."

After Captain Moe left, I was tidying up the kitchen when Ted came up behind me and snaked his arms around my waist. He kissed my shoulder.

"Thank you for dinner. It was terrific," he said.

"Thank you for walking Angus after he ate," I said. "He'd have been content to go back out into the backyard and squirrel hunt, you know."

"I know, but it was starting to rain, and it's time for little doggies to get settled in for the evening."

I laughed at his calling Angus *little.* "You're good with him."

"He's good with me."

I turned in his embrace. "You're good with me too."

We kissed, and then I took Ted's hand and walked into the living room. Angus was already snoozing in front of the hearth.

"I think Captain Moe's visit tired him out," I said as Ted and I snuggled on the sofa.

"The good captain certainly gave me a few new leads to pursue."

"So you really think Ken Sherman might be laundering money for some drug dealer?" I asked.

"It's entirely possible. And it would explain the start-up businesses that he doesn't seem to care whether or not they fail."

I ran my fingers lightly over Ted's hand. "But how will you be able to confirm that? It's not like Mr. Sherman will have accounts labeled JOHN BROWN, DRUG DEALER."

"We'll simply have to investigate all of his clients to make sure they are who he says they are," Ted said.

"And how will you do that without Mr. Sherman becoming suspicious?"

"I haven't figured that one out yet."

I took a deep breath.

"What's really on your mind?" Ted asked.

"Blake . . . and Sadie. You don't think Blake *knew* Ken Sherman is laundering money for a drug dealer, do you?"

"Sweetheart, *we* don't know that Ken Sherman is laundering money for a drug dealer. Right now, it's purely conjecture." He gave me a gentle squeeze. "That said, I don't think Blake would've volunteered the MacKenzies' Mochas logo to someone planning to open a franchise used to launder drug money."

"I don't either," I said. "But I'm worried about their financial situation. They took on the extra work with the Horror Emporium. Blake obviously wanted to pursue this business venture with Keira and her dad. . . . I can't help but wonder how far they are in the red and how far they — or, at least, Blake — would go to get them into the black?"

"You do know that's none of your business and that if you poke that bear, Sadie and Blake are gonna be pretty angry, don't you?"

"Yes, of course, I do. I'm as bad as Todd." I told Ted about talking with Todd about Keira and his asking whether or not I thought Sadie had feared Blake was cheating with Keira before Detective Poston had put that thought into her head. "He said, 'I'd hate to think she killed the competition.' Of course, he laughed as he said it, but I couldn't believe he'd say such a thing even as a joke. I mean, this was *Sadie* we were talking about."

Ted was silent and still.

I was snuggled against him, but I turned

to look at his face. It was a carefully constructed blank mask.

"You don't think Sadie had anything to do with Keira's death, do you?" I asked.

"At this point, I can't say for sure. You know I have to remain objective and that everyone is a suspect right now."

"But you don't think *Todd* actually believes Sadie could've had anything to do with Keira's death, do you?"

"You'd have to ask Todd that," he said.

"I know Sadie . . . and I know Blake," I said. "They might be having money problems, but they're good, honest people. They wouldn't do anything that might get someone else hurt."

They wouldn't. I *knew* they wouldn't. And yet, I was scared.

CHAPTER TWELVE

Angus and I got to the Seven-Year Stitch an hour early because I was so anxious to talk with Sadie. I called her and asked if she could come over.

"Um . . . yeah. . . . We're really busy, Marce, but I'll be there as soon as I can spare a few minutes. Is anything wrong?"

"No, everything's fine."

"Want me to bring you anything?" she asked.

For once, I passed on the low-fat vanilla latte with cinnamon. That's how Sadie knew something was wrong, pulled one of her waitresses from the floor to help Blake behind the counter, and hurried to the Stitch.

"I got here as quickly as I could," she said as she hurried through the door. "What's going on?"

"Let's sit down."

She followed me over to the sit-and-stitch

square. "I thought you wanted to talk about your menu, but when you refused your usual latte, I knew something was up."

"I'm worried about you . . . and Blake."

Sadie's face tightened, and I knew she'd gone into defense mode.

"Just hear me out," I said. "As Riley and I were leaving yesterday, we saw — and heard — Ken Sherman in the alley yelling at Blake. He was blaming Blake for Keira's death."

"I know. The man is grieving. He's blaming everybody right now."

I leaned forward and placed my hand on Sadie's arm. "That's not the only thing. Captain Moe told us that Mr. Sherman has a bad reputation . . . that he might not be a completely legitimate businessman."

"I'm way ahead of you on that too, Marcy. Blake had heard the rumors, and he broke off the deal last Monday. That's another reason why he hadn't felt the need to go into everything with me. He figured what was the point since he'd already backed out."

"That's a valid argument . . . but I know you're angry that he didn't tell you he was still considering the deal with Mr. Sherman and was hoping to persuade you to change your mind," I said.

"I was angry, but I'm not anymore. I'm over it. I blew it all out of proportion." She shrugged. "I do that sometimes. Now . . . about your menu."

Since Sadie had effectively ended the discussion of Ken Sherman, why he blamed Blake for Keira's death, and Blake's reasons for not telling her about everything up front, we spent the next fifteen minutes finalizing the menu for the anniversary party. I wanted to ask if she and Blake were okay financially and to offer help if they needed it, but the stony set to Sadie's face told me it would do no good to try to talk about that today. She was shutting me out . . . just as Blake had shut her out. Granted, secrets between a husband and wife were entirely different from secrets between best friends — generally, besties *knew* each other's secrets — but her putting a wall between us stung.

After Sadie left, I called Ted.

"Good morning, sunshine," he said.

I laughed softly. "Thanks. I needed that this morning."

"Well, it's so dreary in Tallulah Falls today that you're the only sunshine around."

"I'm glad you think so." I told him about my conversation with Sadie. "So if Blake broke off the deal the Monday before Keira was murdered, do you think maybe that affected Ken Sherman's customers in some way?"

"It could have. If one of the drug cartels was already planning on laundering money through Keira's MacKenzies' Mochas franchise, then that certainly would've thrown a wrench into their plans."

"But couldn't Mr. Sherman have still opened a coffeehouse for Keira under a different name?" I asked. "Although why he would want to launder money through his daughter's business is beyond me."

"I'm looking into all of his business ventures today. Meanwhile, Inch-High, stay out of it . . . *please.* If what Captain Moe told us is true, then Ken Sherman is a dangerous man."

"I'll be careful," I said. "You be careful."

"Always."

After talking with Ted, I went ahead and opened the shop. Then I took my tote bag from behind the counter and sat on the sofa facing the window looking out onto the street. I took out the ribbon embroidery bouquet project I was making to give as a door prize. I really needed to get busy on it since I intended to have it framed by Friday.

Angus, too, had been in the mood to look outside this morning. He was lying in front of the window. It was his excited bark that brought my attention to the fact that Christine Willoughby was walking past.

She waved at Angus and me through the glass, and then held up her index finger to suggest she'd be back.

A few minutes later, she returned with a MacKenzies' Mochas cup and, after greeting Angus, joined me in the sit-and-stitch square. She sat on the sofa across from me and sipped her drink.

"I'm sorry," she said. "It was rude of me not to ask if you wanted anything from MacKenzies' Mochas as I walked past, especially knowing that I was coming right back here."

"That's fine," I said. "I'm good. How are you holding up?"

"Well, as you can see, I'm scatterbrained. My nerves have been a wreck since I found out about Keira and that key ring."

"About the key rings . . . Riley Kendall and I counted them yesterday, and there were only four ninety-seven in the box."

Her eyes widened. "That means I didn't have the only one!"

"It at least gives you reasonable doubt. Do you have an attorney yet?"

"Not yet," said Christine. "To be honest, I can't really afford it. Jared offered to get a loan against his business for me, but I can't let him do that. What if they find me guilty anyway, and Jared would lose his mother *and* his business?"

"We're not gonna let that happen. If you'd like, I can call Riley and see who she recommends from legal aid."

"Would you?" she asked. "I'd appreciate that so much."

I'd picked up the phone to call Riley's office when a customer came in. I stood, set aside my ribbon embroidery, and greeted the man.

"Hello! Welcome to the Seven-Year Stitch. I'm Marcy."

"And who is this?" he asked, stooping slightly to pet Angus.

"That's Angus."

The man wore a tan trench coat and a brown fedora, and he somehow seemed to have stepped out of another era.

"I'm looking for a gift for my granddaughter," he said. "When I saw the name of your shop, I just had to come in. Marilyn Monroe . . . she was one of the greats."

"She certainly was."

"Lovely woman . . . curvy. . . . Advertisers don't seem to appreciate women with any meat on their bones anymore, but the men still do."

I laughed.

"I'm sorry, my dear. I didn't mean to be indelicate. I just simply don't understand the direction the world has taken," he said.

"That's quite all right. What did you have in mind for your granddaughter?"

"I have no earthly idea. I was hoping you'd help me come up with something."

He told me her age — ten — and I walked him over to the children's crafts. He chose a beginner's cross-stitch kit, a friendship bracelet kit, and a latch hook kit.

"Surely, she'll like one of these," he said.

"I'm betting she'll like them all." I rang up his purchases, placed them in a bag, and invited him to bring his granddaughter to our anniversary party on Friday evening. "I'll be giving goodie bags to everyone, and there will be plenty of door prizes too."

"Sounds fun. I'll see if I can't get her to be my date."

As the man headed off down the street, I rejoined Christine in the sit-and-stitch square.

"He seemed awfully nice," she said.

"He did." I paused. "Speaking of people *seeming* nice, did Jared ever say anything about Keira's dad?"

"No, I don't think so. Why?"

"I've heard some rumors that his business ventures might not all be legitimate," I said.

"Of course, it could simply be the gossip mill speculating about Keira's murder."

"I'll ask Jared if he ever heard anything, but you know how people talk. When someone is rich and powerful, folks sometimes like to cut them down." She frowned. "Then again, he did have all that money, and Keira would still take loans from Jared. Maybe he isn't a very good person after all."

"Maybe not. Ted and I saw Jared when we were out to dinner on Saturday."

"He told me about that," she said. "Jared has been dating Adalyn for a couple of weeks. I don't think it's anything serious yet, but it was a major step for him in getting away from Keira."

"Did Keira know Jared was seeing Adalyn?"

"I don't know. Maybe."

"If she did, that would explain why Keira hadn't wanted to work concessions at the Horror Emporium," I said.

"I suppose so. But, as I said, there's nothing serious between Jared and Adalyn yet . . . at least, not as far as I know."

"Still, with Keira, everything was serious when it interfered with her getting what she wanted." I explained about how she'd considered me a threat when she liked Todd Calloway. "The girl detested me and would do anything she could to get my goat."

"You don't . . ." Christine bit her lower lip. "You don't think . . . Adalyn and Keira might've . . . fought . . . do you?"

"I doubt it," I said. "I'm merely speculating. Let me go ahead and call Riley to see who she recommends at legal aid."

I called Riley's office. Riley was in court, but her administrative assistant, Julie, said that Riley had a list of people she recommended. The first person on that list was Sean Clay. I passed his information along to Christine, and she said she'd call him as soon as she got home.

Christine left, and I resumed my work on the ribbon embroidery bouquet. Once again, I wished there was some way I could talk with Ken Sherman. I felt that if I could speak with him — even for a minute — I could get a better handle on what kind of person he was. I already knew that Ted didn't get a good vibe from the man. I wanted my own first impression.

Keira had died on Thursday. Had this been a normal death, her funeral would have likely taken place on Sunday. I knew that the autopsy would hold up any memorial services, but the coroner's office *had* to release the body to the family soon . . . didn't they?

■ ■ ■ ■

By the time Ted brought lunch, I'd finished the ribbon embroidery bouquet. Now to iron it and have it framed. But ironing could definitely wait until after lunch.

Today, Ted brought Caesar salads and breadsticks from our favorite Italian restaurant on the outskirts of Tallulah Falls.

"Wow, you had to go out of your way today," I said as I placed the clock on the front door.

"I thought it would be worth it."

I smiled. "It totally is."

"And, to be honest, I was in the area anyway."

"Chasing down a bad guy?"

"Chasing down a lead," he said, following me into my office. "One of Ken Sherman's franchises is out that way. It's a café that specializes in hot dogs."

"Bob's Big Dogs?"

"That's the one." He handed Angus a breadstick, and the dog wolfed it down.

I took two bottles of water from the mini-fridge. "Sorry. This is all I have. I need to go by the grocery store and restock after work."

"You probably need to restock at home

too. Your mom comes in tomorrow, doesn't she?"

"She does," I said.

"I thought maybe we could get our moms together for dinner before your class on Wednesday." Ted opened his salad and sprinkled the packet of Romano cheese over the top. "That way, we'll have only an hour. If it's awkward, we have an excuse to duck out."

"Smart thinking. I knew I loved you for more than your brawn." I smiled as I dug into my salad.

"Have you told your mom very much about mine?"

"Not a lot. You?"

"Not too much. She knows she's a costume designer and that she lives in San Francisco."

"Mine knows Veronica once put a federal agent in time-out," I said.

Ted laughed. "Yeah, I suppose she did."

"Um . . . not to change the subject, but I guess I'm really *not* changing the subject but rather changing it back —"

"We have only half an hour, you know."

"I know," I said. "I was wondering what — if anything — you learned from Bob's Big Dogs."

"I learned that those hot dogs were definitely not what we wanted for lunch," he said. "And I'm not joking. There were several patrons in the place, but the majority of them had sodas. That was it. I can see going to a coffee shop to enjoy a beverage and a chat with some associates but not a hot dog place."

"I agree. Those fountain sodas are hit-or-miss. So you think they were up to something nefarious?"

"Hard to say," he said. He ate his salad for a moment and thought this over. "They weren't *doing* anything nefarious while I was there, but they could very well have been plotting up something."

"So how did you wander around in the restaurant without making anyone suspicious?" I asked.

"I didn't. I asked for the manager, introduced myself, and told him we were talking with people who knew Ken Sherman to determine if anyone could help us identify his daughter's killer."

"Whoa. . . . I imagine you could've heard a hot dog drop in there after you made that announcement."

"Well, yeah. And then the manager took me into his office and told me what a bad decision he'd made when he'd agreed to allow Ken Sherman to finance this venture for him. He said his business had started out fairly strong but that now it was going downhill fast," said Ted. "He said, 'You see the people out there. How many of them are eating?' I asked if he knew *why* they weren't eating, and he either suddenly forgot how to talk or remembered who his patrons were."

"Then doesn't that kinda confirm what you went there to learn?" I asked.

"It does, but *kinda* doesn't hold up in a court of law."

"I was just thinking earlier that I'd love to talk with Ken Sherman . . . get a feel for who he is, what makes him tick, you know?"

Ted leveled his steely blue gaze across the desk at me. "No."

"No? You don't know what I mean? Well, I'm talking about seeing what kind of first impression he makes on me. I know he didn't leave you with a very good one, so —"

"Marcy, this is not a joking matter."

"And I'm not kidding! I truly want to meet the man," I said. "I'll tell you what I *really* want. I want to go to Keira's funeral. On television, the killer always shows up at the funeral. If we were there, we could see who showed up, I could say a few words to Mr. Sherman, and —"

184

"I *am* going. In fact, Manu and I are going."

"Then Reggie and I should go too. If you and Manu go by yourselves, then it's going to be obvious that you're there as police officers. If you guys take Reggie and me, then everyone will think you're there as concerned members of the community." I let my words sink in for a minute. "Please?"

He blew out a breath before biting into a breadstick.

Good stalling tactic. He couldn't talk with his mouth full.

"When is the service?" I asked.

He swallowed. "This evening."

"They've finished the autopsy already? That was quick."

"We asked that Keira's autopsy be made a top priority."

"What was the official cause of death?" When he hesitated, I reminded him that the death certificate would be a matter of public record.

"I could suggest you look it up," he said dryly. "But I might as well tell you — the cause of death was heart failure from venom toxicity. She was poisoned."

I gasped. "So it *was* the rattlesnake?"

He shook his head. "The puncture wounds are inconsistent with the distance between

185

the snake's fangs."

I frowned. "But —"

"I've said too much already."

"Okay. So what time is the service tonight?"

He took a long drink of his water. "Let me talk with Manu. I'll call you later this afternoon and give you all the details."

Chapter Thirteen

Ted picked me up at six p.m. That had given me only little over a half hour after getting home to feed Angus and get ready for the funeral. I hadn't had time to stop by the grocery store, but I figured drinking water for one more day would do us good. When Ted arrived, he'd changed into a black suit, gray shirt, and dark gray tie. He looked gorgeous.

I was wearing a long-sleeved black dress with a high-necked lace bodice and black heels. I'd curled my hair and pinned it back off my face with rhinestone clips. My platinum locks were short but versatile, and I felt this style made me look more serious.

"You look beautiful," Ted said as he helped me into my cobalt blue coat.

"Thank you."

I left the living room and hall lights on for Angus and turned the porch light on for Ted and me.

When we arrived at Tallulah Falls's one and only funeral parlor, Manu and Reggie were waiting for us in their car in the parking lot. We parked beside them and got out.

"Do I look all right?" Reggie asked, indicating her simple white tunic and slacks. "White is what we wear to funerals in India. I couldn't find anything black that was appropriate."

"You look lovely," I said.

Manu looked nice too. He wore a black suit, cut much like the one worn by Ted, a white shirt, and a white pocket square. I liked how he'd managed to comingle the mourning colors of his native land and America's.

"I don't really know what to say to anyone," Reggie said. "I barely knew Keira at all."

"We're here to express our respect and regrets to her family," said Manu. "I didn't know the girl either."

A shadow passed over his face, and I imagined he was remembering how he'd found her and tried to care for her when we'd come upon her on the sidewalk.

I squeezed Ted's hand. I didn't tell him often enough how much I appreciated his job and his skill in taking care of others.

He smiled down at me. I hoped he could

guess at what I was thinking . . . or that I could remember to tell him later.

We walked inside to the cloying scents of carnations, mums, and roses. There was a small dish of wrapped peppermints in the foyer. I took one, unwrapped it, and took a deep breath to savor the smell of the candy before I popped it into my mouth. I looked around for a wastepaper basket but couldn't find one.

"Be right back," I said to Ted.

I stepped into a hallway that opened up to a larger room. I saw a small garbage can discreetly placed near an end table in that room. I hurried over and tossed in my cellophane wrapper.

I raised my head, and it occurred to me that I'd walked into the room where the casket was — or, at least, where a casket was. I didn't know if this was the room set aside for the Sherman family or not.

There were a few people mingling around, but I didn't recognize any of them. Some were giving me curious glances, so I made my way slowly to the casket.

Inside was Kiera in a long-sleeved yellow dress with a white lace overlay on the bodice. Her long dark hair was spread out on the pillow, and she reminded me of one of those princesses asleep in a fairy tale. I thought maybe if Jared came and kissed her, she'd open those smoky gray eyes and sit up.

A wave of sadness swept over me, and my eyes filled. A tear escaped down my right cheek.

Someone came up beside me and offered me a tissue.

"Thank you," I said, dabbing at my eyes. When I turned, I was surprised to see that it was Ken Sherman who'd given me the tissue. "Oh . . . Mr. Sherman. . . ."

He smiled slightly. "I'm sorry. Your name escapes me."

"I'm Marcy Singer," I said. "We've never met. I just . . . um . . . recognized you from seeing you with . . . Keira."

"I see. Well, we've met now."

I nodded. "I'm so sorry for your loss."

"Thank you. How did you know Keira?"

"I knew her from MacKenzies' Mochas," I said. "I didn't know her all that well . . . and I regret that now." I really did regret that. After what Jared had told me, it seemed Keira could've used a few more friends.

He shook his head slightly and stared at his daughter lying in her casket. I patted his arm.

"Dad . . . are you all right?" The smooth,

cultured voice came from behind Ken Sherman and me.

Mr. Sherman turned. "Yes, darling. Come here and meet Marcy. She used to work with Keira."

"Um . . . actually, we didn't work together," I said. "I have the embroidery shop down the street from MacKenzies' Mochas."

"Oh," said the sophisticated young woman who was apparently Keira's sister. "The Seven-Year Stitch. I've been meaning to stop in."

"Marcy, this is Bethany," said Mr. Sherman.

Bethany and I shook hands. Hers were long, thin, and well manicured. I remembered what Jared had said about her — gorgeous and brilliant. I couldn't attest to the brilliance yet, but Bethany was stunning. She looked similar to Keira; but where Keira reminded me of a Disney princess lying there, Bethany reminded me of a supermodel. There was nothing princess-y about her. She was all sleek lines and . . . well . . . hard edges. I could easily believe Jared had been right about her dual degrees too.

"Do you embroider?" I asked. It sounded lame, but she'd said she'd been meaning to visit the Stitch, and it gave me something to say.

"Some of the women in my circle knit," said Bethany. "I've been thinking of picking it up."

"Well, if you do, come and see me."

"I certainly will." She turned to her dad. "I just wanted to make sure you're all right. I left some people in the other room. I need to get back to them." She glanced over her shoulder at me. "Nice meeting you, Marcy."

"It was nice meeting you too," I said.

Bethany strode away, and Mr. Sherman smiled at me, pride shining in his eyes.

"Isn't she something?" he asked.

"Yes, she is. She appears to be holding her emotions in check well."

"Oh, that Bethany is a rock," he said. "She takes care of everyone else, leaving herself for last. It makes me worry about her sometimes."

My eyes cut to the room across the hall from us where Bethany was throwing her head back and laughing at something someone had said. Either she wasn't really all that broken up about her sister's death, or else she was hiding it awfully well.

"What does she do . . . for a living, I mean?" I asked.

"She's a criminal attorney in a prestigious

firm in Seattle," he said. "She also has a doctorate in psychology, so she has an edge over other lawyers in the courtroom."

"I imagine so. That's wonderful."

"It is." His eyes misted. "I'm so proud of her. Poor Keira. . . . We couldn't even persuade her to go on to college. She was so lazy and unmotivated. She thought I'd give her everything until she could find a man and get married."

The conversation was getting more and more awkward, and I just wanted to get away. I felt sorrier for Keira than ever.

"I guess maybe she thought her strengths lay in becoming a homemaker," I said.

"Who knows? I cut her off and made her get a job, hoping she'd come to her senses," he said. "When she didn't, I thought I'd buy her a business. I thought she could maybe make a go of that."

"Excuse me, Mr. Sherman. I need to speak with someone," I said. "Again, I'm truly sorry for your loss."

"Thank you, Marcy."

I hurried into the foyer where Ted, Manu, and Reggie were waiting.

"Where've you been?" Ted asked. "We were getting concerned about you."

"I went to throw away my candy wrapper

and wound up in the room with . . . with Keira."

"Let's step out into the fresh air," Reggie said.

"Good idea." I hurried out the front door, and they followed closely behind me.

"What happened?" Ted asked when we got to a relatively secluded area.

"I spoke with Mr. Sherman." I blinked back the tears that suddenly burned my eyes. "I wish we could just leave. I know it was my idea to come here, but . . . but poor Keira!"

"I can drive you home," Ted said. "I can still get back in time for the funeral."

"No," I said. "I'll see this through. Besides, I feel like *someone* has to be here for her. I mean, I think her dad cared about her . . . but not as much as he loves her sister and — and maybe even his business."

"Are you sure?" Ted asked. "We've got this if you'd like to go home."

"We do," said Manu. "We know the boyfriend, his new girlfriend, his mom . . . all the major players. We even know some of the people who might've been working with Mr. Sherman."

"No." I lifted my chin. "I'm not gonna bail on you guys." I took a deep breath. "I'm feeling better now. I just . . . I know exactly what you mean about getting a weird vibe from Mr. Sherman now."

We went back inside and sat down in the chapel. The casket was wheeled from the viewing area to the front of the chapel before the service began. We were the only ones not socializing in the other two rooms when the coffin was brought into the chapel. Reggie, Manu, Ted, and I sat on the back row where we could observe everyone.

Blake and Sadie came in, but they didn't seem to notice us and sat in the middle on the side opposite us.

The Atwoods came in. Not surprisingly, they looked as if they'd just come off the set of a comedic horror show. Claude wore a black tuxedo with tails, a ruffled black shirt, black bow tie, and black top hat. He even walked with a black cane with a gold handle. From where we were sitting, I couldn't be sure, but the handle looked like the head of an eagle. Priscilla wore a long, Kelly green gown with a matching headband that held a large flower. Her hair was curled into an intricate updo. When she walked, I noticed there was a thigh-high slit in the gown and groaned aloud before I'd realized what I was doing.

Ted raised a brow at me.

"Sorry," I whispered. "That's just . . . inappropriate."

"Agreed."

"Definitely," Reggie said from my other side. "Disgustingly immodest."

"Oh, it's not that bad," said Manu, and earned an elbow to the ribs from his wife.

Ted chuckled into his fist.

Several of the Horror Emporium actors trailed in after the Atwoods and sat with them — or near them, when they ran out of room on the pew. I saw the one who was afraid of dogs, the one who'd done a monologue from *Hamlet* . . . and Adalyn Daye. Adalyn wore a tasteful black suit and black flats. Her hair was held at the nape of her neck by a black ribbon. She appeared to be very quiet and reserved, especially in comparison with the Atwoods and the rest of their entourage.

Todd came in, spotted us, and came to sit in the row in front of us. He turned to say a hushed hello.

"I'm glad you're here," I whispered.

"I'm glad you guys are here," he said. "I feel really uncomfortable being at Keira's funeral, but I felt like I should come."

Christine Willoughby walked in, her blue purse clutched to her chest. Her eyes darted right and left, and she went up the left side between the pews and the wall. She sat in a pew about a third of the way from the front.

She looked miserable. I supposed she was here for Jared, but where was he? I kept thinking he'd join her any second, but he never did.

Manu, Reggie, Todd, Ted, and I had agreed to meet at the Brew Crew for a drink. Since Ted and Manu were driving, they had sodas. Reggie had a white wine. And, since I felt depressed, I had a decaffeinated coffee with Irish cream.

"Where was Keira's mom?" I asked to no one in particular.

"She died when Keira and Bethany were young," said Todd.

"And Mr. Sherman never remarried?"

He shook his head. "From what I hear, he keeps a few girlfriends on the string but didn't want to risk his wealth by marrying again."

"What did you guys think of Bethany?" I asked.

"The stunner sitting beside Ken Sherman?" Todd asked. "Wow. I'd heard about her from Keira, but she exceeded even Keira's exaggerations."

I slapped Todd's arm lightly.

"Ouch! What was that for?"

"Well, maybe if everybody didn't feel like Bethany was so perfect, Keira would've gotten more attention and been a better, happier person."

"Everyone deals with sibling issues, dear," said Reggie. "I have two sisters — one younger and one older. We had our differences growing up. Each of us thought another of us was our mother's pet or our father's favorite. We got over it. It's what you do as you mature."

"What about you?" I asked Ted. "Did you and Tiffany have any issues growing up?"

"Of course. We used to fight all the time. We didn't stop until I went to college and we didn't live in the same house anymore," he said. "We don't talk every day or anything like that, but we each know the other would be there if needed."

"I not only had to deal with siblings, but I had plenty of cousins to compete with," said Manu. "We loved one another, we hated one another, but at the end of the day, we were family."

"That sounds great. I never had siblings or cousins," I said. "But I never felt that I was missing out on anything. I just wish things had been different for Keira. Even standing there at her casket, her father was comparing her unfavorably to Bethany —

and he was talking to *me* . . . a stranger!"

"That is sad," said Reggie. "But we can't know what he's feeling. Maybe he was talking that way to hide his grief."

"Maybe," I said.

I glanced at Ted and he shrugged.

"I'm sorry I slapped your arm, Todd." I took a sip of my coffee.

"That's all right. I'll send you the bill for the X-ray." He winked.

"Christine looked so scared when she walked in," I said. "I should've gone and sat with her, but I kept thinking Jared would join her."

"She did look frightened," said Manu. "It took a lot of courage for her to come to that service, especially given the fact that she's our primary suspect."

"Wonder why Jared *didn't* join her?" Reggie asked. "He had been dating the girl, hadn't he?"

"Yes," I said. "They were off and on, but still. . . ."

"For his mother to come *and* the woman he's currently dating to be there as well . . ." Ted frowned. "It looks suspicious that he didn't show."

CHAPTER FOURTEEN

I got up early Tuesday morning to prepare the guest room — that also doubled as my office — for my mom. I put fresh sheets on the bed, dusted, vacuumed, and put a small crystal bowl of foil-wrapped chocolates on the chest of drawers. I'd have put the chocolates on the nightstand, but I was afraid a certain curious dog would find them.

Once the pillows were fluffed and lavender sachets put in the dresser drawers, Angus and I headed for the Seven-Year Stitch. I'd barely shrugged out of my jacket when Jared Willoughby came in. Surprisingly, he was dressed in khakis, a red knit sweater, and a navy blue sport coat.

"Hey, Marcy, are you alone?" Jared asked as Angus loped over to say hello.

"Not anymore." I tried to force a smile, but the fact was that I didn't want to be here alone with Jared. Not that I thought he was a killer . . . but deep down I was no longer so sure of his innocence.

He ruffled Angus's ears before going over to sit on the sofa. "Come talk with me for a minute. Please?"

"Sure." I placed my jacket on the counter and sat on one of the red club chairs near Jared.

"I wanted to explain to you about Saturday," he said. "About Adalyn. It probably looked bad for me to be out on a date when my ex-girlfriend was . . . you know. . . ."

"Dead?"

"Yeah. I guess it made me look callous. But I haven't been seeing Adalyn for that long, and I didn't want her to think I still had feelings for Keira."

"Is that why you didn't come to Keira's memorial service?" I asked.

He bit his lip and he stared down at his clasped hands. "The truth is I *do* still have feelings for Keira. Or, I did. I don't know. Either way, I simply couldn't bring myself to see her that way." He sighed. "I'd told Mom I'd meet her there, but in the end, I just couldn't do it."

"You know, Adalyn — and everyone else — would've understood if you'd come to the service and been upset. I mean, you and Keira were close."

"Yeah, I know. It was cowardly of me . . . especially to ditch Mom that way." He stood. "I did go to Keira's interment this morning. There weren't very many people there for that. Well, I need to get home and change and get to the garage. I just wanted to explain."

"Of course. Well, have a good day."

"Thanks. You too." He patted Angus's head. "See ya, buddy!"

As Jared left, I wondered why he'd felt it necessary to tell me why he'd been with Adalyn on Saturday and why he *hadn't* been at the funeral the night before. Had he thought I'd report what he'd said back to Ted — which, of course, I would — to supply answers to questions the police might have? If that had been his intent, he might've raised more questions than he'd answered.

I took my jacket and hung it up on the coatrack in the office. Angus went with me, knowing that's where I kept his granola treats. I gave him one, and he hurried back into the shop to lie down by the front window to eat it. I retrieved my ribbon embroidery project — the second one — and returned to the sit-and-stitch square to get to work.

I glanced up, and the sidewalk on both sides of the street appeared to be flooded with people. I quickly put my project under the counter and grabbed Angus's leash. *Tour bus.*

"Come on, baby," I said to him. "Let's get you into the bathroom." I spotted his Kodiak bear lying near the hallway and snatched it up as I begged him to cooperate with me. I finally muscled him into the bathroom, unsnapped the leash, and tossed him the bear. With the final promise that I'd get him as soon as the tourists left, I pulled the door shut. He barked, whined, and scratched the door.

I hated putting him in there, but I felt it best that he not be around that many tourists. Some were probably elderly, and I was afraid one might trip over Angus or that he'd accidentally knock someone down.

People were already milling around the shop when I got back from the bathroom.

"Welcome to the Seven-Year Stitch!" I called over the cacophony. "I'm Marcy. Sorry for all the noise. That's my dog Angus — he should quiet down soon. Please let me know if you need help finding anything."

A middle-aged woman in a green shaker-knit sweater came up to the counter. "I was interested in the aromatherapy shop. Why is it closed?"

I had no idea why it would be closed. Nellie should be fine now. "The owner took a spill last week. She must still be recovering."

"Oh." The woman ambled away to half-heartedly look at yarn.

Amid all the mayhem, Vera strolled into the Stitch. Her eyes widened as she came to join me behind the counter. "What in the world?"

"It must be a tour group."

One of the tourists overheard me and smiled. "It is," he said. "We're touring small towns up and down the Pacific coast from Washington to California."

"How fun," I said.

"It has been. But between you and me, I'm about ready to get to California. We're going to see a Giants game in Candlestick Park. That's the only way my wife was able to talk me into this trip."

I laughed. "May I get you some coffee?"

"Nah, I'm fine. That couch looks awfully comfy, though."

"Help yourself."

As the man wandered over to the sit-and-stitch square, I looked at Vera. "Would *you* like some coffee?"

"And have you leave me here to man the counter by myself?" she asked. "No, thanks."

I lowered my voice. "Someone said Nellie's shop is closed. Isn't she well enough to be at work yet?"

"I don't know, but I'll find out. What time will your mom be here?"

"She should be in late this afternoon. Her flight gets in about three o'clock, and she's renting a car," I said. "She doesn't like being without wheels you know."

"I'll see what I can learn about Nellie, and I'll drop back in later." She looked around at the crowd as more tourists poured through the door. "Good luck, kiddo."

After the tourists left, I let Angus out of the bathroom. He gave me an accusing stare, and then got up, trotted past me, and went into the shop to sniff around and see what he'd missed. I began straightening bins of floss. The bells over the door jingled to let me know someone had arrived.

"Be right with you!" I called.

"Looks as if you could use a hand."

"Mom!" I hurried to the front of the shop and flung my arms around my mother. "I wasn't expecting you until later!"

"I got an earlier flight." She laughed. After hugging me, she embraced Angus, who was dancing around us excitedly.

I took her hand. "Let's sit down."

"Not until after we've cleaned up. What happened?"

"Tour bus."

"I hope you made lots of sales," she said. "Especially with them leaving the shop like this."

"I did, Mom. In fact, I'll need to go to the storeroom once I've seen what I need to restock."

"Great. I'll help."

I started to protest but recognized that look on her face. "Would you mind straightening the books and making sure they're all in their proper places?"

"I can handle that."

"How was your flight?" I asked.

She did her Bette Davis impression. "It was a bumpy ride."

I didn't know whether or not the flight really was bumpy, but I was certainly glad she was here. "I've missed you."

"And I've missed you. Get to cleaning so we can catch up."

I returned to my floss bins, but called Ted as I worked.

"Hey, sweetheart," he said.

"Hi. I've called to ask a favor."

"That's funny because I was just getting ready to call and ask *you* for a favor."

"What's your favor?" I asked.

"You go first."

"I was going to ask you to bring an extra lunch. Mom got an earlier flight. Now you."

"Okay. I was going to ask to bring a couple of extra guests. My mom wants to bring Clover to visit Angus."

"Okay." I drew out the word.

"Are we good?" he asked.

"Yeah. It'll be great for our moms to get to know each other."

"I agree. See you in about forty-five minutes."

"See you then." I wondered if Ted realized how nervous I was about our mothers meeting. Of course, he did. He didn't get to be head detective on the basis of his striking good looks.

I finished tidying the bins and making a note of what flosses needed to be replenished. As I went through to the stockroom, I saw that Mom had put straight anything she'd found askew including the candle-wicked pillows on the sofa. Then she'd sat down on a red club chair, propped her feet on the ottoman and was petting Angus's face while talking to him.

"I called Ted and asked him to bring extra lunch," I said. I went into the stockroom with my basket and gathered the necessary flosses. As I passed back by the sit-and-stitch square, I tossed over my shoulder, "And by the way, he's bringing his mom too . . . and Clover. You remember Clover, the bunny? Angus loves her."

"Get back here."

Her voice stopped me in my tracks. I turned, innocent look firmly in place, basket on my arm, probably looking very fairy tale–like guileless, if I do say so myself.

"Marcella, did you and Ted just decide to spring this meeting on me without giving me a chance to properly prepare?"

"No, ma'am, we did not. As I told you, I thought you'd be in on a later flight. And until talking with Ted moments ago, I had no idea his mother had planned on coming today," I said. "So she'll feel as ambushed as you do."

The idea of Veronica Nash ever feeling ambushed struck me as preposterous. Then again, I couldn't imagine Mom ever feeling that way either.

"I will admit to ambushing you — for lack of a better word — with the whole actor thing," I continued. "But I wanted you and Veronica to meet under more ideal circum- stances — dinner at an elegant restaurant when you were both looking forward to it."

"Ah, well, maybe this way is best," Mom said. "And I'm looking forward to seeing

Angus and his bunny friend playing together."

"Yeah! It'll be great!" I wished I felt as
confident as I sounded.

Ted, Veronica, and Clover arrived at a
quarter past one. Mom was in the bathroom
"freshening up" — making sure she looked
perfect despite having been traveling since
five a.m.

I hugged Veronica, gave Ted a quick kiss,
and placed the clock on the door saying I
would be back in a half hour, even though
we were going to be sitting in the sit-and-
stitch square, the door would be unlocked,
and customers would see that I hadn't gone
anywhere. But that was okay. I thought I
might welcome an interruption at some
point during this meal.

Veronica wore a blue silk pantsuit that
matched her eyes almost perfectly and carried Clover in a white-and-navy-striped
tote. Veronica's silvery gray hair was cut in a
stylish angular bob, and she wore taupe
pumps.

Angus didn't approach Veronica, but he
loped up and leaned his head against Ted.
The dog stretched his neck in the direction
of Veronica's tote and sniffed.

"Yes, your friend is in here," said Veronica. "Would you like to play?" She sat the tote on the sofa — Ted had placed our food on the maple coffee table — and gently took the large brown and white bunny out and sat her on the floor.

Clover went to Angus, stood up on her hind legs and waited for him to lower his head to hers.

"How precious!"

The three of us turned to Mom, who'd emerged from the bathroom looking as if she'd just stepped out of the hair and makeup trailer. She'd changed into a black jersey dress and black pumps and had pulled her hair into a chignon at the nape of her neck.

She extended her hand to Veronica. "I'm Beverly Singer. How do you do?"

"I'm Veronica Nash. It's a pleasure to meet you, Beverly. And I'm ravenous. How are you?"

Mom smiled. "Starving. Let's dig in."

Ted and I glanced at each other and let out a breath I don't think either of us had realized we were holding as we sat down around the table and unpacked the food. Ted had brought taco salads as well as chips and *queso* from our favorite Mexican restaurant.

"I hope this is all right with everybody," he said.

The rest of us agreed that it looked wonderful, and we began eating. Angus and Clover kept us entertained by chasing each other around the shop until they tired themselves out and plopped down in front of the window to rest. Clover took her usual spot between Angus's huge front paws.

"That's adorable." Mom raised her phone and took a photo.

"How long are you in town for, Beverly?" asked Veronica.

"I'll be here for a week."

"Fantastic. I know you'll be busy helping Marcy prepare for Friday's open house, but maybe after that you and I can have lunch one day — just the two of us."

"I'd like that."

Ted and I exchanged nervous glances again. Having our mothers together without our being there to chaperone and to hear what was being said about us? That was even more nerve-racking than this!

I decided to change the subject. "Jared Willoughby came by this morning. He'd attended Keira's interment this morning but wanted to explain why he was with Adalyn on Saturday evening and why he didn't go to Keira's memorial service last night."

Ted arched one dark brow. "And why did he feel the need to confess all of that to you?"

"I've given that some thought, and I think he told me believing I'd tell you," I said.

"Fancy that," Veronica murmured.

Ted smiled. "And what feeling did you get from the young man, Inch-High?"

"I'm not sure. He's wishy-washy. He claims to still have feelings for Keira even though they'd parted ways and he was seeing someone else." I inclined my head. "Of course, anyone would be affected by the death of someone they'd once cared for . . . especially if that person died tragically. But why wouldn't he want Adalyn to know? Is she so hard-hearted that she wouldn't understand Jared's mourning his ex-girlfriend's passing?"

"There's more to this than meets the eye," said Veronica. "It sounds as if Jared is the sort of man who wants to have his cake and eat it too. Perhaps he'd begun seeing Adalyn while he was still supposed to be dating Keira."

"Regardless, she should understand his need to attend Keira's memorial service," Ted said. "After all, Adalyn was there."

"That's just it — he claimed he couldn't bear to go to the funeral," I said. "And yet, he went to the graveside service this morning."

"I'm wondering if he truly mourns Keira's death, or if he only wants it to appear he does to certain people," Mom said. "Like Veronica pointed out, he might be playing both sides. He didn't go to the funeral where the majority of Keira's acquaintances turned out, but he attended the interment where it was probably only Keira's family and closest friends who were present."

"Excellent observation!" Veronica exclaimed.

"So who is Jared Willoughby trying to impress and why?" Ted asked.

CHAPTER FIFTEEN

After Ted, Veronica, and Clover left, Mom asked me why I looked so relieved.

"I don't know," I said. "I just really wanted you and Veronica to get along. And you're both such strong-willed women and devoted mothers . . ." I shrugged.

She smiled. "We want the same things — for our children to be happy. She seems like a lovely woman."

"She is. And so are you."

"Flatterer. About Keira's murder, do you really think Jared Willoughby is a viable suspect? It worries me that he came and visited you while you were here alone this morning."

"Well, I wasn't entirely alone. Angus was here."

At the sound of his name, Angus raised his head and wagged his tail.

"But I find it hard to believe that Jared would knowingly implicate his mother in

Keira's death," I continued. "I suppose that key ring lying beneath her body could've been a coincidence, but I can't help but think the killer left it there on purpose. Riley and I counted, and there are three missing from the box. I'm thinking someone came in while I was walking Angus and took the other two, and I believe *that* person killed Keira."

"And you think the key ring was left to implicate . . . who? You?"

"I don't know, Mom. I guess if that's the case, whoever did it didn't realize I was with both Ted and Manu when the murder occurred."

"How well do you know Christine?" she asked. "Are you absolutely certain she didn't kill Keira in a fit of rage?"

"Almost a hundred percent," I said. "I've canceled tonight's class so I could be with you, but you'll probably meet Christine at the class on Thursday evening. She's one of the nicest people you'd ever want to meet. Plus, if she'd lashed out at Keira in a rage, I don't believe she would have hit her with something that would cause two puncture wounds — *and* the police believe Keira was poisoned through those wounds, which would make the murder premeditated."

"So then the question is who knew where

and when Keira would be alone that evening?"

I blew out a breath. "This is so frustrating! The obvious suspect is Jared . . . but I honestly can't see him being a killer."

"How well do you know him?"

"I'd only spoken with him at length once before this morning."

"Then you don't know him at all," she said. "And his behavior concerning Keira's memorial service and interment is suspicious."

"True, but playing devil's advocate, let's say he was sincere." I picked up the second ribbon embroidery project to give myself something to do with my hands and because I needed to get it finished before the anniversary party on Friday. "Let's say he didn't want to attend the more public memorial because he didn't want to be perceived as the grieving boyfriend. Maybe he simply wanted to express his condolences to the family and say his good-byes privately."

"Possibly . . . but it could be that he only wanted to be there to suck up to Keira's father. Didn't you tell me he was a powerful businessman? Maybe Jared's business is struggling."

I looked around to make sure no one was

about to enter the shop. "Actually, it has been rumored that Ken Sherman launders money for criminals. What if he's using Jared's garage to launder money? I mean, according to the grapevine, Mr. Sherman tends to favor food places, but most good businessmen diversify, right?"

"Now, Marcella, you know better than to believe everything you hear from the gossip mill."

"I know, but the police are discreetly investigating Mr. Sherman, so it could be a possibility." I put ribbon leaves on a rose stem. "Right?"

"I suppose, but don't put stock in rumors until they're confirmed."

Thank goodness that conversation was brought to an end by a phone call from Vera.

"Hey, Marcy! I checked on Nellie. She has a couple of bumps and bruises still, but the reason she wasn't at work today was because she's considering putting her inventory up for sale to another retailer and hightailing it to Arizona."

"What? Are you kidding me?"

"No, hon. She's dead serious."

"Is it because she really believes Claude and Priscilla are vampires?" I asked.

"I'm not sure she'd admit to that, but given the fact that Keira had two puncture wounds on her neck, it *does* back up Nellie's theory. And, no, I'm not saying I think the Atwoods are creatures of the night. I'm just telling you that Nellie is freaking out."

"Maybe I should go talk with her," I said. "Would you mind giving me directions to her house?"

"Are you sure that's such a good idea?" Vera asked.

I glanced at Mom's wide eyes and decided she was thinking the same thing.

"Mom got here early, and I'd already canceled classes anyway," I said. "Maybe if I just go by there, I could talk some sense into her. If nothing else, I could fire her up and give her a reason to stay."

"You mean, she'd stay to spite you?" Vera chuckled. "Why would you *want* her to stay? She's been nothing but mean to you since you stepped foot in Tallulah Falls."

"I know. But having her get scared off just seems wrong to me."

She sighed and gave me Nellie's address. "It's your funeral, dear."

"I hope not."

"You say your mom's there already?" Vera asked. "Is she upset with me?"

"Of course not. But, then again, the actors haven't started pestering her yet."

Vera was quiet.

I laughed. "I'm *kidding.* If she's going to be upset with anyone, it'll be me. It was my idea, remember?"

"Okay. I'll try to get by the shop and visit with her tomorrow. Let me know how it goes with Nellie." She paused. "Maybe I should check in with you later . . . in case you don't make it back."

"It'll be fine. All she can do is refuse to let me in, right?"

"Or shoot you."

"Or that," I agreed.

I ended the call and looked over at Mom. "I know you heard most of that."

She nodded. "I take it Vera asked why you'd want Nellie to stick around."

"She did."

"I'm proud of your answer. I'll go with you to visit her. You might need a witness."

I smiled. "Would you like to go home and take a nap? Your room's all ready for you."

"No, I'm not an old lady, you know. Is there anything useful I can do to help you?"

"Would you mind stuffing some of the open house giveaway bags while I work on this ribbon embroidery?"

"Not at all."

I went to the storeroom and got Mom the bags and the items she'd need to put in them. When I returned, I explained that all the coupons were different.

"That was actually Vera's idea. Everyone gets a little something — say, ten percent off or even a free item of ten dollars or less — and I don't go bankrupt."

"That's a clever idea," Mom said.

As she stuffed bags, Angus snoozed by the window, and I stitched, we caught up on all the Tallulah Falls and San Francisco news. It was nice and peaceful, and I was able to put Keira's murder and my upcoming visit to Nellie Davis out of my mind for a few minutes.

We'd been working for about a half hour when an attractive dark-haired woman walked into the store.

I set my ribbon embroidery project aside and went to greet her. Angus beat me to it, and she patted his head.

"Welcome to the Seven-Year Stitch. I'm Marcy, that's Angus, and there on the sofa is my mom, Beverly."

The woman smiled. "I'm Jaya. It's a pleasure to meet all of you. I'm looking for a book on Lambani embroidery."

"Lambani?" I frowned over my shoulder at Mom. "I haven't heard of that. Have you?"

"No, I haven't."

"My great-grandparents were Lambanis

and originally lived in southern India," Jaya said. "They were a tribal people who practiced a traditional form of embroidery that utilizes mirrors. I'd love to find some old patterns to try to get in touch with my heritage."

I invited her to have a seat in the sit-and-stitch square while I grabbed my laptop. I heard Mom explaining that she was making goodie bags for the open house on Friday and inviting the woman to attend.

When I returned, Jaya was sitting on a red club chair, and Angus was sitting happily at her side. I sat on the sofa and did a search for Lambani embroidery.

"It says here that Lambani embroidery is a mixture of cross-stitch, mirror work, quilting stitches, and appliqué. These examples are beautiful." I turned the laptop so Mom and Jaya could see the screen.

I couldn't find any books that predominately offered Lambani embroidery patterns.

"Do you know Reggie Singh, the librarian?" I asked Jaya.

She shook her head.

"Let me give her a call. If anyone will know where to find a book on Indian embroidery, it's Reggie."

Reggie told me that Lambani embroidery

was also known as Banjaras. Given that information, we were still unable to find Jaya any books, but we did discover several video tutorials and Web sites with information on the art.

"Thank you so much!" Jaya said. "I'll go home and study these — after I go by the library and thank Mrs. Singh personally — and I'll be back on Friday to get some materials so I can start my own project."

"Great," I said. "It's been a pleasure meeting you, and I look forward to seeing you again."

Jaya had barely gotten down the street before Claude and Priscilla swept into the Stitch. Today Priscilla wore a purple pantsuit with a large white silk orchid in her upswept hair. Claude wore a black tux with tails and a purple sequined vest to match his wife's ensemble. Surprisingly, there was no orchid in his lapel, but he was sporting his top hat.

Claude swept off the hat and bowed. "Good afternoon, Marcy . . . Mr. O'Ruff. . . ." He turned his eyes to the sofa. "And who is this lovely creature?"

As if.

"Claude, Priscilla, this is my mother, Beverly Singer. Mom, Claude and Priscilla Atwood. They own the Horror Emporium."

Mom rose and shook hands with the Atwoods. "It's a pleasure to meet you."

"The pleasure is all ours," Priscilla gushed. "Marcy had told us you were coming in for her open house gala, but we didn't realize you'd be here so soon."

"Yes, well, I'm hoping I can help out a bit before the big day," Mom said.

"We do hope that while you're here, Ms. Singer, you'll regale us with some of your Hollywood anecdotes," Claude said.

"Please call me Beverly. And, of course, I will. Perhaps we can have lunch one day before I return to San Francisco."

"Oh, that would be absolutely divine!" Priscilla beamed. "And, in the meantime, we'll try not to let the other talent at the Horror Emporium know you're here yet. We'd like to keep you all to ourselves for a day or so."

Mom smiled slightly. "Yes, well, I'm not really here to scout for actors. I'm here for Marcy."

"Of course," Claude said. "And we wouldn't dream of imposing."

"But, then, if you *do* know someone looking for diverse talent, we have quite the résumés," Priscilla added.

"Wonderful. We'll talk about that when we have lunch." Mom cut her eyes to me.

She's gonna kill me. But then, she's *the one who volunteered to have lunch with them. I had nothing to do with that.*

"By the way," Mom said, "I'm terribly sorry for your misfortune the night of your grand opening celebration."

Priscilla flicked her wrist. "That's okay. The whole ordeal has actually been a boon for business. I mean, I feel awful about the girl — Keira? — naturally, but if it was her time to go, then what better place than in front of a haunted house, right?"

"Well." Mom returned to the sit-and-stitch square and resumed stuffing the giveaway bags. "I've kept you from your business long enough."

"We didn't really want anything . . . other than to pop in and say hello," said Claude. "We'll be on our way for now. Good day, all."

He and Priscilla left, and I returned to the sit-and-stitch square.

"They're . . . um . . . something, aren't they?"

"Something?" Mom scoffed. "That Priscilla is one of the most boorish women I've ever met. Does she even realize how insensitive she is?"

"I don't know. That's what turned me off to them too. At first, I thought they were quirky and kinda fun. After seeing their reaction to Keira's death, I haven't liked them very much."

I dropped Angus off at home and fed him before heading to Nellie Davis's house. Mom brought the rental car and parked it in the driveway.

"Are you sure you want to go with me?" I asked before we got into the Jeep. "I'll be fine."

"I'm sure I want to go with you, because I'm not so sure you'll be fine. That spiteful little woman might have you arrested for trespassing or something."

"Do you think I shouldn't go then?"

"If it's on your heart that you should go, then go. Just be prepared for whatever reception you get."

"With Nellie, I'm always prepared for the worst," I said.

Nellie lived on a quiet street in a small teal Cape Code home with white trim. The lawn was neatly manicured, and as I pulled over to the curb, I could see that the house was larger than I'd originally thought. I glanced over at Mom and took a deep breath.

"Ready?" she asked.

"As I'll ever be."

We got out of the Jeep and went to the door. Before I could even knock, Nellie flung it open, nearly dislodging the fall wreath of maple leaves, sunflowers, and lavender.

"What are you doing here?" she demanded.

I held up my hands. "I'm just here to check on you."

"You can see for yourself that I'm fine."

"Vera told me you were thinking of leaving Tallulah Falls," I said.

"I am," she said. "You should be glad."

"Maybe I should be. But I'm rather disappointed. I never thought you'd be a quitter, Nellie."

"I'm not a quitter. This town has just got to be too much for me." She glanced at Mom, making me think she'd have added *since you came here* had Mom not been with me.

"You don't honestly believe the Atwoods are *vampires,* do you?" I asked.

It had started sprinkling rain as we drove up, and there was no roof to speak of over Nellie's front stoop. I decided I needed to get Mom back home. Vera had been right. Coming to speak with Nellie had been a lost cause.

I turned to tell Mom we should go when

Nellie invited us inside. Mom and I exchanged glances. Was this a trap? Was she going to shove us into an oven? Or would she lure us into a cage so she could lock the door behind us and fatten us up first? There went my wild imagination again.

I stepped inside and looked up at the ceiling to ensure steel bars didn't surround us. There was only white tile. I felt relatively safe.

Nellie led us to her living room, a cozy space with a floral sofa and matching chair and a picture window that looked out upon the ocean. Thankfully, Nellie sat on the chair, leaving the sofa for Mom and me.

"I'm not a nutcase," Nellie said. "I don't know *what* the Atwoods are besides a couple of weirdos, but I feel like a cat that's on its eighth of nine lives. Look how many near misses I've had in the past year! How many times I could've been killed!"

"But you haven't been killed, Nellie. You're a survivor," I said.

"Vera mentioned you were thinking of going to Arizona," Mom said. "Do you have family there?"

"No."

"Then why are you going, Nellie?" I asked.

"It's a warmer, milder climate. . . . I'll get to know people." She shrugged her bony shoulders. "It'll be good for me."

"You're scared," I said. "So am I. But I know the Tallulah Falls Police Department is working day and night to find Keira's killer . . . and they will. And then we'll be safe again."

"Until the next time something happens." Nellie briefly closed her eyes. "And then what? We're back where we started."

"Bad things happen everywhere, dear," said Mom. "I do a lot of traveling in my line of work, and scary situations aren't exclusive to Tallulah Falls. What will you do when something bad happens in Arizona?"

"You'll be alone there. You won't know anyone," I said.

"And who do I have here?" she asked.

"You have a lot of friends, Nellie. You know you do." I went on to tell her about the tour bus group that came into town today. "The tourists were terribly disappointed to find Scentsibilities closed."

"Well, I *do* have the nicest shop on the street," she said.

"It is a nice shop," I agreed.

"I don't know that I'd call it the absolute *nicest,*" Mom said. "I mean, there are a variety of different shops on Main Street, and that's what gives the place its charm."

"That's true," Nellie said quietly. "Marcy

has a . . . an okay shop also."

It was as close to a compliment as I could ever hope to get from Nellie Davis.

"I hope your shop will be open tomorrow," I said as I stood. "But if you don't reconsider, I wish you the best of luck in Arizona."

"So do I," Mom said. "We'll see ourselves out."

Nellie got up from the chair. "I . . . appreciate your coming by."

I had no idea what Nellie would decide to do. Either way, my conscience was clear.

CHAPTER SIXTEEN

After going to Nellie's house, Mom and I stopped by the market and got the few things I needed for the shop and for home. On the drive to my house, I asked Mom what she'd like for dinner.

"You know what I'd really like that I haven't had in ages?" she asked. "A deep dish pepperoni pizza."

"Ooh, that sounds good. And I know just the place." I handed Mom my phone, told her the name of the place and that it was in my contacts, and asked her to call in the order.

When we got home with our pizza, we left the box in the unheated oven — I was afraid to trust Angus with a pizza on either the kitchen table or the counter and he refused to go out until we'd eaten and given him a bite or two. Mom and I both hurried upstairs and slipped into our warm fuzzy pajamas. Hers had matching slippers but I simply wore thick socks.

We ate at the kitchen table with Mr. O'Ruff sitting on the floor nearby watching us as if we were playing a tennis match. If a single pepperoni were to hit the floor, he'd be on it in a second.

Mom laughed softly. "I remember when you first got him. He was the scrawniest little beast I'd ever seen."

I'd rescued Angus from a puppy mill. My intention had been to get a Yorkie or some other small dog. Instead, I'd brought home the big-eyed, even-bigger-footed Irish wolfhound.

"Remember how concerned Alfred was?" I asked, with a smile. "He didn't think I realized how big Angus would get."

"Did you? Truly?"

"Well, I knew he'd be big. . . ."

Alfred Benton was Mom's attorney and had been for the past thirty years. My dad had died when I was too young to remember him, so Alfred had been like a surrogate father to me.

"How *is* Alfred?" I asked. "Is he dating anyone?"

I'd always kinda hoped Mom and Alfred would find their way to each other someday . . . somehow. They'd always been the best of friends. Mom was a widower, Alfred was divorced, and Alfred was a silver fox — tall, fit, white hair in a neatly trimmed military cut.

"He's wonderful, and I don't believe he's seeing anyone. Not seriously, anyway."

"Mom, why didn't the two of you ever give something more than friendship a chance?"

She shrugged and stuffed a slice of pizza in her face to keep from having to answer.

I wasn't willing to let the matter go that easily. "*Did* you ever try?"

She swallowed and took a drink of her soda before answering. "I believe we were both afraid dating would ruin our friendship, so we kept our relationship platonic."

"But, Mom, he's perfect for you."

She blushed. "He's my best friend and has been for three decades. We've been through so much together. I don't want anything to ruin our relationship."

"You don't think you could go back to being friends if you didn't work romantically?" I asked.

"Tell me about you and Ted. How are you getting along?"

"We're doing great. He makes me so happy."

She smiled. "I'm glad. And I realize that's why you're playing matchmaker. Happy people in love want everyone else to be happy and in love."

"Oh, hey," I said, "I saw where *Trouble's Door* is coming on tonight."

"Really?" She shook her head. "I had a lot of fun on that one. Jack DeLong played such a serious character, but he was a clown when the camera wasn't running. He kept the crew in stitches."

"But not the director so much, if I remember correctly."

She laughed. "You do! What time does it start? I'd love to see it."

"I think it was coming on at either seven thirty or eight." I awarded Angus's patience with a piece of pizza crust.

The movie started at eight. When it came on, Mom and I were cuddled under a green fleece throw on the sofa, and Angus was snoring softly by the hearth.

Trouble's Door was nearly ten years old. Jack DeLong didn't make many movies anymore, and when he did, he played taciturn bit-part characters like judges and corrupt politicians.

I asked Mom why Jack didn't act as much as he used to.

"He made a small fortune off *Trouble's Door,* and I suppose he took care of it. For all his kidding around, he was serious and knew to wisely manage his money. He realized he wasn't as young as he once was."

"Still, he's fantastic . . . and looks great," I said. "I'd love to see him get some meaty part in a television series or something."

"So would I." She winced and placed her hand on her chest.

"Are you all right?"

"I'm fine. Now, be quiet and watch Jack."

Trouble's Door was about a wise-cracking detective named Abe Ponitello — nickname, Pony. Pony was the first person on the scene of a homicide of a beautiful young woman. Her lovely older sister arrived moments after Pony did and sobbed into Pony's arms. She was Pony's love interest and was played by an unmemorable actress. I couldn't recall anything she'd appeared in either before or after *Trouble's Door*. Of course, she turned out to be the murderess — she'd killed her sister for their inheritance — and had broken Pony's heart.

We were watching the scene in which we — the viewers — discovered the sister's treachery. She was murdering her sister's boyfriend after planting evidence implicating him in the crime. She wasn't strong enough to overpower him, so she used a Taser on him and suffocated him while he was dazed from the electrical current.

Mom caught her breath.

I turned to stare at her sharply. Sure, the movie was suspenseful, but we'd seen it before. Besides, she'd worked on it for eight months. There were no surprises here.

She was holding her chest and struggling to breathe.

"Mom, talk to me!"

"It'll be all right."

I was already reaching for my phone. "Have you ever had pain like this before?"

She shook her head. "It's probably . . . indigestion. I'll . . . be . . . fine. Put . . . down . . . the. . . ." She pressed her lips together.

I could see how much pain she was in. I called nine-one-one and told them my mother was having chest pains.

"They're sending an ambulance right out."

In the commotion, Angus came over to lick Mom's face.

"Angus, please," I said, gently pushing his head away.

He whimpered and lay down at her feet.

"I'm sorry," I whispered. I wasn't sure if I was talking to the dog, to Mom, or to both of them.

Mom took my hand. "It's . . . okay."

■ ■ ■ ■

I managed to get Angus into the backyard before the ambulance came. After the paramedics got Mom outside, I let Angus back in, slipped on a pair of loafers and a jacket I kept in the hall closet, and rode with Mom in the back of the ambulance.

It dawned on me as we raced to the hospital that I'd left the television on. Not that it mattered. Not that anything mattered except that my mom was okay.

I wanted to hold her hand but one paramedic was taking an electrocardiogram and another was drawing blood.

At the hospital, Mom was rushed into the emergency room. I stayed out of the paramedics' way but followed as closely as I could.

I was able to hold back my tears until I heard Ted's breathless voice from behind me.

"Marcy."

I turned and practically dissolved into his arms.

He held me and let me sob for a minute or two. Then he held me slightly away from him and wiped my tears. "Sweetheart, we need to get in there to your mom. She's going to be worried about where you went."

"I know. . . . You're . . . right." I hugged him again and took a deep, steadying breath. "I'm fine." I looked up at him. "How did you know?"

"The call came over the police scanner. I recognized your address."

I gulped. "Thanks for being here."

"Where else would I be?"

Ted took my hand and led me to the bay where the paramedics had just gotten Mom settled onto a bed.

"Look who I found," I said to her.

"Oh, goodness. I know I look horrible." She glanced at me. "And you don't look much better."

"Gee, thanks."

"You both look beautiful," Ted said. "How're you feeling?"

"Like my daughter overreacted," Mom said. The grimace that followed belied her words.

A nurse hurried in and asked us to wait outside. The little area *was* getting pretty crowded.

"I should call Alfred," I said quietly as we stepped out into the hall.

Ted's eyes widened. "I might have to agree with your mom about your overreacting."

"Not because he's her *attorney,*" I said.

Ted had met Alfred on more than one occasion. "He's her best friend. He should know."

"Don't you think you should have a diagnosis before you call him? Otherwise, he'll be as panicky as you are."

"That's true. I hadn't thought of that." I slumped against his chest. "I can't think of much of anything. I just want to *do* something. I want to fix this somehow. Please tell me she'll be all right."

"She'll be fine." He kissed the top of my head. "Even if she *is* having a heart attack — and we don't know that yet — she's here where she can get the best care possible."

"I know. I know." I knew I was trying to reassure myself. But it had to be true. She had to be fine.

I heard the clip, clip, clip of non-nurse shoes coming up behind me at a rapid pace. I turned to see Vera hurrying toward us with her arms spread wide. Paul Samms followed in her wake.

"Oh, poor darling!" Vera enveloped me in a perfume-scented embrace. "How's Beverly?"

"She's having some chest pain," I said. "And shortness of breath. I'm really scared."

"She'll be okay, darling. She's strong and healthy."

I started to ask how Vera had known but then I remembered that, as a reporter, Paul often listened to the police scanner. They, too, had apparently recognized my address.

Paul patted my shoulder. "I had something like this happen myself a year or so ago. Turned out to be a false alarm. It's good you had your mom brought in though, Marcy. People often refuse to seek care, and then they don't get the help they need. But Beverly will be right as rain before you know it."

I knew everyone was trying to make me feel better with their reassurances, but I wasn't going to quit worrying until Mom was back at home with me chiding me for worrying too much.

The nurse came out.

"May we go back in now?" I asked.

She frowned. "I'd prefer that only one of you go at this time. Are you her daughter?"

"Yes."

"The rest of you may wait here in the hall."

I went back into Mom's room. "Hi. Vera and Paul are here."

"Great. My little misadventure will be a headline in tomorrow's paper."

"Everyone's just worried," I said.

She reached for my hand. "I know. I'm

just still not accustomed to this small town. In San Francisco, I could fall down the stairs and break a leg and even if I was able to call an ambulance, none of my friends would know for days unless I called them. In Tallulah Falls, you suspect something might be amiss, and the whole town turns out in the hospital waiting room."

"Well, not the *whole* town."

She smiled. "I'm happy you have such good friends."

"They're your friends too."

The doctor came in. She was a young woman with light brown hair and tortoise-shell glasses. She didn't look old enough to have completed medical school, but I knew I was being critical because I wanted the top heart doctor in the world — one with at least twenty years' experience, but not one so old he or she had become dotty — to treat my mother.

"Hi, I'm Dr. Jacobs. Ms. Singer, I've looked over your reports. Your ECG doesn't show any signs of heart attack, and your troponins are not elevated." She looked at Mom's chart. "I see here you're vacationing from California. As soon as you get back home, I want you to make an appointment with a heart specialist just to make sure everything is all right. For now, I'm going to order you some nitroglycerine for the angina."

"Will she get to go back home tonight?" I asked.

"If her chest pain subsides, she certainly will. The nurse will be back in with your medicine in just a moment." Dr. Jacobs smiled at us both and then left the room.

I released my breath. "Thank God."

"I told you it was a false alarm."

"Oh, admit it, you were scared too," I said.

"Maybe a little."

When the nurse returned, I went back out into the hallway to give the good news to Ted, Vera, and Paul.

Once Mom was released from the hospital, Ted drove us home. Vera and Paul tagged along to make sure we didn't need anything.

"We're good," I said to Vera. "I'm going to close the shop tomorrow, so I can stay here and look after Mom."

"You most certainly are not," Mom said. "I'm not an invalid. I had a little chest pain. It was no big deal."

"The doctor ordered you to rest for the next couple of days and to see a heart specialist when you return home," I said. "That doesn't sound like *no big deal* to me."

Paul and Ted turned their attention to Angus, who was thrilled to see all the guests who'd come to his midnight surprise party. It was especially a surprise to Angus.

"Darling, go ahead and open the Stitch tomorrow," said Vera. "You still have to get ready for the open house on Friday. I'll come by and stay with Beverly. And, Beverly, if and when you feel up to it, I'll drive you into town."

"I appreciate the offer, Vera," I said. "But Mom's health is more important than the open house."

"I will *not* ruin this open house for you," Mom said. "If you're going to cancel everything — work, your classes, and even your open house — for me, then I'll get on the next flight back home."

"Oh, no, you will not! I —"

"Ladies, please!" Ted finally stepped in to bring order to the situation. That sort of thing happens when you're dating a cop. "Marcy, accept Vera's generous offer. You'll have your phone with you and can check on Beverly throughout the day. And, if Beverly feels up to it, she can join you at the shop. You'll know your mom is being looked after, and she'll know that you're going about your business as usual."

"Okay," I said. "You're right."

"Thank you, Ted," said Mom.

"Yeah . . . thanks. And, thank you, Vera."

"Anytime." She beamed at Mom. "We'll have a delightful time tomorrow. I'm looking forward to having you all to myself. We'll watch some television, and you can give me insight into the costuming world."

"That'll be fun," Mom said, stifling a yawn.

"You guys should get in the bed," Ted said. "You, too, Vera and Paul. We all have to be up early tomorrow morning."

"Aye, aye, sir," I said.

He dropped a kiss on my lips before taking my hand and leading me out of the living room. "Don't stay up all night worrying. She'll be fine."

"I'm going to insist that she sleep with me."

"All right. Call me if you need to." He grinned down at my disheveled appearance. "This isn't what you're wearing to the open house, is it?"

"Of course!" I smiled. "Wanna bet that Priscilla Atwood would wear something even more outrageous?"

CHAPTER SEVENTEEN

The next morning, I left Mom sleeping upstairs. I had been able to talk her into sleeping in the bed with me. She'd balked at the idea, but she finally decided she didn't want me sitting in my office chair all night watching her sleep in the guest bed. I don't think either of us slept that well. I kept jerking myself awake and checking to make sure Mom was still breathing. That would usually wake *her* up and she'd reassure me before turning over and going back to sleep.

I was in the kitchen making coffee, and Angus was outside for his morning romp, when Sadie came to the door.

"I just heard," she said, giving me a one-armed hug because she was holding a basket of goodies in the other hand. "Paul Samms came in to get some coffee and he told Blake and me all about what happened to your mom."

"Come on into the kitchen," I said. "You look exhausted."

"I am. We didn't get home until after midnight, but I tried not to sleep because I was afraid . . ." My eyes swam with tears.

"Oh, Marce." Sadie put the basket on the counter and gave me a proper hug. "Paul said everything was going to be fine."

"I suppose it is. But it was so scary."

"I brought her some oatmeal walnut and blueberry muffins — both kinds are really good for your heart."

"Thanks." I nodded toward the coffeepot. "I just made this. Would you like some?"

"Please."

I got us both large mugs of coffee and set the cream and sugar on the table. "I've got a feeling I'm going to need an IV of this stuff to get me through the day. Plus, I've got the combined class tonight that Mom refuses to let me cancel."

"She doesn't want you fussing over her." Before I could protest, Sadie held up her hand. "Admit it, you're the same way."

"I know. But she's my *mom.* She's the only family I have. Last night, I thought I was going to lose her."

"But you didn't, Marce. And she's okay. I know it's hard, but you can't treat her like a child."

I gave Sadie a half smile. "It's funny how your roles reverse as you get older, isn't it? You start to feel like the parent."

"We wouldn't have to if parents would stop acting like kids."

"While it's just you and me talking, how well do you know Jared Willoughby?" I asked.

She shrugged. "Not very. He came to the coffee shop to see Keira on occasion or to pick her up from work, but we didn't really engage each other in conversation. Why?"

I told her about his visit to the Seven-Year Stitch yesterday morning. "I used to think he was a super-nice guy — and felt bad that he got involved with Keira — but I realize now that I don't really know him at all. You don't think he could've killed Keira . . . do you?"

"I doubt it. Like you said, he seems like a good kid." She sighed. "But I suppose you never know."

"Do you think he was working with Mr. Sherman?" I explained how Jared had told me he'd gone to the interment, and Mom and I thought maybe he'd gone to impress Keira's father.

"Again, I don't know. When Mr. Sherman was courting Blake, Blake didn't fill me in on any of the particulars." She slowly shook her head. "I think Ken had Blake convinced that this was a really good deal and that Blake and I could make money for practically nothing. Blake knows better than that — never trust a deal that's too good to be true. Or, at least, investigate it a little further."

"Mr. Sherman might be one of those people who could sell ice to Eskimos. *You* don't fall for anything, but then, you're in the minority. You're tougher than most people."

She smiled. "So you're saying I'm just smarter than my husband?"

"I did *not* say that, and don't you dare tell Blake I did! I'm just saying you're not as . . ." I struggled for the right word.

"As gullible."

I covered my face with my hands. "I just keep making this worse. I'm going to shut my mouth now."

Sadie laughed. "Oh, come on. It's just us girls. Blake *is* more naive than I am. He's sweet and lovable and always sees the best in people. That's one of the things I adore about him. But he can fall for a sales pitch in a hurry. He keeps me on my toes."

"He just wants the best for you," I said. "And he thought Ken Sherman could put him a step closer to being there."

"Yeah." She sipped her coffee. "But I got a bad vibe from that man from the moment we met. There's something dangerous about him."

Todd sauntered into the shop minutes after Angus and I arrived and asked, "How's our girl?"

"I'm fine. Thanks. A little sleepy, but I'll be okay."

He shook his head. "I'm not talking about you, silly. I mean your mom."

"Oh. Of course. She's fine too. The doctor wants her to check with a heart specialist when she gets back home, but she didn't seem to think Mom has a heart condition. She definitely didn't have a heart attack."

"That's good." He sat on the sofa and patted the cushion beside him. "Come sit down."

I joined him, and Angus sat on the floor at Todd's other side.

"You are wiped out, aren't you? Why didn't you stay home today?"

"Mom wouldn't let me." I yawned. "Excuse me."

"Hey, I understand. Are you all right . . . really? I know that must've been quite a scare."

I nodded. "I'm just glad she's okay. Let

me guess — Blake?"

"Yeah. He heard the news from Paul Samms, of all people. Then again, Paul seems to know everything."

"If he doesn't know, he can sure find out," I said. "Hey, do you know whether or not Jared Willoughby and Ken Sherman had any kind of business arrangement?"

"I have no idea, but the more I'm finding out about Ken Sherman, the more I'm thinking it's best to steer clear of him." He patted Angus's head. "You especially need to be careful."

"Why do you say that?"

"I saw him leaving the alley behind your shop on my way home last night . . . or, rather, this morning — it was around two a.m."

"Why in the world would Ken Sherman be here at two o'clock in the morning? All the businesses were closed." I stood. "I'm going out there to see if there's any clue about what he was doing."

Todd stood too. "No, you're not! If I let anything happen to you, Wyatt Earp will have my hide."

"You're not letting anything happen to me. I seriously doubt the man is there now. You said you saw him leaving."

"Well, he wasn't skulking around in a

black suit and twirling his mustache, so I can't say for sure that he was up to anything disreputable."

"Mr. Sherman's mustache is trimmed too close to twirl." I headed for the back door.

I heard Todd's growl come from behind me. "Let me go first."

I didn't obey. If anything happened to Todd, I didn't want it on my conscience. Besides, if I was responsible for getting Todd hurt, Audrey Dayton would have *my* hide.

I stepped out into the alley. As I'd suspected, Ken Sherman was not there. Nor were there any obvious signs of . . . nefariousness? Was that a word?

"Where exactly was he?" I asked Todd.

"He was pulling out of the alley in his car. You aren't going to find anything — damning or otherwise."

I spotted a dime on the pavement and picked it up. "I beg to differ." I handed the coin to Todd. "There. Don't say I never gave you anything."

"Wow. I'll try not to spend it all at once."

I walked slowly around the parking area, keeping my eyes on the ground in front of me.

The back door opened, and I whirled around to see Ted coming through it.

"What's going on?" he asked. "I came to

check on you, found the place empty, and Angus crying at the back door. You nearly gave me a —" He caught himself before finishing the sentence.

"Todd saw Ken Sherman leaving here at two this morning," I said. "I came out to see if I could find any evidence as to what he was doing lurking around in the alley."

"So far, she's found a dime," said Todd. "Would you be jealous if I told you she gave it to me?"

"I'm devastated," Ted said.

Unlike Todd, he began helping me look. I was glad. He was a seasoned clue finder. If Ken Sherman had left anything behind, we'd certainly find it now.

I spotted a white rectangle of paper lying about a foot away from the Dumpster. I walked over and picked it up. It was a business card from Sal's Exotic Pets in Pacific City.

"What've you found, Inch-High?" Ted asked.

"I'm not sure." I took him the card.

Todd stepped up to look over Ted's shoulder. "It's from a pet shop. Maybe you stopped there once to get something for Angus."

"Why would Marcy stop at an *exotic*-pet

shop to get something for her dog, you twit?"

"Well, excuse me," Todd said, holding up his hands. "But Angus looks pretty exotic to me."

Ted shook his head and took out a small evidence bag. "I don't know if this is worth anything, but I'll follow up and see if these people know Ken Sherman. Good work, Inch-High."

"Hey, what about me?" Todd asked.

Ted arched a brow.

"He *did* tell me about Mr. Sherman being in the alley," I said.

"Fine. Way to go, Inspector Clouseau. Happy?"

Todd smiled. "Yes. Thank you. I'll get back to the Brew Crew now."

"You do that," said Ted, placing a hand at the small of my back. "Think there's anything else to find out here?"

"No . . . and I need to get back into the shop myself. Jill isn't so hot with the customers."

"Really? I see Calloway talking to her all the time."

"Hardy har har," Todd said. "See you guys later. Marcy, let me know if you and your mom need anything."

"I will. Thanks, Todd."

"You're really kinda mean to him some-times, you know," I told Ted after Todd had left.

"He wouldn't have it any other way." I smiled. "You're probably right."

"I've already checked in with Vera," he said. "Your mom is doing great. She's get-ting tired of everyone fussing over her, which is too bad, because Mom is headed over there now with brunch."

"Your mom cooks?"

"No. But the condo association has a couple of really good chefs on staff." He kissed me. "I'm sorry to hurry off, but I'll be back at around one with lunch. What're you in the mood for today?"

"An energy drink?"

He smiled. "So . . . something not too heavy. Gotcha."

After Ted left, I was glad to have a few customers wander in. Business was slow, even for a Wednesday. I helped my custom-ers find patterns and flosses, canvas and needles. There was one who wanted only to browse, but I told her about the upcoming open house and invited her to attend.

When the store was empty again, I went to the storeroom and got the box with the giveaway bags and the bag stuffings. Mom made quite a bit of progress on these yesterday afternoon, but there was still a lot of stuffing left to do.

I debated about whether or not to call Mom. Vera was right — Mom didn't like to be fussed over as if she was a child. And Veronica was going over with food. I should wait a little while to check on her. She was in good hands.

I was sitting on the sofa facing away from the window while stuffing the bags. I normally sat facing the window because I liked seeing what was going on outside — the people on the street, the cars passing by, the birds flitting from tree to tree — but today the glare bothered my sleepy eyes. My sleepy eyes, which seemed to be getting heavier and heavier. I rested my head against the back of the sofa for one second and closed my eyes . . . for one second.

I was transported to the set of *Trouble's Door.* I walked into Jack DeLong's office. But instead of Jack DeLong, it was Ted sitting behind the desk. He wore a dark suit and a fedora. He looked good in a fedora. Somehow I realized I'd set the movie nearly sixty years back in time. I myself was wearing a formfitting black dress and a wide-rimmed black hat, and I carried a cigarette in a long black holder.

Ted adjusted his tie and stood. "What can

I do for you, doll?"

I took a puff off my cigarette and blew the smoke over my shoulder. "You can find the man who wants me dead."

"Who'd want you dead? I think you'd be much more fun alive." He turned to look directly into the camera and to speak to the viewer. "Who'd want to kill this dame?" he asked the viewer. "Look at her. She's gorgeous and has pins for . . . well, not for miles by any stretch of the imagination . . . let's go with feet. No, that doesn't sound right. Let's just say she has some good-looking gams."

"Over here, handsome," I said. "You gonna help me with my problem or not?"

Ted turned back to me. "How could I refuse?"

"So what's it gonna cost me?"

"It might cost you a kiss." He moved out from behind the desk and stepped up to me.

"And it might cost a lot more." I tossed my head back and looked at him, my lips parted expectantly. "I've known guys like you before."

"I doubt that. But you obviously want to be kissed. I won't disappoint you, sweetheart." When he said *sweetheart,* he sounded like Humphrey Bogart. He lowered his mouth to mine.

Suddenly, I was standing in the rain outside the Horror Emporium. The female lead from *Trouble's Door* was there. I was still dressed in my noir outfit, sans cigarette, but she was dressed as she had been in the movie — a tight jean skirt and an even tighter red T-shirt.

"You think you can take what belongs to me," she said. "Well, you can't. No one can!" I noticed she had a sack beside her. She reached into the sack and got a rattlesnake. It had a collar around its neck that read SAL'S. She held the rattlesnake out and it bit me. I collapsed onto the sidewalk.

As I lay dying, Ted raced up. Everything else disappeared — the actress, the sack, the snake, even the buildings around us.

Ted leaned over me. "I love you." And then he licked my cheek.

My eyes flew open. Angus was licking me. I hugged him and kissed the top of his head.

"Thank goodness that was a dream," I said. "A weird, whacked-out dream."

Angus hurried to the counter. He needed to go out.

I grabbed his leash, put the clock on the door saying I'd be back in five minutes, and took Angus to the square. Passing by the Horror Emporium and its Lair of the Serpent, I kept my eyes up and straight ahead.

CHAPTER EIGHTEEN

A sideways glance let me know that Scentsibilities was open for business today. I hid a smile. So I guessed Nellie was staying in town after all. That was good . . . I supposed. What's that old saying — better the devil you know than the devil you don't? And who knew what devil might move into Nellie's shop? Besides, there was always the slim chance that Nellie and I would become friends. Yeah . . . right.

What if some *angel* were to move into Nellie's shop, we really would become friends, and all would be well? What if by convincing Nellie to stay, I'd blown my chance at a nicer neighbor? Oh, well. I decided to go with my first thought — that someone even worse than Nellie could move into her vacated shop — and be glad Nellie had opted not to move to Arizona.

I walked Angus on up to the square. He immediately went to every dog's favorite spot — the base of the wrought-iron clock — sniffed, and peed. He looked up as if to tell me he was finished, and we headed back to the Seven-Year Stitch.

I made a concerted effort not to look at Nellie's shop. I wanted to peep in and wave to her, but I didn't dare.

We were walking past the Horror Emporium when Priscilla opened the door.

"Well, hi," she said. "How are you guys this morning?"

"I'm still trying to wake up," I said.

She laughed. "I know what you mean. We had a fantastic crowd last night and stayed open later to accommodate everybody."

"That's good."

"It is, isn't it? Hey, I know you and your mom are super busy getting ready for the open house, but Claude and I would love to bend her ear a teensy bit. We promise not to take up too much of her time."

"I'm sorry, but Mom isn't feeling well and didn't come with me today," I said.

"I guess the trip was a bit much for her."

She apparently wasn't in the small-town loop yet, and I didn't want to elaborate. "I suppose so. By the way, I saw you, Claude, and some of your staff members at Keira's memorial. I thought it was awfully nice of you to go."

"Well, she was . . . lost . . . while doing work for us," Priscilla said. "So, naturally, we wanted to be there for Ken Sherman . . . and the rest of the family . . . and for MacKenzies' Mochas too, since she was one of their own." She lifted her shoulders. "What a tragic loss for . . . for everyone."

"Yes, it truly was." I noticed someone crossing the street as if she might be heading for the Seven-Year Stitch. "Well, I'd better go. Drop in anytime."

"You do the same." She waggled her fingers good-bye at me before closing the door to the Horror Emporium.

As it happened, the woman wasn't coming to the Stitch. She walked toward MacKenzies' Mochas. So I had time to contemplate the conversation I'd just had with Priscilla.

Had I misjudged her? I wondered as I unsnapped Angus's leash and put it back behind the counter.

Angus trotted back to the office to get a drink of water, and I sat back down to work on the open house bags.

For days after Keira's death, I'd been appalled at how unfeeling she and Claude had seemed about the whole thing. They'd actually spoken about the murder being good for business, that is, after they'd worried that too many people had seen their actors in costume on the street. I guessed they could've been trying to make the best of a bad situation. Maybe they simply hadn't known how to behave or what to say about a young woman getting killed while helping out at their grand opening party. Or maybe by now Priscilla had finally processed the killing.

The bells over the door jingled letting me know a customer had come in. Angus wandered out of the office to see who was there. Since it was an elderly woman, he obediently walked over to the window and sat down.

"What a nice dog," she said.

"Thank you. His name is Angus. I'm Marcy. Is there anything I can help you find?"

"I'm really just looking. But I was at my friend's house the other day, and she was doing something that was like a bunch of French knots."

I picked a pillow up off the sofa and turned it toward her. "Did it look something like this?"

"Yes, that's it! What is that?"

"It's called candlewick, and you use Colonial knots rather than French knots. I can show you how, if you'd like."

"Yes, please."

I got a piece of linen, an embroidery hoop, and some white floss and joined the woman in the sit-and-stitch square. I had to demonstrate the Colonial knots only a time or two before she got the hang of it.

"Oh, I like this," she said. "Do you have any pattern books?"

"I do." I led her over to the candlewick books.

She picked out a book, floss, linen, an embroidery hoop, and some pillow stuffing. I rang up her purchases and invited her to the open house. She said she'd be there, took her periwinkle bag, and turned to go.

I was surprised to see Nellie Davis coming into the shop with a small bag. She held the door open for my customer and wished her a good day.

"Hi, Nellie," I said. "I'm glad to see you're working today."

"Well, I've decided to stay a bit longer. No one wants to be trying to move in winter, and it's setting in quickly."

"That's true."

"I called Vera Langhorne to tell her that I have her lavender essential oil in — I'd run out when she came by last week. People must be having trouble relaxing and getting to sleep at night. I know I have been." She shook her head slightly as if to reorganize her thoughts. "Anyway, Vera was at your house when I reached her. She told me about your mother." She placed the bag on the counter. "This is for her. It's a bottle of bergamot essential oil and a diffuser. She should diffuse the oil for no more than twenty minutes at a time." She patted her chest. "It's for her heart."

"Thank you!" I stepped around the counter and started to give the frail little woman a hug, but when she saw what I was about to do, she said good-bye and hurried out the door. I had to throw both hands over my mouth to quiet my laughter.

I called Mom to tell her that Nellie had brought her a gift.

"Is Vera bringing you to the shop when she goes to Scentsibilities to pick up her lavender oil?" I asked.

"She isn't going for a while yet. She, Veronica, and I are playing gin rummy and enjoying a chat. We're staying put for now . . . unless, of course, you need me to help you with something."

"No," I said. "I'm fine. I just wanted to check on you and let you know about Nellie's gift. I'll bring it when I come home for dinner."

"All right, darling. See you then."

Vera, Veronica, and Mom . . . chatting while playing cards. Would I want to be a fly on the wall for that conversation or not? Probably not.

I was surprised to see Adalyn coming in.

"Hi," I said. "Didn't Priscilla tell you my mom isn't here today?"

"No, I don't go into work until later this afternoon." She bent and hugged Angus. "Besides, I'm here because I'd like to learn to cross-stitch. I was looking at the stuff in here the other day, and I think it's really cool."

"Oh. That's great. Come on over, and let's find you a kit." I led her to the beginning cross-stitch kits. "I think it's best to start with a simple kit so you can decide whether or not you like it before tackling anything too difficult."

She picked out a fox. "This is adorable! Do you think I could do this one?"

"Of course, you could. I can get you started on it now, and then you can come back by if you need any more help."

I rang up her kit, and then we went over to the sit-and-stitch square to open it and begin. I showed her how to start in the center of the pattern.

"You can either cross the stitches as you go, or you can do a line of half stitches in a particular color and cross them as you come back," I said. "That's the way I usually work."

Soon she was comfortably making the stitches on her own.

"This isn't hard at all," she said.

"I knew you'd catch on quickly." I decided this was a great opportunity to talk with Adalyn about Jared and Keira. I couldn't think of any casual way to bring them up, so I had to use the blunt approach. "You and Jared seemed happy at dinner the other night."

"We were. We *are*," she said. "He's such a sweetheart. He deserves better than . . . well, than how he's been treated in the past."

"Do you mean Keira or Susan?" Susan was Jared's ex-wife.

"Both. Neither was very good to him from what I've heard."

"I believe Christine would agree with you," I said. "Have you met Jared's mom?"

"Yeah. She's a treasure. I think it's awful that she's got this stress about killing Keira hanging over her head. You don't think she did it, do you?"

"No, I don't. Adalyn, do you know whether or not Jared has any business dealings with Keira's dad?"

She looked up from her needlework. "I

don't know. Jared is hoping to expand. He's been saving and is looking to add another bay or two onto the garage . . . maybe even hire another mechanic. I think that'd be super, don't you?"

"I do." Adalyn was still young enough to want everyone to agree with her. "Progress and growth is almost always good."

"Why *almost* always?" she asked.

"Well, I wouldn't want to grow the Stitch right now because I wouldn't want to take on more than I could handle. But, unlike Jared, I'm not looking to hire a helper either. Right now, I'm happy with my shop being small."

"Yeah. But, you know, if you decided you were ready to settle down and have a family, then you might change your mind about that."

"I might indeed." Hadn't she and Jared been dating for only a couple of weeks? Surely they hadn't talked about marriage and a family already.

"Jared is always thinking about the big picture. He was really glad when I told him I'm studying to be an accountant. I mean, I enjoy acting, but I don't think it would be a suitable career for me."

"I don't know," I said. "You're awfully good."

"Thanks." She smiled. "I might be good enough for community theater, but I'm not a silver screen kinda gal."

"So is Jared already thinking of making you his bookkeeper?"

"Maybe. It's hard to say what the future holds, but I like him. I like him a lot."

I was delighted — and so were my stomach and Angus — to see Ted walk in with lunch. He'd brought chef salads and milk shakes.

"Milk shakes?" I asked with a bemused smile.

"Sure. It's for energy. Plus, you've got protein from the eggs and meats in the salad. And it's not a heavy meal. Well, not entirely." He put the bag and the drink carrier on the counter and swept me up into his arms. "How's that for a pick-me-up lunch?"

I laughed. "Wait! I have to put the clock on the door."

He set me down, and while I fixed the clock, he carried the food into the office. Guess which one of us Angus went with? If you guessed Ted, you were right.

As we ate, I told Ted about how his mom, my mom, and Vera were spending the day playing cards and chatting.

"I wouldn't be surprised if they're having

a little wine too," he said.

"Does that make you nervous?"

"The drinking part — not so much. The chatting — a little bit."

"Me too. You know they're talking about us," I said.

"And yet, if either of them could hear us speculating on what they're talking about, they'd say we're flattering ourselves." He mimicked his mother's voice. "We're intelligent women. We have much more interesting things to discuss than our children."

I smiled. "You're right."

"No, *you're* right — they're definitely talking about us. But they'll never admit it."

"Are you having a good day?" I asked.

"Yeah. I followed up on that pet store lead. The owner swears he's never heard of Ken Sherman, but he could either be lying or Ken could be using an alias with some of his clientele. How about you?"

"I've had a day full of surprises." I told him about how Nellie had brought a gift for Mom. "I was so touched that I went around the counter to give her a hug, and she practically ran out of the store."

He chuckled. "I can't get over *anybody* turning down a Marcy hug. She doesn't know what she's missing."

I huffed.

"What? I'm not kidding!" He laughed again. "You said you had more than one surprise?"

"I have. Believe it or not, I think Priscilla might have a heart after all. When I mentioned seeing her at the memorial, she talked about Keira's death being a *tragic loss* instead of *good for publicity.* And then Adalyn came in to learn cross-stitch."

"Adalyn? Is that the girl we saw with Jared Willoughby at dinner Saturday night?"

"It is," I said. "And, although they've only been dating a couple of weeks, it must be getting serious." I told Ted about Jared's plan to expand his business and the possibility of making Adalyn his bookkeeper. "When I told her I wanted to keep my business small for now, she said I might change my mind when I got ready to start a family."

He dabbed at his mouth with his napkin. "Jared appears to be quite a few years older than Adalyn."

"I'd say he's about five to seven years older. That's not a terrible gap." I drew my brows together. "Why? What're you thinking?"

"I'm wondering if Adalyn has come up with these fanciful ideas on her own, or if Jared truly feels like putting up the white picket fence after being burned so badly two times in a row."

My frown deepened. "Oh. You're right. I hadn't thought of that." Ted had raised some good questions. Had Adalyn set her sights on Jared to the point that she'd decided to give up her dream of acting and go into a profession that could benefit him? Or had Jared gone that quickly from one serious relationship to another? It's possible that Adalyn had been telling me the truth — that she didn't feel she was cut out for Hollywood. But, if she hadn't been serious about acting, why had she auditioned for Vera and me in the hope of meeting Mom?

We ate in silence for a few minutes, each of us lost in our thoughts.

"I did ask Adalyn if Jared had any business dealings with Keira's dad," I said at last.

"What was her response?"

"She said she didn't know, but then she started talking about Jared's plans for expansion."

"We're already looking into whether or not Jared is working with Ken Sherman," Ted said. "She said he'd been saving for this expansion?"

I nodded.

"I wonder if Jared is simply imagining the

business he could possibly have someday, or if he's found an investor willing to make it happen."

"Or *was* willing to make it happen," I said. "Would Ken Sherman still want to help out Keira's boyfriend now that she's gone?"

CHAPTER NINETEEN

I was delighted to see Captain Moe stroll into the shop shortly after lunch. He boomed a hello to Angus, who romped over to greet him, and then he gave me a hug.

"I was in town visiting Camille and the baby, and I heard about your mother," he said. "Is she all right?"

"I believe so. It was quite a scare." I motioned for him to accompany me to the sit-and-stitch square.

"I'm sure it was." He sank onto the sofa.

"The doctor told her to see a cardiologist when she gets back home, but she thinks Mom's heart is fine." I sat on the red club chair I'd recently vacated.

"Good to hear, Tink." He nodded toward the goodie bags. "For the upcoming celebration?"

"Yes. Will you be able to make it?"

"I'm afraid not," he said. "I'll be working."

I handed him one of the goodie bags with my compliments.

"Thank you very much." He smiled. "Has it been a year already?"

"It has." I chuckled, remembering the first time Angus and I met Captain Moe. "I met you on a Sunday . . . The diner was closed, and yet, you fed us anyway."

"How could I not? Two wee strays . . . Well, one wee stray and a big furry beastie!"

Angus wagged his tail.

As we were laughing, the bells over the door jingled. I looked up to see Priscilla walking into the Stitch with a potted amaryllis and a DVD.

"Hello." I was getting ready to introduce Priscilla to Captain Moe when he spoke.

"Well, as I live and breathe. Priscilla Morris! What brings you to Tallulah Falls?" He got up and crossed the room to give her a brief hug, which she awkwardly accepted.

"My husband, Claude, and I are running the Horror Emporium next door. You should come and check us out some evening."

"I'll do that. How's Jim?"

She pressed her lips together into a thin line before answering. "You know my father." She turned to me. "I have to get back and get ready for tonight's performance. I just wanted to drop these off for your mom. Tell her I hope she feels better soon."

I thanked her and took the items from her. "I'm sure she'll appreciate your thoughtfulness very much."

"Tinkerbell, I need to leave also." Captain Moe gave me a hug and patted Angus's head. "Priscilla, I'll see you out."

Outside on the sidewalk, Captain Moe and Priscilla spoke briefly before going in opposite directions. Captain Moe looked faintly troubled as he walked away. I turned from the window so he wouldn't think I was watching them.

I looked down at the DVD Priscilla had brought. *The Amazing Atwoods.* I shook my head. She was determined to audition for Mom.

The DVD didn't look like a top-notch professional production. I wondered how famous the Atwoods had been.

I went to the office and got my laptop. I did a search for the Amazing Atwoods. Some links advertising performances came up but not much more than that. I then searched for Claude Atwood and Priscilla Atwood separately. Again, not much turned up. And, from what I could see, it didn't appear the two had been performing but for the past two to three years.

Oh, well. The video would make for interesting postclass entertainment later tonight. Given the Atwoods' flair for the dramatic, I was looking forward to seeing what they did when they were full-out *trying* to put on a performance.

While there was a lull in customers coming into the Stitch, I called Alfred. His secretary put me right through to him.

"Marcy, dear, is anything the matter?"

"No . . . I don't think so."

"Out with it." Alfred Benton had put on his surrogate father voice.

I told him about Mom's trip to the emergency room. "I just need to know if anything like this has happened before. Is there anything I should know — anything she hasn't told me about?"

"Not that I'm aware of," said Alfred. "My guess is that the stress of travel plus the heavy meal simply took its toll. I'll make sure she is seen by a cardiologist as soon as she returns to San Francisco. In fact, I'll have my secretary make the appointment."

"No, please don't. She'll kill me for snitching on her."

"Well, too bad."

"At least, call and talk with her first," I said. "For all I know, she's already called and made the appointment today."

He deftly changed the subject. "How are preparations for the anniversary celebration coming along?"

"They're coming along well. I'm just finishing up the goodie bags. Sadie and Blake will be bringing over refreshments tomorrow."

"Something delicious, I'm sure."

"Some crudités, a cheese platter, some cookies . . . things like that. I wish you could be here."

"I will be . . . in spirit, at least." He chuckled. "I hate to rush off, my dear, but I have a meeting."

"Okay. If there was anything you thought I should know about Mom, you'd tell me . . . wouldn't you?"

"You know I would."

I took Angus home at five. I gave Mom her gifts from Priscilla and Nellie and told her how many people had been in to check on her.

"That's awfully sweet," she said. "Had I been to the emergency room at home, no one would've known unless I didn't show up at work the next day . . . other than Alfred, of course. It seems Alfred knows just about everything. Even *he* had heard of my misadventure."

"I'm sorry, but I needed to know if you'd had anything like that happen before," I said. "I knew you wouldn't tell me because you wouldn't want me to worry, but Alfred would shoot straight with me."

"It's all right. I just hate to cause him undue concern."

Taking a page from Alfred's book, I changed the subject. "Check out this DVD Priscilla Atwood sent you. And, by the way, I don't think they're as famous as they let on. I did an Internet search for them, and it appears they've only been performing for a couple of years."

"Or maybe they only recently adopted the stage names Claude and Priscilla Atwood." She shrugged. "There's a famous story about Walter Matthau where he was credited for a cameo appearance in *Earthquake* using the name Walter Matuschanskayasky. Fans assumed this was Matthau's real name, but it wasn't. It was Walter Matthow. He changed it to Matthau because that was the current American spelling of the name. Incidentally, his nickname was Jake."

"Okay. Well, maybe we can watch the DVD when I get home. Or you can go ahead and watch it if you'd rather." She was obviously miffed at me for calling Alfred, so who knew what she'd do?

"We'll see."

I fed Angus, grabbed a protein bar, and headed back to work.

Mom had texted me before class was over and told me she was tired and was going on to bed. Although I understood, I was a little hurt by it. Was her health worse than she'd led me to believe? Had even Alfred kept me in the dark about her true condition? Or was she merely in a snit because I'd called Alfred to tell him about her trip to the emergency room? I hated that we hadn't had much time together since she'd been here.

I called Ted and asked if he'd like some company. He said he'd love some.

He met me at the door with a slice of chocolate cheesecake and two forks. "You sounded a little down over the phone."

"You always know how to make me feel better."

We went on into his kitchen and sat down at the table in the breakfast nook. Ted's kitchen had a more modern decor than mine. The appliances were stainless steel, the countertops were dark gray granite, and the cabinets were a glossy black with silver handles. Skylights and recessed lighting over the island and a chandelier over the table kept the room from being too dark.

"Coffee?" he asked.

"Do you have decaf? I don't want it keeping me awake all night."

"Of course." He made the coffee, poured us cups, and then sat down at the table where we savored the cheesecake.

"This is fabulous," I said.

"Thank you. I keep it on hand for the occasional bout of the blues."

I smiled. I'd never known Ted to have "the blues." He must've been referring to my blues.

"It's not that bad really. I just . . . Well, Mom isn't doing what I'd like her to do."

"Parents. You do your best to raise them right, but you're never quite sure how they'll turn out."

"Ha-ha. I missed her at the store today. I mean, I'm glad she was able to spend time with Vera and your mom, but I thought that at least we'd have some time this evening." I explained how she'd seemed upset with me for calling Alfred.

"What's the deal with those two anyway?" he asked. "Lifelong friends only? Romantic spark?"

"I don't know. I've always thought Alfred would be perfect for Mom. Of course, he was married when Dad died. I think his marriage had been in trouble anyway, and it fell apart a few years after Dad's death. Neither he nor Mom ever remarried."

"Have Alfred and your mom ever dated?"

"No . . . not that I know of. I did bring it up with her just the other night." I lifted and dropped one shoulder. "She said they're afraid that if they'd date, they'd end up ruining their friendship."

"Maybe. But it might be worth the gamble — don't you think?"

"*I* think so, yes. As for what Mom thinks . . . Who knows?" I took a bite of cheesecake and savored the rich, velvety chocolate. "And while I love being here with you, I'd really wanted to spend some time with Mom tonight. Priscilla brought over this DVD called *The Amazing Atwoods,* and I thought she and I would get a kick out of watching it together."

"Sounds like a winner. Do they sing, dance, do a variety show?"

"I think it's some sort of magic act." I shook my head. "I looked them up after Priscilla brought by the DVD but couldn't find much about them. According to the information I could find online, the two of them have only been performing — at least, as Claude and Priscilla Atwood — for the past two or three years. Did Priscilla mention to you or Manu that she's originally from this area?"

"Manu interviewed her, so I don't know. I can check her statement tomorrow to see. Why?"

"Captain Moe was in today, and he recognized Priscilla. He asked about her father. She didn't seem terribly friendly with Captain Moe and made an excuse to leave as soon as she'd dropped off the DVD and a flower for Mom."

"Who doesn't like Captain Moe?"

"That's what I was wondering myself. It made me really curious as to what Priscilla's story is . . . and Claude's too, for that matter. Where are they from? Who are they really? And what are they hiding behind those outlandish outfits they always wear?"

By then, we'd polished off the cheesecake. Ted took our plate and forks to the sink, rinsed them off, and then put them in the dishwasher.

"They're personas," Ted said. "I suppose we all are in a way. The Atwoods are just more obvious about theirs. Maybe Priscilla didn't want Captain Moe to blow her exotic cover. For the Horror Emporium to be a success, I believe that Claude and Priscilla feel they have to portray themselves as eccentrics. For Captain Moe to recognize her as a small-town girl might've been a threat to her facade."

"You're ever so deep, Detective Nash."

He sat back down at the table and took a sip of his coffee. "As for your mom, she might be scared. I don't think she'd intentionally hide anything from you, but she wouldn't want you to worry either. You know how that is. I've seen you do the same thing with her."

"That's true. But that's different."

"Of course it is." He smiled. "Now about that video . . . you don't happen to have it with you, do you?"

"I don't, but I promise we'll watch it together soon."

"Are you ready for Friday?" he asked.

"Yep. The goodie bags are all stuffed and in a basket in the storeroom. I'll put the basket on the counter Friday afternoon. The door prizes are finished, framed, and wrapped. And, I'm sure Sadie has the food under control."

"No nervous jitters? No nightmares about your first party at the Seven-Year Stitch?"

"No . . . not really. I mean, no nightmares. Plenty of jitters. It sounds bad to say this, but I feel like the worst thing that could happen this year has already happened," I said. "What could be worse than Keira's death?"

"Shhh. Don't jinx it."

My eyes widened.

"I'm kidding," he said.

"I know you really can't talk about it, but do you have any leads in Keira's murder?"

"We're still following the leads we have, but we do have a couple of new developments. I can tell you with the utmost certainty that vampire fangs did not make the puncture wounds in Keira's neck."

"What about Detective Poston?" I asked. "Is he still on the case?"

"He is. Why?"

"I didn't care much for him. He was too abrasive."

"I knew you didn't like him. That's why after the initial interview, we didn't have you talk with him anymore. Besides, you'd been with Manu and me. You weren't a suspect."

"For a change." I gave him a wry smile.

He lifted my hand to his lips. "Poston is currently investigating business owners who might be linked to Ken Sherman. We think one of those people might've killed Keira or know who did."

"Including Jared Willoughby?"

"I've said too much already," he said.

"I know. We should stop all this talking." I leaned in for a kiss.

CHAPTER TWENTY

When I got up on Thursday morning, I heard Mom messing around downstairs. From the scents of bacon and maple wafting up the stairs, I deduced she was making breakfast. I quickly showered, dressed, and joined her in the kitchen.

"Good morning, darling," she said.

"Hi. Are you feeling better?"

"I am. I made you pancakes, eggs, and bacon. Angus has already had his bacon and eggs and is outside. He also enjoyed half of the banana I put on my oatmeal."

"Mom, you had oatmeal, and you made me all this?" I gestured toward the table.

"Well, it isn't *all* for you. I invited Ted, but he can't get away. So I asked Todd to come by. He should be here —"

Before she could finish her sentence, the doorbell rang.

"Come on in!" she called.

Todd came in, strode into the kitchen, and

swept Mom up into a hug. "Good morning, ladies! Thanks for thinking of me, Ms. Singer."

"You're welcome. You two go ahead and sit down."

Todd and I sat down at the table, and like siblings, reached for the same pancake.

"I'm the guest," he said.

"I'm the girl. Guys are always supposed to defer to the girl."

"Well, if you want that giant pancake on your hips . . ."

I glared at him. "Fine. Take it."

"Oh, no. Go ahead."

"Children." Mom stood with her hands on her hips looking at us. "There's enough to go around."

"Yes, ma'am."

Todd and I spoke in unison, and then laughed.

"So how are you feeling, Ms. Singer?" he asked.

"Much better . . . and it's Beverly. Ms. Singer makes me sound old." She got herself some coffee and joined us at the table. "Did you know that Marcella actually called and told on me to Alfred last night?"

Todd looked at me. "Tattletale."

I poked my tongue out at him and then poured syrup on my pancake — the one *under* the one Todd had claimed. "I just wanted to find out if anything like that had happened before. You know you wouldn't tell me if it had, Mom."

"I wouldn't want you to worry . . . especially not right now when you're getting ready to celebrate the Seven-Year Stitch's anniversary." She sipped her coffee. "But nothing like that *has* happened to me before. And I'm sure I'll get a clean bill of health from the cardiologist."

"I should take off and go with you to that appointment," I said.

"No, you should not. I promise I'll tell you if anything's wrong." She turned to Todd. "Do you argue like this with your parents?"

"Of course. It's an adult child's job. It keeps you guys on your toes."

"Gee, thanks. So our children are trying to keep our old minds sharp, is that it?"

Todd looked at me. "I did not say that. Now I see where you get it."

I smirked at him.

"By the way, Todd, I'm sorry about Keira," Mom said. "I know the two of you weren't together anymore and that you'd both moved on, but it still must've been quite a shock for you when she died."

"It was. Thank you."

My mind raced. Had I even thought of Todd during this ordeal? Not really. Not as someone who had dated Keira in the past. Granted, they'd dated only casually and just a time or two, but she'd been crazy about him.

Todd silently read the expressions flitting across my face and winked. "Now aren't you glad you let me have the biggest pancake?"

"Yes." I pushed my plate over. "You can even have the rest of mine."

He pushed it back. "No, thanks. I don't want your cooties."

Mom laughed. "You two are impossible."

I had a sudden thought. "Did Keira's dad ever try to invest in the Brew Crew?"

"He bought a couple of beers one night. Does that count?"

"No." I explained Adalyn's tale about Jared wanting to expand his business. "Given Mr. Sherman's penchant for trying to get people to franchise, I thought he might've approached you."

"Not me. And I'm glad of it given everything I'm hearing about him now. Besides, I've always been a stand-on-my-own-two-feet kinda guy."

"Me too. I mean, I told Adalyn I was happy with the Seven-Year Stitch the way it

is now and that I didn't see myself expanding anytime soon."

"What did she say to that?" Mom asked.

"She said that I might change my mind
whenever I decided to have a family."

Todd shrugged. "She's got a point. As nice
as Jill is, I don't think she'd be the world's
best nanny."

I had a fleeting thought of my mannequin
turning into Mary Poppins.

"Maybe by then, I'll be ready to give up
showbiz," said Mom.

"I doubt that." I dug back into my pancake
before realizing Todd and Mom were staring at the top of my head. "What?"

"Is there some news you'd like to share
with the rest of us?" Todd asked.

"No, there isn't." I simply couldn't see
Mom ready to give up show business before
I was ready to have a child. In fact, I
couldn't see Mom *ever* ready to give up her
career.

Mom, Angus, and I barely had time to get
into the Stitch before actors started coming
in. The young man who was afraid of dogs
basically said hello and left. But the others
lingered. In the sit-and-stitch square. For
hours.

Priscilla and Claude came in wearing

matching black tuxedos. At first, they acted as if they were disappointed that their actors had come over to "bother Ms. Singer" and were going to herd them back up the street, but then they joined the party. Priscilla stood at the prime spot to Mom's right until the girl sitting there moved and let her boss have her seat. The girl promptly plopped onto the floor at Mom's feet.

While I waited on customers, Mom entertained the neighbors with Hollywood anecdotes. I heard snatches of conversations now and then, but mostly I restocked bins and waited on needle crafters. I'd been afraid all the attention would wear Mom out, but she seemed to be really enjoying herself.

When they all finally left, I asked Mom if she'd found any budding talents among the actors.

"Maybe," she said. "I told them I'd keep my eyes open, and I steered them toward some reputable agencies."

"That's good."

"Yeah." She brushed at the sleeve of her sweater. I didn't see any hair or lint there, so I wasn't sure what she was doing. Finally, she spoke again. "Does Tallulah Falls have a community theater?"

"Probably. If not, I'm sure there's one not terribly far from here. Why? Are you thinking the actors need more practice?"

"No, I was thinking about what you said this morning at breakfast about starting a family . . . How you felt like that would happen long before I retire."

I sat down beside her. "And?"

She shrugged but still didn't meet my eyes. "I don't know. I wouldn't want to miss spending time with my grandchild while I was off on first one movie set and then another. I made that mistake when you were growing up."

"I think I had a terrific childhood."

"Still. . . . Maybe the other night was a wake-up call. Maybe it's time to start thinking about retirement."

"Mom, that would destroy you," I said. "I saw what a wonderful time you were having with those actors. You need that in your life."

"But I need you too."

I took her hand. "And you've got me. You'd never be happy doing community theater."

"I might."

She looked at me, and I arched a brow.

"Or I might not," she admitted. "But I'd be willing to give it a try."

"You're really concerned about your health, aren't you?"

"No. I'm worried that I won't be here for

you when you need me." She quickly corrected herself. "I don't mean *be here* as in living. I mean *be here* as in Tallulah Falls."

"You've always been around when I needed you, Mom. And you always will be."

She smiled softly and lowered her eyes.

"And I want to be there for you," I continued. "Let me go with you to the doctor when you get back home. Or let me make an appointment for you with a cardiologist here in Oregon. Then you'll at least have a better idea of your condition."

She shook her head. "I'm fine, darling. I think I'd know if there was something wrong with my heart. And I think the ER doctor would too. Had she suspected anything truly serious, she'd have either kept me in the hospital or referred me to a cardiologist right away. She wouldn't have advised me to wait until I got back home."

"Fair enough. Then why are you so down today?"

"I don't know. I guess I just don't want to miss anything," she said. "I mean, I know you have your own life, but —"

"You won't miss a thing, Mom. I promise."

I was really glad that Ted came in with lunch and put an end to our awkward chat. I didn't like to see Mom melancholy. It was

291

so out of character for her. Had my leaving San Francisco last year taken such a toll on her? I didn't think so. She'd been here to visit several times — and I'd been home to visit too — and we'd both been busy with our work. Was she more scared about her health than she wanted to admit? Or had something that she, Vera, and Veronica talked about yesterday reminded her of how fast time was flying past?

I rose to greet Ted with a kiss. Then I put the clock on the door and suggested that we move into my office before any more of Mom's fans came to visit.

"I take it you've been mobbed by actors today?" he asked.

"Yes. They were all really sweet though," she said. "I enjoyed talking with them."

For today's lunch, Ted brought cedar plank grilled salmon and green beans. It was delicious.

"We should have this more often," I told him. I turned to Mom. "We have salads and chicken salad croissants from MacKenzies' Mochas fairly often, but this salmon is a really nice change."

"I was afraid it'd be cold by the time I got here with it. It came from that seafood place we like in Lincoln City." He nodded toward Mom. "We'll all go there before you leave, if you'd like — you, Marcy, Mom and me."

"That'd be nice. I really like your mother. We had a lovely time yesterday."

"She said she enjoyed it too." He glanced at me, and I knew we'd compare notes later. The bad thing was I didn't have any notes to compare. Mom had said very little about yesterday.

I fed Angus a small bite of my salmon.

"I spent the morning with one of your favorite people," Ted told me.

"Nellie Davis?" I asked.

He laughed. "No. Mark Poston."

I explained to Mom that Detective Poston had been called in to help with the investigation since so many people were in the area when Keira was found.

"Plus, he questioned those of us who were together that evening and recorded our statements," Ted said. "Marcy found him to be rather harsh."

"Ted says he's one of the best interrogators with the Tallulah County Police Department, but I don't think he's ever heard the old adage about catching flies with honey."

Ted grinned. "He's not catching flies, babe. He's catching criminals. And he's doing a good job getting information about the people Ken Sherman is in business with."

"Has he found any evidence to support the suspicion that Ken Sherman is laundering money for criminals?" I asked.

"You know I'm not at liberty to say."

I smiled. "I know. I just want this case to be solved."

"So do I. But I know your Mom doesn't want to hear shop talk."

"You should've heard *her* shop talk this morning." I looked over at Mom. "Did you watch the Atwoods' DVD before you went to bed last night?"

"No. I wanted to wait and watch it with you."

"I'd love to talk with Captain Moe about Priscilla and see what she was like growing up," I said.

"Maybe you can ask him tomorrow," said Mom.

I shook my head. "He has to be at the diner tomorrow night and can't come to the open house. I gave him his goodie bag yesterday. But I'm sure I'll get the opportunity to talk with him soon."

We finished our meal and walked out of the office. Mom and I thanked Ted for bringing lunch, and I noticed that Christine Willoughby was standing outside on the sidewalk.

I hurried to the door. "Christine! Hi!

Come on in."

"I can come back if this isn't a good time." She twisted her scarf in her hands.

"No. We were just in the back eating lunch. You should've come on in."

"I didn't want to intrude."

"I'm just leaving." Ted kissed my cheek, nodded to Christine, and gave Mom a brief wave before stepping out onto the sidewalk.

"Christine, I don't think you've met my mom, Beverly Singer."

The two women shook hands.

"It's nice to meet you," Mom said.

"Then, obviously, Marcy hasn't told you about me."

I ushered Christine over to the sit-and-stitch square. "Don't be silly. Mom and I both have been in the position you're in right now, and we know it's no fun."

"And we also know that you'll be exonerated."

"Thank you. I wish I could be that sure." Christine sighed. "I came by to tell you that I'd still love to come to class tonight, but I understand perfectly if you'd rather I skip it."

"Of course I want you to come to class! Why wouldn't I?"

"Because I'm a suspect in a murder case."

"Please, Christine, I know you're innocent," I said.

"The police don't think so."

"Ted always tells me that everyone's a suspect, but I don't think they give you any more weight than anyone else currently under investigation in Keira's homicide." I placed my hand on Christine's arm. "Just be patient. Ted and Manu are wonderful detectives. They'll find the real killer."

"I hope you're right."

"I know I am. Now let's talk about something more pleasant . . . at least, I *hope* it's more pleasant. Have you met Adalyn?"

"The girl Jared's been dating?" She nodded. "She seems sweet. I worry that she's a bit young for him."

"Adalyn told me that Jared is thinking of expanding the garage," I said.

She sighed. "He's mentioned it, but there's no way he could afford an expansion right now. I'm afraid he could simply be telling this girl what she wants to hear."

"Or she could be projecting her wishes onto him," Mom said. "I think girls these days move a little too fast sometimes. It seems they're so desperate for a happily ever after, they try to orchestrate situations to bring about the result they desire."

Christine leaned forward. "That's exactly it. I'm not saying Jared is innocent of filling these girls' heads with white picket fences, but Keira was the same way. In fact, I don't think Jared ever even considered expanding his business until Keira started talking about it. For goodness' sake, they should date a while and get to know each other before they begin making all these grand plans."

"Did Keira ever offer to have her dad invest in Jared's business?" I asked.

"I don't know. When I disagreed with Jared about the need to build onto the garage, he got angry with me and refused to discuss it with me anymore. Why do you ask?"

"Apparently, that's something that Mr. Sherman does." I shrugged. "He was trying to get MacKenzies' Mochas to allow him to franchise another coffee shop for Keira."

"I imagine it would've been nice for the girl to have had her own business, but — and I hate to speak ill of the dead — I seriously doubt she'd have been mature enough to operate it on her own," said Christine. "Maybe her dad planned to help manage it."

"Maybe so," I said.

"Well, I'd better go." She smiled. "Thank you for letting me attend tonight. I'm really enjoying this class."

"I'm enjoying having you in the class," I said. "And I hope you'll come to the open house celebration tomorrow too."

"I'm planning on it."

After Christine left, I turned to Mom. "So what do you think?"

"I think Christine Willoughby is a smart woman and that it's likely her son refused to discuss his business dealings with her because he realized she was right but didn't want to admit it."

"I'm wondering if Ken Sherman was offering to pay for the garage expansion. If so, then Jared would feel obligated to him — even more than for the cost of the add-on."

Mom nodded slowly. "Mr. Sherman might've even insisted on a partial ownership of the business."

"And then he could carry out whatever dealings he wanted, and there would be nothing Jared could do about it."

"Exactly." She frowned. "Jared is still talking about the expansion even though Keira is no longer a part of his life. That makes me feel that if there *is* a business agreement of any sort between Jared and Mr. Sherman, it was independent of Jared's relationship with Keira."

"I wonder if Keira knew that."

CHAPTER TWENTY-ONE

A small group of coworkers came into the Stitch. They each wanted to make a cross-stitch or embroidery panel and then turn the panels into a quilt for a friend who was retiring from the company. I began asking questions about what sort of theme they were interested in. Did they want something vintage? Was there a hobby their friend had always liked that they could incorporate into the quilt?

Angus went to the door.

"I'll take him," Mom said, getting the leash from behind the counter and taking Angus up the street.

The coworkers — one of whom was a man — went back and forth between Sunbonnet Sue and Sam, flowers, and birds. They finally decided on the flowers. Since there were six of them, they each took two flower patterns to make the embroidered quilt squares. They said they'd return when they got the squares completed to get what they'd need to complete the quilt. I invited them back to the anniversary open house and put flyers in their bags advertising the current classes.

After they left, I began to get concerned about Mom. She should've been back by now. I stepped out onto the sidewalk and looked up the street. She and Angus were standing on the sidewalk in front of Scentsibilities talking with Nellie. I went back inside.

I decided that after talking with Nellie, Mom might need a stiff drink. I made a fresh pot of coffee.

"Mmm, that smells delicious," she said when she returned. "Thank you for making it. I got cold while I was standing there talking with Nellie Davis."

Angus muscled past me to get a drink from his water bowl as I put two cups, the coffee carafe, sugar, and creamer on a tray and took it into the sit-and-stitch square. Mom had already sat down on the sofa facing the window and stretched her legs out in front of her.

"So, how did you find yourself chatting with Nellie?" I asked. "Did she stop you as you walked by?"

"No. Actually, I stuck my head inside the

door and called to her." She stirred creamer into her coffee. "I wanted to thank her for the diffuser and the bergamot."

"Did you try that, by the way?"

"I did. I don't know what health benefits it was supposed to have had, but it was a pleasant, refreshing citrusy smell. I liked it." She sipped her coffee. "Back to Nellie. While I was thanking her, she came to the door to talk. I don't know whether she's lonely or not in the loop where the town's gossip is concerned or what, but she wanted me to tell her what was going on with the investigation of Keira's murder."

"What did you tell her?"

"The truth — that I don't know a thing." She leaned back against the sofa cushions. "I know she's frightened. That's why she was considering leaving. But she's not as intrepid as you are. I think the thought of leaving everything familiar to her is even scarier than having a murderer in her midst."

"She thinks the murderer is in her midst?"

"The murderer *is* in her midst, darling. Yours too."

"Well, yeah." I shrugged. "But by now, I'm kinda used to it."

"That concerns me more than you could possibly know."

■ ■ ■ ■

I had to hurry to get back to the Stitch and get ready for class, so Mom and I had grilled cheese sandwiches and tomato soup for dinner. Mom said she didn't want to return for the class — that she'd prefer to relax and read for a while — so I left Angus with her. I also left her with strict instructions to call me if she needed anything. I was still concerned that she wasn't feeling a hundred percent, but she assured me that she simply didn't want a repeat of this morning.

"I felt like I disrupted your work this morning when all those actors came in," she said. "People will be there tonight to take your class, not visit with your mother. I'll talk with them tomorrow at the open house."

I parked in one of the spaces in front of the building when I got to the Seven-Year Stitch rather than going around back. I was surprised to see a man standing on the sidewalk in front of the shop peering inside. I was even more surprised when the man turned and I saw that it was Ken Sherman.

I got out of the Jeep and walked over to the sidewalk. "Mr. Sherman?"

He smiled. "Hello, Marcy! I thought I'd missed you."

"I typically close at five, but I teach needlework classes on Tuesday, Wednesday, and Thursday evenings." I unlocked the door. "You wanted to talk with me?"

"I . . . ah . . . just wanted to drop by and thank you again for your thoughtfulness the other night. I realize you didn't know Keira all that well, but it meant a lot to me and Bethany that you came and expressed your condolences."

"Well, I truly am sorry for your loss."

We were still standing on the sidewalk. I didn't particularly want to take Ken Sherman inside with me. I mean, if he *did* associate with criminals, then I wasn't sure I would be comfortable being in the shop alone with him.

"May I come in and see your shop? I know Bethany has been talking about stopping in."

Great.

"Of course," I said, walking into the Stitch. "Come on in. The students will be arriving soon. Do you mind if I tidy up while we talk?"

"Not at all." He wandered over to Jill.

I went a few feet away from him and tidied the embroidery floss bins. They didn't really need to be straightened up, but I wanted some distance between the two of us.

He laughed and I started.

"I love your mannequin," he said. "What a beaut!"

"Thank you."

"You have a nice little shop here, Marcy." He blew out a breath. "I wish Keira had been interested in allowing me to set her up in business before . . . well, before." His shoulders slumped. "She was always so flighty going from one thing — or one boy — to another. She was never settled and sure of herself like Bethany."

"Bethany appears to be quite an accomplished young lady."

"She is. She's extraordinary really. Do you have any sisters or brothers, Marcy?"

"Nope, I'm an only child."

"I imagine your parents are very proud of you," he said.

"I believe my mother is. My father died when I was young."

"I'm sorry to hear that."

"You know, I think Keira would have really made a go of the MacKenzies' Mochas franchise," I said.

"You heard about that?"

I smiled. "Hey, it's Tallulah Falls. There aren't any secrets here . . . not for long anyway."

"I suppose that's true. But, you know, some of the tales being told around here aren't true."

My smile faded and my heartbeat quickened. Still, I tried to keep the conversation light. "Oh, I know! Ms. Davis who owns Scentsibilities has said time and again that she believes my shop is cursed and that I'm bad for everyone else's business." I lifted and dropped one shoulder. "I've had my share of things go wrong around here. Some people tend to get panicky."

"I understand that you have friends on the police force."

"Um . . . you mean Manu? I think he's friends with everybody. And, of course, I'm dating Ted Nash." I glanced toward the door. Surely one of my students would be here any second now.

"I loved my daughter with all my heart," said Mr. Sherman. "I wanted desperately to see her succeed at something — anything — and now I'll never have that opportunity. I'll never be able to help her succeed."

"I . . . I know. That's t-terrible."

"Do you know who killed my daughter, Marcy?"

"No, sir. I don't have the foggiest idea," I said.

"None of your police friends have discussed any of their theories with you?"

"No, they haven't. They take their oath of confidentiality seriously." I wondered if police officers *did* take an oath of confidentiality. I kinda doubted it, but I liked the sound of it. It was nicer than telling Mr. Sherman that Ted and Manu weren't in the habit of spreading dirty laundry all over town.

"I'm sure they do, but you seem to be the kind of girl people are drawn to — that they'd share secrets with."

"They haven't, Mr. Sherman. I assure you that you likely know much more than I do about your daughter's murder and the person or persons responsible," I said.

"Well . . . thank you for your time."

"You're welcome. I'm sorry I couldn't help."

As he left, I went into the office for a moment. I needed to collect myself before my students got here. I didn't have time to converse with Ted, but I sent him a text:

Ken Sherman was just here at the Stitch. He wanted to know if I knew anything about his daughter's killer. I told him I don't, and he left. Everything's okay, but he kinda gave me the creeps. Don't say anything in front of Mom about him being here.

He immediately texted back:

You're there alone? Is Angus with you? I'll be right over.

I called him. "Hey, sweetheart, there's no need to come over. Ken Sherman is gone, and my students are" — I heard the bells over the door jingle — "they're coming in right now."

"I'll still be by. I'm just getting off, and I'm going to be there when you leave the Stitch this evening. I won't have you harassed."

"He didn't harass me, he just —"

Christine called from inside the shop. "Marcy, are you here?"

"Yeah, Christine! Be right there." To Ted I said, "I really need to go."

"See you in a bit."

His protectiveness gave me the warm fuzzies. "Thank you."

"Always."

I went back into the shop.

"Are you all right?" Christine asked.

"Yes, I'm fine. I'd just stepped into the office to talk with Ted for a sec."

"I saw that man leaving — Mr. Sherman — and when I didn't see you right away, it scared me."

"He kinda gave me the creeps too, but it's okay. He just wanted to talk about Keira." I didn't go into the specifics.

"But I didn't think you knew her all that well."

"I didn't . . . and I told him that. I suppose he's just grieving and trying to express himself," I said.

"Be careful around that man." She looked down at the floor.

"Why? Christine, do you know something I should know?"

She rubbed her face with her fingertips. "I just . . . Jared had mentioned once or twice that he could be . . . um . . . gruff with Keira."

"You mean like abusive? Did he ever hurt her?"

Before Christine could answer, another student arrived. And then another and another. I was hoping I could catch a spare moment to quietly question Christine again — maybe before she left. But she was the first one out the door after class was over.

True to his word, Ted was outside the shop about a quarter of an hour before class was over. He waited until the last student left, and then he came inside.

"Did you have a good class?" he asked.

"Yeah, I did."

"And yet that little frown right there" —

he gently rubbed the area between my brows — "tells me something didn't go the way you'd planned."

"Well, when Christine got here, she saw Ken Sherman leaving. She told me to be careful of him. I asked why, and she said Jared told her that Ken was *gruff* with Keira," I said. "I realize most parents need to be gruff or at least strict at times, but the way Christine was acting made me think it was something more. I asked Christine if Ken was abusive to his daughter. She didn't answer me because other students began arriving, and she left before I could talk with her after class."

"Sherman doesn't have a record of any kind, including domestic assault," Ted said. "I can tell you that much. Granted, that doesn't mean he's never *done* anything, but he doesn't have a record. Did he frighten you?"

"Not really. At first, I was confused about why he was here. Then he began talking about Keira, and I realized he was fishing for information. I suppose he thought that since you and I are dating and I'm friends with Manu and Reggie that I might know something that had been withheld from him. But he wasn't threatening."

"He'd better not be."

I linked my arms around his neck. "He wasn't. I think he's just desperate for answers. I get the impression that Bethany was the favorite child. Now she's the only child. Mr. Sherman has to have some guilt over that, don't you think?"

"That's possible." Ted kissed me gently. "You're awfully down tonight. Would a walk on the beach cheer you up?"

I smiled. "I think it would. Let me call Mom and let her know I'll be a few minutes late."

When I spoke with Mom, she told me she'd been reading all night and to take my time.

"I'm comfy and cozy and curled up with a good novel."

As soon as Ted and I stepped outside the Seven-Year Stitch, it started to rain.

"There goes the trip to the beach," Ted said.

"Still, Mom isn't expecting me home for a little while, why don't we go to Captain Moe's for a milk shake?"

He narrowed his eyes. "You want to go all the way to Depoe Bay for a milk shake when MacKenzies' Mochas is just down the street?"

"MacKenzies' Mochas doesn't make milk shakes." I grinned. "And I *really* want a

310

chocolate milk shake . . . and to find out what Priscilla was like as a child."

CHAPTER TWENTY-TWO

There were few cars in Captain Moe's parking lot when we arrived, probably because it was near closing time. Ted parked his red Impala, came around and opened my door — a true gentleman — and we hurried inside out of the rain.

Captain Moe looked slightly perturbed at the sound of customers coming in at the last minute until he turned and saw it was us. Then his broad face broke into a smile.

"What a surprise! What brings you two scamps to my door so late?"

"A craving for the best chocolate milk shake around," I said.

"She's also wanting some information," Ted said.

"Surely not our wee Tinkerbell. She never concerns herself with gossip or rumors or the affairs of others."

Both men laughed.

I put my hands on my hips. "Hey! So I

happen to be curious. Sue me."

"I would, but I can't afford to hire my niece," said Captain Moe.

"She'd never let you take me to court anyway." Brave words. I *hoped* she wouldn't let him, but I couldn't be certain. I supposed it would depend on the circumstance.

Captain Moe patted the countertop. "Come on over and tell me what's on your mind."

Ted and I sat at stools in front of Captain Moe, who called over his shoulder for someone in the kitchen to make two chocolate milk shakes.

"I had no idea you knew Priscilla's dad," I said. "I just have to know if she was always as —" I struggled to find the proper word.

"Weird?" Ted asked.

"Kooky?" Captain Moe contributed.

"Eccentric," I said.

Captain Moe drew his brows together. "I'd say that especially compared with the rest of the family, Priscilla was a bit *out there.* Jim and the two younger children were as down-to-earth as a family could be. They were humble, unassuming people."

"Were the other kids boys or girls?" I asked.

"One of each."

The guy in the kitchen brought out our

milk shakes. Captain Moe thanked him and set the drinks in front of Ted and me before continuing his story.

"Of course, the other two children might've been more reserved because their mother was sick and died not long after the youngest one turned three. So Priscilla had to be a mom to her brother and sister from the time she was seven or so."

"That's sad," I said.

"And a huge responsibility for a seven-year-old to try to take on," Ted added. "Didn't the family have a grandmother or aunt or someone who could've come in to help care for the children?"

Captain Moe shook his head. "I guess not."

I took a sip of my milk shake. "I imagine Priscilla was adorable as a child. Those tangerine corkscrew curls . . ."

"Straight, lank brown locks," Captain Moe said with a smile. "But she could sure strut out some wild outfits — plaids with paisley or floral prints, sweaters with halter tops over them, purple shorts, green tights, and an orange shirt. You just never knew what that child would tromp out in from one day to the next. It was always interesting to see Priscilla."

"It still is," I said. "It sounds as if she's

actually toned things down a bit since growing up. It'd be fun to know what Claude was like as a child."

"I never met him," said Captain Moe. "I suppose he must be from somewhere in the Midwest or something. I remember Jim telling me Priscilla had gone off to college in Ohio. I think she wound up dropping out though. Maybe meeting Claude and joining his . . . act . . . was the impetus for that."

"Poor Priscilla. I can't imagine it was easy for her to go off to school and leave the kids she'd practically raised," I said. "I mean, I'm sure her dad worked outside the home, didn't he?"

"Yeah. He had Jim's Lobster Shack. In fact, I told you about him the last time you were in here."

Ted leaned forward. "He's the one whose business Ken Sherman ruined?"

"He sure is," said Captain Moe.

"I wonder if Priscilla knew Keira was his daughter?" I asked.

"I doubt it." Captain Moe flipped up his palms. "If she had, she'd have likely requested another waitress. Jim was pretty bitter toward Ken. I can only imagine the rest of his family was too."

I took another drink of my milk shake and tried not to make an obnoxious slurping noise, since I was getting close to finishing it. "When you and Priscilla stepped outside and you talked there on the sidewalk, you looked troubled when you walked away."

Ted pushed his empty glass away. "Nope. Marcy isn't nosy at all, is she?"

Captain Moe chuckled. "Nah."

"I didn't come right out and ask!" It was a weak defense, but it was all I had.

"No, but I am guessing you'd like to know." Captain Moe's shoulders shook with his suppressed laughter. "It wasn't anything terribly important. I merely asked her for her father's phone number. The last time I tried to call him — oh, I'd say about two or three months ago — I got a recording telling me the number was no longer in service."

"So you and Priscilla's dad still keep in touch?" I asked. "Has he been to the Horror Emporium?"

"Well, that's what I was getting ready to tell your impatient little self."

I blushed.

"Priscilla said her father had been admitted to an assisted-living facility. I started to ask her which one, but she said she had to run and would talk with me later." All traces of his smile vanished. "I need to stop in and ask her the next time I'm in Tallulah Falls.

I'd like to check on Jim and see how he's doing."

"If I see her before you do, I'll ask her," I said.

"Maybe that's not a good idea, sweetheart." Ted placed his hand gently on my back. "Captain Moe might not want Priscilla to know he was talking about her and her family. She might misinterpret our conversation."

"Oh, that's true. I never thought of that, Captain Moe. I'm sorry."

He waved away my apology. "I know you well enough to realize you're only trying to help. But I'll see Priscilla soon enough."

Ted drove me back to the Seven-Year Stitch to get my Jeep, and then he insisted on seeing me home.

"You're sweet," I told him. "When we get there, you can come in and —"

"No," he interrupted. "I don't want to come in and disturb your mom. I'll just see you to the door . . . get a good-night kiss."

I leaned over and kissed him. "Just one?"

"One is never enough with you."

I smiled as I opened the car door and slid out. Ted had stopped in the middle of the street right beside my Jeep, so we couldn't linger long. How bad would it look for the

Tallulah Falls Police Department's head detective to be holding up traffic while his girlfriend stole a kiss?

"See you in a few!" Ted called as I got into the Jeep.

I started the Jeep and pulled out in front of him. Nothing looked amiss in the semi-darkness of the Stitch. I'd left the hall light on in the back for extra security. Jill happily looked out upon Main Street. Everything was set for tomorrow. I was both happy and nervous about the day ahead.

The first thing I saw when I pulled into the driveway was Angus's wiry face looking out at me. I waved to him as I waited for Ted to park behind me. He woofed, but the sound was muted by the closed window and the fact that I was still inside the Jeep. I hoped Mom wasn't asleep.

Ted got out of his car and came up beside the Jeep. He opened my door and I slid out and into his strong arms. We kissed, and then he walked me to the door . . . where we kissed some more.

It wasn't until Angus barked at the window again that I said I really should go inside. "Won't you reconsider coming in with me?"

Ted shook his head. "Your mom might be sleeping. And, if she isn't, you two need this time together."

"Have I told you how much I love you?"

"Not in the past half hour." He smiled and kissed me gently. "Now, go on inside so I can be a hundred percent sure you're safe."

"All right." I started to tell him he shouldn't worry so much, but I actually liked that he was so caring. I went inside and shut and locked the door.

I smiled to myself as I heard Ted's car drive away, and then I hugged Angus who was thrilled that I'd finally came in to tell him hello.

"Marcella, is everything all right?" Mom called from the living room.

"Yeah, Mom. Everything's fine." I walked into the living room and dropped onto the chair near the couch where she was stretched out reading.

"Nothing happened to your car, did it?"

"No." She was wondering why Ted had followed me home. I'd better come up with a satisfactory story. "It started raining, so Ted and I went out for milk shakes instead of going to the beach. When we got back to the Stitch, he insisted on following me home because . . . well, because there's still a murderer on the loose, I guess." *Oh, sure, that'll make her feel better.* "I mean, he's protective . . . that's all."

"Okay."

She was looking at me suspiciously, but she didn't come right out and ask if Ken Sherman had dropped by the Stitch, so I didn't need to say anything about that . . . right?

"So," I said, "it looks like you've made quite a bit of progress in your book. It must be pretty good."

"It is good," she said. "Why didn't Ted come in for a while?"

"He didn't want to disturb you. Plus, he said we needed time together — you and me — just the two of us."

"That was thoughtful of him."

"He is very, very thoughtful," I said.

She placed her bookmark in her book, closed it, and laid it beside her. "What aren't you telling me?"

"Not much. Nothing really."

"Marcella . . ."

And then after asking Ted not to tell Mom about Ken Sherman coming by the shop, I told Mom about Ken Sherman coming by the shop. It was out of my mouth almost before I knew what I was saying. It was the *tone.* I've never been able to endure the tone. It was like she'd already looked into my soul and knew what I wasn't telling her and was just waiting for my confession.

"Wouldn't it have been simpler to have told me this in the first place?" she asked.

"Well, yeah. But I didn't want to worry you. I'm still concerned about your heart."

"My heart is fine. Was this man threatening to you? Is that why Ted was concerned?"

"No. Mr. Sherman just weirded me out." I shrugged. "He's probably only mourning his daughter and desperate to know who killed her. And since I'm dating Ted and am friends with Manu and Reggie, I guess he thought I might know something that had been kept from him . . . which is ridiculous because they're going to keep her next of kin informed way before they tell me anything. And I'm not privy to any confidential information."

"Calm down, darling. You don't have to sell me on the fact that you don't know who killed Keira."

"I know. I just . . . That's why I think he was at the Stitch. But, on the other hand, I was kinda scared because it's rumored that he's mixed up with criminals. Of course, he told me that not all the stories told in a small town are true."

Mom's eyes widened. "You didn't actually ask him if he consorted with criminals, did you?"

"No! I'd never come right out and ask him that . . . I mean, I don't think I would. Maybe if I thought he was going to hold me hostage or something, but —"

"Why did he tell you the stories weren't true?" Mom asked, rubbing her forehead.

"Well, I told him that I'd heard he was going to open a MacKenzies' Mochas franchise for Keira and that I thought she'd have done well with it," I said. "He seemed surprised that I knew about that, and I told him that was the nature of a small town like Tallulah Falls — no one has any secrets here, at least, not for long. And then he said that not all the stories that are told are true."

"Again, he wasn't threatening toward you, was he?"

"Not at all. And I texted Ted as soon as he left . . . which is why Ted was there when class was over and why he followed me home."

"So Ted is worried that this man might hurt you." She expelled a long breath.

"Ted is just a super-caring boyfriend." I wanted desperately to change the subject. "Which is why he took me all the way to Captain Moe's to get a chocolate milk shake."

She leveled her gaze at me. "You drove almost half an hour for a milk shake?"

"Well, that and to see Captain Moe. Guess what. He knew Priscilla when she was young. He said she wore some outlandish outfits even as a child."

Her stare didn't waver. "I know you're just trying to change the subject."

"Not entirely. Apparently, Priscilla's dad was in business with Ken Sherman."

"And you think Priscilla's dad is a criminal?" she asked.

"No. I don't think so." I frowned. "I guess he could be. I never thought of that. But he and Captain Moe are friends, so I doubt he's a criminal."

"Captain Moe's brother is in prison," Mom reminded me.

That was true. Captain Moe's brother — Riley Kendall's father — Norman Patrick was serving time for fraud. He too had been a lawyer. He was nice . . . even though his smile reminded me of the shark Bruce in that popular kids' movie about the missing fish. I knew Mr. Patrick had done some bad things, but I didn't feel that he was a bad person. He'd simply made a few mistakes. And he was paying for them now.

Still, I didn't defend him to Mom. I merely nodded.

Angus got up, stood and looked at me for a moment, and then headed for the kitchen.

He needed to go outside. Saved by the dog.

"I'm going to get a bottle of water while I'm in the kitchen," I said. "May I bring you anything?"

"No, thank you."

I let Angus out into the backyard. Thankfully, it had stopped raining, and I could let him play for a few minutes. He ran off the porch and then stood stock still, staring and sniffing the air. I didn't know if he thought there was something out there or if he was merely making sure there wasn't. After a few seconds, he trotted over to his favorite tree, and I went back inside.

I got my water and returned to the living room. Mom was looking down at her hands.

"Mom? Are you okay?" I hurried over to her side.

She raised her head. "I'm fine, darling. Just lost in thought."

"What're you thinking about?"

"The movie we just wrapped," she said.

I returned to the chair, kicked off my shoes, and put my feet up on the ottoman. "Tell me all about it."

She looked wistful. "It was wonderful. I loved the director . . . the producer . . . the cast."

"*Everybody* in the cast?" I asked. There was usually at least one person who acted poorly toward Mom or his or her other cast-mates and gave Mom something to complain about — and relay funny stories about — during the entire shoot.

"Every single person. You know how you hear actors talk during their promotional tours about the cast being one big happy family? In this case, it was true." She smiled. "One of the secondary characters — a young woman who played a harlot — knitted scarves for all of us."

"That was sweet."

She nodded. "Everyone raved over their costumes. It was wonderful."

The reason for her pensive stare dawned on me. "And you're afraid that in comparison the next set will be a nightmare."

"So far, there isn't another set."

"What?" I paused with my water bottle halfway to my lips.

"I don't have another job lined up yet."

Usually, by the time one movie wrapped, Mom was already contracted for another. I didn't know how to express my concern without making her feel worse. I figured it was better to show optimism.

"Enjoy the break," I said. "You'll have another job before you know it."

Was the lack of work the real reason she'd expressed interest in moving to Tallulah

Falls and working with a community theater?

"Sure, I will."

She'd tried to sound convincing, but her
words fell a little flat.

"I'm absolutely certain you will, Mom.
You're one of the most talented costume
designers in the business. And as soon as
word gets out that you aren't currently
working — and are looking for another
movie or television show — your phone will
be lighting up."

"Yeah. I know. And I *am* enjoying my
vacation." She gave me a smile that didn't
quite reach her eyes. "I'm so glad I'm able
to be here for your celebration."

I went over to the sofa and gave her a hug.
"I'm happy you're here too."

CHAPTER TWENTY-THREE

Friday morning I woke with a major case of nerves. I hadn't slept well the night before because I really wanted to sleep well and be rested for the big day. I should've simply got up and stayed up for all the good tossing and turning in bed did me. Angus had even deserted me to go sleep in the guest room with Mom.

I took a quick shower, dressed, and styled my hair. I carefully applied my makeup to try to look as if I'd had more than four and a half hours of sleep last night, and then I went downstairs.

I wandered around in the kitchen. I peered into the cabinets, the refrigerator, and then back to the cabinets. Maybe I'd missed something on the first pass, or something had magically appeared since I last checked. I wondered what on earth I could eat without upsetting my already queasy stomach.

The doorbell rang. Out in the backyard where Angus was playing, he sounded the alarm. I didn't know who in the world would be coming by unannounced this early. Maybe it was Ted. He'd know I'd be feeling nervous this morning. After all, the last time I celebrated my shop, I wound up with a dead body in my storeroom.

I opened the front door. I could barely see the delivery guy behind the spectacular display of red roses, baby's breath, and sprigs of lavender.

"Are you Marcy Singer?" the man asked.

"Yes, sir. Wait right there." I traded him a tip for the vase of flowers.

I carried the flowers into the kitchen, set them on the table, and retrieved the card.

Good morning, beautiful. Congratulations on your one-year anniversary with the Seven-Year Stitch. It's going to be a great day. I love you — Ted.

Tears sprang to my eyes, and I quickly dammed them with my index fingers so I wouldn't ruin my makeup.

It was at that moment that Mom came into the kitchen. "Darling, what are you doing?" Then she noticed the flowers. "Oh, aren't they gorgeous!"

Well, that made it even harder for me to dam up the tears. I hurried over to the counter and tore a paper towel off the roll and pressed it under my eyes until I could get my emotions under control. When I turned back to Mom, she held out her arms for a hug.

I shook my head. "Not yet. Let me pull myself together first."

"Why are you such a wreck?" she asked with a bemused grin.

"I could hardly sleep at all last night thinking about today and this evening's celebration. I mean, you know what happened last year. And then, Ted sent me this beautiful bouquet to let me know he's thinking about me, and —" I had to put the paper towel back in place.

The doorbell rang again. And, once again, Angus began barking, though not as much as before.

"I bet that's Ted."

"I'll let him in," Mom said. "You finish pulling yourself together."

Pulling myself together would be a lost cause as soon as I saw Ted and dissolved into a puddle of goo. Oh, well. I supposed looking well rested wasn't everything.

From the foyer, I heard Mom's exclamation of surprise and hurried to see what was going on. It wasn't Ted but Alfred Benton who was at the door.

"Alfred!" I ran to him and hugged him tightly.

He held me at arm's length. "Let me look at you, Marcy girl. You get more beautiful every time I see you." He looked past me. "Just like your mother."

"Come on into the kitchen," I said. "I was getting ready to make some coffee."

"I'm fine," Alfred said. "Could I speak with your mom alone for a second?"

I looked from Alfred to Mom and back again. "Okay. Um . . . I'll grab Angus and go on into work. I'm not feeling much like breakfast anyway."

"Wait until you see the flowers Ted sent her," Mom told Alfred. "They're stunning."

"It sounds as if this young man is getting serious about our girl," Alfred said. He tried to look stern, and that made me laugh.

But his wanting to talk with Mom alone was deadly serious — I could see it in his eyes. And I was scared.

On my way to the Seven-Year Stitch, I called Ted to thank him for the flowers. He must've been in a meeting because my call went directly to voice mail.

As soon as Angus and I arrived, I took the

witch costume off Jill. I thought that in keeping with the name of the shop, I'd outfit her in a white halter dress like the one in Marilyn Monroe's iconic subway grate photos.

Vera came in before I'd got the mannequin dressed. "Jill! You're indecent!" She laughed, covered her eyes, and peeped between her fingers.

"She's almost ready," I said with a grin as I pulled the dress down over Jill's head and zipped the back.

"That looks great," Vera said. "You know what would make it even better? A tiny fan at her feet to make the dress billow out."

"I think I have one in my office."

While Vera played fetch with Angus, I went into my office and got a small pink fan out of the closet.

"Do you think this will work?" I asked.

"Let's try it." Vera took the fan, plugged it in at the floor outlet behind the counter, and turned it on.

The dress immediately blew up over Jill's head. Vera and I succumbed to a fit of giggles.

Vera turned the fan down to its lowest setting, and the effect was just as we'd hoped. The dress blew out and made the skirt full, but it didn't expose Jill's unmentionables.

"Where's Beverly this morning? I hope she's not feeling bad again."

"No, actually, Alfred Benton — her attorney and one of our oldest friends — came to my house this morning. He said he'd like to talk with Mom alone. I called him after Mom had her health scare the other night, and she got angry because I did so. But now I'm afraid there's something really wrong with her . . . something neither of them wants to talk with me about. Why else would he come all the way here?"

Vera looked down at the floor.

"You know, don't you?" I stepped closer to her. "Whatever it is, she talked to you about it day before yesterday, didn't she?"

She still wouldn't meet my eyes. "I'm sure she'll talk with you about it when she's ready."

I grasped her arms. "Vera, if you know something, please tell me. *Please.*"

She slowly raised her eyes. "All right. But you have to swear not to let on like you know."

"Of course, I won't let on that I know." I desperately hoped I could keep that promise. As I examined Vera's eyes for worry or fear, she gave me an impish grin.

"He kissed her."

"What? Who? Who kissed who?"

"Alfred kissed your mother."

"Alfred kissed my mother?" I blinked. "Are you sure?"

"Positive. She talked with Veronica and me about it over cards."

"Why didn't she tell me?"

"She wasn't sure how you'd feel about it." She shrugged. "Heck, she wasn't sure how *she* felt about it."

I released Vera, staggered over to one of the club chairs, and sat down. "For years, I've wished my mom and Alfred would get together."

Vera came over and sat on the sofa. "That's probably why she didn't tell you, hon. She didn't want to get your hopes up if things didn't work out."

"Was this kiss a onetime thing, or did Mom talk like the relationship was going somewhere?"

"From the way she was mooning over that man, I'd say she's been in love with him for years," said Vera.

"Then why did it take them so long to do something about it?"

"Sometimes people don't realize how deep their feelings are until — bam! — they get hit with them like a pie in the face. And, too, she didn't want a fling to ruin a lifelong friendship and business relationship."

"So Mom thinks this . . . thing . . . with Alfred would only be a fling?" To me, that was sad. I didn't want the special relationship they shared to be turned into something fleeting. I wanted theirs to be a love they would cherish for the rest of their lives — just like their friendship had always been.

"I don't think so, hon. But I believe she's afraid of her feelings."

"Me too," I said softly. "I know it sounds selfish, but Alfred has been like a surrogate dad to me since I was a little girl. I don't want to lose him because he and Mom have suddenly made their relationship awkward."

"Well, that's between the two of them. I don't think Alfred would stop loving you if he severed ties with your mother. I believe he'd still be a part of your life. And, if he wouldn't, then he's not the man you think he is."

Vera had an excellent point, and I told her so.

"Thanks, kiddo. I'd have been a great mom, don't you think?"

"I know you would have." I gave her a hug.

"Is there anything I can help you do before I leave?"

"Nope. I think I have everything under control," I said. "I'm excited about tonight, but I'm also a nervous wreck."

"Don't be." She smiled brightly. "History wouldn't be so ordinary as to repeat itself, would it?"

"I certainly hope not."

I spent the first half of the day waiting on regular customers as well as my favorite visitors. Sadie brought me a low-fat vanilla latte with cinnamon and a pumpkin muffin from MacKenzies' Mochas. Todd brought a six-pack of apricot ale for the anniversary party — or the after-party. He said it was whatever I wanted to do.

And Reggie brought me a beautiful midnight blue silk blouse on which she'd embroidered the collar and cuffs with *chikankari*. For the second time already today, I was so overcome with emotion that I nearly cried. I promised her I'd wear the blouse to the party tonight. She acted modest, but I could tell she was touched by my praise of both her thoughtfulness and her workmanship.

I was ringing up a hardanger embroidery kit for a woman when Mom and Alfred came into the Stitch. Angus ran to greet them. I completed the customer's transaction and invited her to attend the anniversary celebration this evening. She said she'd try to attend.

Mom and Alfred took a seat in the sit-and-stitch square. I slowly walked over to join them.

"What's up?" I asked.

"I realize I probably alarmed you this morning when I told you I wanted to speak with your mother alone, especially given your concern over her health," said Alfred. "I apologize if that's the case."

"That was the case. I was afraid you'd come to discuss her living will or something." I crossed my arms. "So which of you wants to tell me what's going on?"

"I will," Mom said. "You know what close friends Alfred and I have been over the years."

"The best of friends," Alfred added.

"And we've decided . . ." She looked at him and then back at me. "We've decided to see if there might be something more there . . . between us."

Alfred cleared his throat. "How do you feel about that, Marcy?"

"I feel like it's about time." I uncrossed my arms and stood.

Mom and Alfred stood too, and we all hugged.

"Just . . . if this . . . romance . . . doesn't work out," I said, "please don't throw away what you had before."

"We won't," Alfred said. "That's what we've been discussing at your house."

"We plan to move slowly," Mom said. "We're not going to rush into anything."

"Except lunch." Alfred grinned. "We're heading off down the street to get something now. May we bring you something?"

"No," I said. "Ted should be here soon."

Mom hugged me again. "We'll talk more later."

I nodded.

I had to smile as I watched them walk hand in hand down the street. They looked like a couple of kids. Why did it take them so long to find each other when they'd been right there together all along?

When Ted came in a few minutes later, he'd brought fettuccine Alfredo for three. He'd thought Mom would be there.

"Thank you for thinking of her, but she and Alfred Benton are having lunch at MacKenzies' Mochas."

"Okay. Well, Angus, this is your lucky day."

Angus thumped his tail on the floor.

"Did you know Alfred was coming?" Ted asked.

"No. I was totally surprised when he was the second visitor at my door this morning." I leaned over and kissed him. "Thank you again for the flowers."

"You're welcome. And I'm sorry I didn't get time to call you back, babe. I've been in one meeting after another."

"I understand. Anyway, Alfred showed up totally out of the blue and said he wanted to speak with Mom alone. It scared the dickens out of me. I thought he was here about her health problems."

"But that's not it, is it?"

"No. He and Mom are now officially seeing each other." I opened my box of fettuccine.

"That's fantastic!" He watched my expression carefully. "Right?"

"I think so. I'm trying to be optimistic about it, Ted, but what if this doesn't work out? Mom and I could both lose Alfred forever. And he's been a huge part of my life since my father died."

Ted broke a breadstick in half and gave part of it to Angus. "They know what they're doing, sweetheart. They're mature enough to handle whatever happens. If a romance isn't in the cards for them, then they'll be able to go back to being friends."

"I don't know. Mom is going through some stuff right now. I'm not sure where her head is at." I twirled some noodles around my fork and took a bite.

"What're you talking about? You mean,

338

her health scare?"

"That's part of it, I think, but it's more than that. She confided to me last night that she doesn't have another job lined up. She even asked a couple of days ago if Tallulah Falls has a community theater group."

"Don't you think she was kidding?"

"That's what scares me. I don't think she was." I bit my lip. "I feel like she's worrying about her usefulness, her attractiveness, her purpose. I don't want her to project those needs onto Alfred and hope he can solve all her problems. These are issues she has to resolve within herself."

"Are *you* afraid she won't get another job?" Ted asked.

"No. I'm fairly certain that she will. I just don't think she's in a good place to be making serious decisions about her life right now. I don't want her to decide in a week or two that embarking upon a romance with Alfred was a mistake and break his heart."

He leaned over and kissed my forehead. "I love you. And it's sweet how you worry so much about other people. But sometimes you need to let them worry about themselves . . . especially when they're two grown people who've known each other since before you were born."

"Good point. But you know me well

enough to realize that that's easier said than done."

Chapter Twenty-Four

After Ted left, but before Mom and Alfred returned, I logged on to my laptop. Since last night, I'd been wanting to find out where Priscilla's father was living. I'd caught a glimpse of Priscilla earlier, but she'd been leaving the Horror Emporium. I thought that while I had a few minutes I'd do some poking around online to see what I could discover on my own.

First I did a search to find out the difference in an assisted-living facility and a nursing home. I learned that assisted-living facilities are more along the lines of supervised communities and that nursing homes are for people who require constant medical care. So if Jim Morris didn't require round-the-clock medical care, why had his phone been disconnected and why was Priscilla reluctant to provide Captain Moe with her dad's phone number?

Then I did a search for James "Jim" Morris with his last-known location — Lincoln City — and I added *Priscilla* to the keywords as a second thought. Maybe if the assisted-living facility had thrown Mr. Morris a birthday party or something recently, it would have been in the local newspaper given the fact that he'd been a successful restaurateur. If by some stroke of fate, I could uncover Mr. Morris's location on my own, then I wouldn't have to bother Priscilla.

The first item in the search engine was an obituary from a Seattle newspaper from June of this year. I thought it *had* to have been another James Morris. If her father was dead, why would Priscilla lie to Captain Moe?

Still, I clicked the link and read the obit:

James "Jim" Morris, 68, of Lincoln City, Oregon, died Thursday of a self-inflicted gunshot wound. Mr. Morris had been the proprietor of the once-popular Jim's Lobster Shack. Mr. Morris is survived by his daughter Priscilla Morris Atwood, son Frederick Morris, and daughter Penelope Morris.

I stopped reading. That *was* the right Jim Morris. Captain Moe's friend had killed himself. How did Captain Moe not know that? And why hadn't Priscilla been honest with him?

Mom and Alfred returned from lunch while I was still staring gobsmacked at the computer screen. I hadn't even paid attention to the bells when they'd opened the door.

Mom hurried over to me. "Darling, are you all right?"

I quickly explained the whole situation with Jim Morris, Priscilla, and Captain Moe. "Why wouldn't Priscilla simply tell Captain Moe the truth?"

"Perhaps she's ashamed or feels guilty," Alfred said. "Survivors of suicide victims often blame themselves. Of course, it's an unreasonable and false accusation, but it appears to be a common feeling among survivors."

"Oh, no. Poor Priscilla. I never even thought of that." I briefly closed my eyes. "I guess it's natural, especially given her childhood, that she'd feel that she could've done something to prevent her father's death. Captain Moe told Ted and me that she had to take on the role of mother to her siblings when she was only seven years old."

"That's sad," Mom agreed.

"Still, Captain Moe should know the

truth," I said. "I'd have thought he'd have heard — but maybe not, since he's in Depoe Bay and Mr. Morris was staying at an assisted-living facility in Washington at the time."

Mom inclined her head. "I think maybe you should talk with Priscilla before saying anything to Captain Moe."

"Your mother's right, sweetheart. At least, let this woman know you're planning on telling Captain Moe what became of his friend. And, who knows? Maybe she'll confide in you, and you can convince her there was nothing she could've done to prevent her father's death."

"You're right. I'll talk with Priscilla the first chance I get."

I closed the shop at five with a note saying I'd be back by five forty-five p.m. for the party. I'd given Sadie my key to the back door in case she and Blake needed it to start setting up the buffet before I returned. I was hoping to make better time, but one never knows what might go wrong.

Mom and Alfred had left for my house at around four thirty. Mom had said she wanted to freshen up for the party. Maybe she or Alfred could feed Angus so I could get dressed quicker.

I drove home with Angus licking the side of my face the entire way. He could tell I was on edge about something, so he hung his wiry head over the divider keeping him in the backseat and gave me kisses to make me feel better. It did make me laugh. And it made me glad I was already planning to redo my makeup.

I parked, got out, and opened the back door of the Jeep. Before Angus could jump out, I attached his leash to his collar. I let him inside before returning to the passenger side of the Jeep and retrieving the gorgeous blouse Reggie had made for me.

When I went into the house, Alfred had already taken Angus into the kitchen.

"I'm taking care of Mr. O'Ruff," he called to me. "Go on upstairs. Your mother is waiting for you."

Mom was standing in front of the closet in my bedroom with both doors flung open. "I thought you could wear this beautiful yellow A-line skirt with your new blouse and these navy platform pumps. What do you think?"

So that was the real reason Mom had left the shop half an hour ahead of me. She'd wanted to get here and pull my outfit together.

"I think that's perfect," I said with a smile.

I'd actually been going to wear a white skirt with the blouse, but the yellow one gave the whole look a bolder, more energetic vibe.

"Good. I'll leave you to get ready then. If there's anything you need, give me a yell."

I hurried into the bathroom and started my bathwater. While the tub was filling, I washed my face so I could start my makeup with a clean slate.

By five twenty-five, I was sprinting down the stairs on my way out the door.

"No running in those shoes!" Mom shouted. "You'll break your neck!"

"Okay." I didn't slow down. "See you and Alfred in a few."

"Be careful!"

I closed the door on her parting words, got into the Jeep, and rushed back to the Seven-Year Stitch.

I parked at the rear of the building this time to give my patrons more space to park in front of the shop. As I was pulling in, I saw Blake carrying a container of food into the Stitch. His back was to me, so I didn't wave or anything. But I was happy to see him. It let me know that he and Sadie had everything under control.

Figuring I'd only be in their way if I went on into the shop before they finished getting set up, I went over to the Horror

Emporium and knocked on the back door.

Priscilla answered my knock. "Marcy! What're you doing here? I thought you'd be next door getting ready for your party."

"Blake and Sadie are busy setting up the food, and I've been wanting to talk with you all day. May I come inside?"

"Of course." She moved aside to let me in, and then directed me a few steps down the hall into the office. "Have a seat."

Priscilla sat behind a scarred-up oak desk, and I gingerly sat on one of the metal folding chairs in front of the desk. I looked around the room. It was cluttered, with knickknacks on every available spot of shelf space and folders, books, and magazines all over everything else — the desk, a couple of chairs, the floor. Priscilla reminded me of a peacock in her bright turquoise-colored blouse as she sat amid the mess.

"What did you want to talk with me about?" she asked.

"Your father."

Her face became a stony mask. "What about him?"

"I was trying to help Captain Moe get in touch with him, so I did an Internet search," I said. "I found his obituary."

"So you know Daddy killed himself."

"I do. But, Priscilla, it wasn't your fault."

"Damn right it wasn't my fault. It was Ken Sherman's fault."

"Captain Moe told me how Mr. Sherman ruined your father's business," I said. "Of course, that was before I knew Mr. Morris was your father. Captain Moe was simply telling me so I could warn Blake and Sadie not to get involved with Mr. Sherman."

"I only wish someone would've warned Daddy."

"Why don't you want Captain Moe to know the truth?" I asked.

"If he cared as much about Daddy as he'd pretended to, he'd have already known, wouldn't he?"

I debated on how to answer that. How *could* Captain Moe have known? Mr. Morris had been living in Seattle. On the other hand, I understood Priscilla's anger that her father's friends hadn't been able to help prevent his death.

As I thought about how to answer Priscilla's question, I gazed around the room again. My eyes came to rest on something that resembled a gun. It was black and yellow and had X26C printed on the side.

My mouth dropped open. "Is that . . . a Taser?"

"Yes. Why?"

"No reason. I just don't think I've seen

one in person before." I stood and so did Priscilla.

"I really need to get back," I said. "I'm sure you've got perfectly good reasons for not telling Captain Moe about your dad. It isn't any of my business. I just thought I could help, that's all."

Priscilla made a lunge for the Taser as I tried to get to the door.

"You aren't going to your party, Marcy." She was pointing the Taser at me now. "You're right. You were messing around where you had no business, and now it's gonna cost you."

"I honestly don't care if Captain Moe finds out the truth about your dad or not. He certainly won't hear it from me."

"This isn't about my dad or Captain Moe anymore, so drop the pretense."

"Fine." I took a step backward. I didn't know how far of a reach that Taser had, but I didn't want to be shocked. "Why Keira? Why not go after Ken himself?"

"What would be the point of that?" she asked. "I wanted him to suffer the way I had suffered."

"I'm truly sorry for your loss. I am. But, again, I won't tell anyone anything. Just, please, let me leave."

"You know I can't. But, hey, at least I'll

give you a fighting chance." She nodded toward the door. "Move."

"How do I know you aren't going to shoot me in the back with that thing as soon as I get in front of you?"

"You don't. I guess you'll have to trust me. My advice is to keep moving and to heed the directions I give you."

"Someone is bound to come looking for me. I should've already been there, and my Jeep is parked out back."

"Walk."

I did as she instructed and walked forward. As I did so, I caught a glimpse of one of the Seven-Year Stitch key rings at the corner of the desk.

Priscilla told me to turn to the left. She was going to lock me in their storage room.

"I imagine *everyone* will be looking for you, dear. But they'd never dream of looking for you in here." She flipped on the light and pushed me forward over another threshold.

I realized too late that the Horror Emporium's storage room had been transformed into the Lair of the Serpent.

"I'd be quiet and still if I were you." She shut and locked the door that led into the enclosure. "That way, you'll at least last long enough to say your prayers."

"But you have a tour coming through soon!"

"Not for an hour," she said. "And when the group *does* come in, I'll be as surprised as everyone else to see you lying in there." She shut the door and left.

I looked at all the snakes slithering nearby and tried to recall any advice that would bring me through this ordeal alive . . . not that I suffered any delusions that Priscilla intended to allow me to live should the snakes fail at killing me. I remembered the time Mom had worked on a movie set in the jungle. I'd become friends with the herpetologist and her son, and they both had taught me a lot about snakes. I could picture the herpetologist and her son in my mind. She'd been tall with an athletic build, and she wore large round glasses. Her son, Steve, had been a few years older than me. He had been thin, with shoulder-length brown hair and green eyes. I'd had a massive crush on him.

I willed myself to be calm. I wasn't planning to move, but if I did, I needed to do so smoothly. Abrupt, jerky movements would stress or frighten the snakes. The only snake that appeared to be venomous was the rattlesnake.

During those few months on set, Steve

had taken me under his wing and impressed me with his knowledge of reptiles. My brain was scrambling to come up with information I could actually use.

Steve had taught me that rattlesnakes were usually docile and shy when left undisturbed and would only strike in self-defense. I looked at the rattlesnake. It appeared to be watching me warily, its tongue darting out every couple of seconds. So it was smelling me . . . trying, I imagined, to figure out what I was doing there.

I'm wondering the same thing, buddy.

I recalled Steve's mom saying that rattlesnakes could strike a distance of two-thirds their total body length. I was terrible at measuring lengths by sight — I'd have thought I'd have gotten better at that after measuring fabric so much over the years — and I had no idea how long this snake was. Furthermore, if it decided to strike, I had very little space in which to retreat. And any sudden movement would frighten the other snakes, and while they might not be venomous, no snake bite — or attack by multiple snakes — would be a pleasant experience.

There had to be another way out. Or, if not, maybe I could get someone's attention and be let out before Priscilla returned. I knew better than to beat on the glass. Even though the sound wouldn't bother them — snakes have no external ears and are essentially deaf — I knew they were very sensitive to vibrations. The pounding would certainly agitate them.

Maybe the door hadn't locked. Maybe I'd only *thought* Priscilla had locked it. I slowly stepped forward. After a few seconds, I raised my hand to the doorknob and turned. Nope. It was locked all right.

I felt something brush against my ankle. Throwing all that good advice I'd received to the wind, I screamed and jerked away. I looked down just in time to see and feel an emerald green snake bite my ankle. My heart was pounding in my chest, and I was on the verge of giving in to hysteria. But I couldn't. If this snake was venomous, then the more upset I got, the quicker the venom would travel through my bloodstream. If it wasn't venomous and I gave in to my panic, I was more likely to be bitten again by one or more of the snakes.

Why did I come here? Why didn't I leave well enough alone? Why wasn't anyone looking for me?

I slowly lifted my hands to cover my mouth and help drown out the whimpers I couldn't suppress.

Claude walked by, casually glanced inside the Lair of the Serpent, and then stopped dead in his tracks. His eyes widened, and his jaw dropped. "Marcy, what're you doing in there?"

Perhaps as curious as but more cautious than the rat snake, the rattlesnake had crawled along a faux branch just above the door. When Claude threw open the door, the rattlesnake fell onto him and bit him between his shoulder and neck. Claude cried out in pain.

Priscilla came running down the hall as I helped Claude from the room and closed the door to the Lair of the Serpent.

"Call an ambulance," I said as Claude slumped to the floor.

Instead, Priscilla hurried over and cradled him in her arms. I'd left my purse and cell phone in my car, so I went into the office and called Ted on the Horror Emporium's landline.

"Marcy?"

I could hear the alarm in his voice. Sparing him the details for the moment, I said simply, "I'm next door. Call an ambulance for Claude and get over here immediately."

EPILOGUE

Both Claude and I wound up in the emergency room, of course. Having been bitten by a Japanese rat snake, I fared much better than he did. I got my wound cleaned with a strong antibacterial cleanser and was instructed to return if I saw any signs of infection.

By the time the paramedics got Claude to the hospital, his trapezius had swelled to more than twice its normal size and was still growing. He was stabilized with antivenin, and then everyone was forced to leave the room so the medical staff could examine him further.

Officer Moore had been called in to keep an eye on Priscilla. I'd told Ted what she'd done to me — which was grounds for arrest on its own — and I'd explained what she'd done to Keira.

"When I saw the Taser, it all clicked into place," I said. "Priscilla had used the stun gun to immobilize Keira and then injected her with poison. She killed her because she wanted to see Mr. Sherman and his family suffer the way her father had suffered when Mr. Sherman destroyed his business and how she'd suffered when her father had committed suicide."

"Actually, it wasn't poison Priscilla injected Keira with," Ted told me. "It was rattlesnake venom, though not the venom of the type of rattler on display in the exhibit. Under Detective Poston's interrogation, Sal — the exotic-pet shop owner — had confessed that a woman fitting Priscilla's description had come into the shop and bought the venom. She'd claimed she was a doctor and needed the venom to make antivenin."

I was surprised. I hadn't thought Keira's murder had been well planned. I'd believed Priscilla had been waiting like a spider for some way to get back at Ken Sherman, and I felt that Keira having to work for the Horror Emporium at their grand opening celebration was merely a fly in her web that Priscilla couldn't pass up. But she'd known who Keira was all along. It was likely the reason the Horror Emporium had approached MacKenzies' Mochas about doing concessions in the first place. And, yet, in the end, Priscilla had been caught in her own web. Her husband was the one suffering for her actions.

Sal, of Sal's Exotic Pets, had recanted his denial of knowing Ken Sherman. He'd told Detective Poston that Mr. Sherman had approached him after Keira's autopsy results were presented to him and asked if anyone had bought venom. He'd told him a female doctor had bought some. When Sal had described the "doctor," Mr. Sherman had put the pieces together and realized that Priscilla had used the ruse to obtain the venom that had killed his daughter. He had no idea Priscilla was the child of Jim Morris, but he blamed Blake for Keira's death because he'd forced her to work at the Horror Emporium the night she died.

After a short while, a nurse came out and told us that Claude had been taken into surgery for a fasciotomy.

Priscilla raised her tear-streaked face and asked what that meant.

The nurse said that since Claude had received a moderate amount of venom in the trapezius muscle, the doctor had to cut the fascia to relieve the pressure and guard against acute compartment syndrome.

"B-but will C-Claude be all r-right?" Priscilla asked.

"We believe so." With that, the nurse returned to her post.

I walked over and patted Priscilla's hand. Yes, she'd shoved me into a literal snake pit and would certainly have killed me had she found me alive before Claude did, but she was a sad, pitiful mess sitting there. Plus, I couldn't help but think about that little girl with the lank brown hair and the outrageous outfits who'd had to become a mother to her siblings when she was only seven years old. Priscilla had been through a lot of pain. Granted, she'd dished out her fair share of hurt too, but the peacock was broken and cornered . . . and about to be caged.

She looked at me in surprise and then crushed me to her ample chest.

Ugh. This is almost as bad as the snakes.

"I'm so sorry, Marcy. I'm so sorry."

"It's okay. And Claude is going to make a full recovery. I just know he is."

"Do you really?" she asked in a tiny voice.

"I do."

Manu and Officer Moore took Priscilla to the police station to charge her on multiple counts, including the murder of Keira Sherman. I asked Manu not to add my kidnapping and reckless endangerment to Priscilla's charges. He gave me a sideways look, shook his head, and said we'd talk about it tomorrow.

Ted took me back to the Seven-Year Stitch. I thought we were only going to pick up my Jeep, but I was deeply touched to see that everyone was still there waiting for me to return. They all cheered when I walked through the door.

Ted gave my hand a squeeze and winked.

"You knew everyone was waiting, didn't you?"

"Maybe." He grinned. "Didn't you think it odd that Manu and I took your statement in the ambulance on the way to the hospital? We didn't want you to miss your big night."

Despite being thrown into the Lair of the Serpent by a madwoman, being bitten by a rat snake, and spending three hours in the emergency room, I had to admit that the anniversary party was a success. Upon hearing why I had been detained, most of the guests had stayed. They were eager to get all the juicy details. I even shared the front page of the *Tallulah Falls Examiner* the next day with Claude and Priscilla.

Fortunately, Claude did make a full recovery and was found to be not culpable in his wife's schemes. He'd bought the Taser gun for the protection of himself, his wife, and their employees; and he'd thought the two

Seven-Year Stitch key rings Priscilla had brought back from my shop the Thursday before Keira's murder were gifts I'd given her.

Mom got a phone call the day before she was scheduled to leave Tallulah Falls. She'd gotten a job doing the costumes for a modern-day interpretation of a Hercule Poirot mystery. Alfred stayed on until she left and gave me his assurance that he'd see to it that she saw a cardiologist as soon as possible. A few days after their return, he called to tell me that she'd received a clean bill of health from the heart specialist.

"I'm guarding that woman's heart with my life, child," he told me triumphantly.

"TMI, Uncle Alfred," I said. "Do you know what that means? Too much information!"

I wanted them to be happy. I didn't want either of them to share all the gory details.

ACKNOWLEDGMENTS

Amanda Lee would like to thank Ken Childress and Lydia Wiley of Bays Mountain Park and Planetarium, Kingsport, Tennessee, for their insights and expertise into snakes. The author is especially delighted that she didn't have to glean any of this knowledge firsthand! That said, any mistakes or misrepresentations about the snakes in the Lair of the Serpent are the author's own.

The author would also like to take this opportunity to thank Captain Charlie Womack of Treasures of the Sea in Lincoln City, Oregon, for his continued support, encouragement, and information.

ABOUT THE AUTHOR

Amanda Lee lives in southwest Virginia with her husband and two beautiful children, a boy and a girl. She's a full-time writer/editor/mom/wife and chief cook and bottle washer, and she loves every minute of it. Okay, not the bottle washing so much, but the rest of it is great.

The employees of Thorndike Press hope you have enjoyed this Large Print book. All our Thorndike, Wheeler, and Kennebec Large Print titles are designed for easy reading, and all our books are made to last. Other Thorndike Press Large Print books are available at your library, through selected bookstores, or directly from us.

For information about titles, please call:
  (800) 223-1244

or visit our Web site at:
  http://gale.cengage.com/thorndike

To share your comments, please write:
  Publisher
  Thorndike Press
  10 Water St., Suite 310
  Waterville, ME 04901